**A soldier had taken hold of her son and was pulling him out of the room.**

"No!" screamed Vera. "What are you doing with my son? Bring him back!"

The colonel nodded to the doctor, who held a needle upward, a clear liquid beading from its pointed tip. The doctor brought the needle down into Vera's arm.

Vera could no longer hold herself upright. Her bones were melting and a black fog was seeping through her mind. As she slipped away, she heard the colonel say, "Vera ... Vera, listen to me. You will know your contact by these two words:

*American roulette ...*"

# THE RED ENCOUNTER

Avon Books are available at special quantity discounts for bulk purchases for sales promotions, premiums, fund raising or educational use. Special books, or book excerpts, can also be created to fit specific needs.

For details write or telephone the office of the Director of Special Markets, Avon Books, Dept. FP, 1790 Broadway, New York, New York 10019, 212-399-1357.

# THE RED ENCOUNTER

**R. D. ZIMMERMAN**

 AVON
PUBLISHERS OF BARD, CAMELOT, DISCUS AND FLARE BOOKS

THE RED ENCOUNTER is an original publication of Avon Books. This work is a novel. Any similarity to actual persons or events is purely coincidental.

AVON BOOKS
A division of
The Hearst Corporation
1790 Broadway
New York, New York 10019

Copyright © 1986 by R. D. Zimmerman
Published by arrangement with the author
Library of Congress Catalog Card Number: 86-90747
ISBN: 0-380-75051-1

All rights reserved, which includes the right to reproduce this book or portions thereof in any form whatsoever except as provided by the U.S. Copyright Law. For information address the Lazear Agency, 3100 Ridgewood Circle, Orono, Minnesota 55356.

First Avon Printing: September 1986

AVON TRADEMARK REG. U.S. PAT. OFF. AND IN
OTHER COUNTRIES, MARCA REGISTRADA, HECHO EN
U.S.A.

Printed in the U.S.A.

K-R 10 9 8 7 6 5 4 3 2 1

For Mom and Sam

# Chapter 1

## Moscow

The men in the black Volga sedan first noticed the defecting Russian because of his shoes. With reddish black uppers and heavy rubber soles, they were the only thing he wore that was obviously Soviet-made. Every other American on the way to the embassy that night wore either running or hiking shoes.

His hand in his thick, curly hair, the leader needed only a glance at the man's face.

"That's not an American. That's our Volodya. Quickly, now," he said to the balding agent seated next to him.

They moved smoothly out of the back seat and into the cool April night. They had no time for subtlety or caution and headed straight toward the defecting cryptologist.

The leader noted how Volodya, in a down coat and jeans, struggled to maintain the appearance of an American on his way to the staff party. He watched as the Russian faltered in his step, aware that he'd been caught. Finally, Volodya turned to run.

The curly-haired man elbowed his partner. They sprang forward and, each seizing a puffy, down-covered arm, were instantly upon Volodya.

"What are you doing?" demanded the cryptologist in heavily accented English.

In Russian, the one in charge said, "Shut up."

Down the street, the black Volga roared to a start. The driver threw the car into reverse and raced backward along the edge of Tchaikovsky Street.

"Let me go!" pleaded Volodya, this time in Russian.

The second agent jabbed a small pistol into the defector's side.

"Silence!"

"But I—"

"Quiet, both of you!" demanded the leader. Steering the defector toward the Volga, he added, "Get in before they spot us!"

The cryptologist froze. "Wh—what?"

His captor turned quickly toward the embassy. The Soviet guards posted in front seemed not to have noticed yet. Certainly, though, the cameras and microwave microphones trained on the embassy were picking up their voices.

"You idiot, I'm American and we've got to get the hell out of here before the KGB arrests us all! Now get in!"

The leader, Richard Stevens, loaded Volodya in the back, then climbed in behind him. The other Russian, Viktor Petrov, sat up front, and the Volga was off, speeding down Tchaikovsky.

As they turned right toward the Moscow River, Richard Stevens checked behind one more time, and said, "Sorry about that, but the Soviet guards knew you were coming. They would never have allowed you into the embassy."

"You . . . you really are American?" asked Volodya.

Stevens reached into his coat and handed over his passport. He watched as the Russian noted his age, forty-seven, and that he was from Minneapolis. After the cryptologist compared Stevens' round, lined face and his curly brown hair to that in the photograph, he closed the book and nodded to the men in the front seat.

"What about them? *Oni Russkie.*" They're Russians.

"Yes, and they're CIA stringers." Stevens tapped the driver. "Turn onto a side street. Stay off the main roads."

Seeing Volodya's doubt, Stevens ordered the two Russians to produce their American pistols and their dollar-crammed wallets. Only when Stevens told Volodya how he intended to smuggle him into the embassy—hidden in a Chevrolet—did Volodya's doubt wane. At last the Russian produced his ticket to America, a two-page list of high-tech equipment—from the latest IBM mainframe computer to the revolutionary Cytel 10418 microchip—that the Soviets actively sought to procure.

Stevens studied the document, which read like a Christmas wish list.

"This is everything?"

*"Da."*

"You're sure?"

*"Da, da, da."*

"Good."

Stevens folded up the paper and slipped it into his coat. At the bottom of the pocket his fingers closed on a small metal disk, which could easily have been mistaken for a retractable measuring tape. It contained, however, a coiled, sharply notched wire that Stevens used for quite a different purpose.

"But let me warn you," continued the American as he released the metal disk and withdrew his hand, "our security people are going to search you, and if they find anything else—anything at all—that you've been keeping from us, you won't be going to the Big Apple. Instead, they'll dump you back on the streets of the Big Potato, naked right in front of the Lubianka."

More accustomed to dealing with codes than with people, Volodya's face flushed in panic. "That's it, I swear. I have nothing else. Nothing!"

Stevens glanced out the window of the moving car. "Except for one thing. The name of the Soviet agent who is to steal the specs of the GALA-1 computer."

"But . . . but . . ." mumbled Volodya as if he had just lost his last hope.

"You don't have the name written down anywhere?"

"No, but if—"

With chilling politeness, Stevens raised his hand and spoke further of the computer that was to run the space-weapons program.

"No, Volodya, don't tell me. My government desperately wants to identify that agent. So hang on to that name. Between you and me, you'd be a fool to tell any of my people before they take you to New York."

Volodya was stunned with gratitude. "Thank . . . thank

you, Mr. Stevens." A true Russian, he could not contain his emotion and, his down coat squishing and hissing, he reached over and affectionately squeezed the American's arm. "I have always liked the United States. You are a very wonderful people."

"I'm glad to hear that." Stevens slipped his hand back in his pocket. "Now, the Chevrolet's right up here. It won't be long."

The driver turned down an empty lane and pulled the Volga to a service gate at the rear of a two-story structure. A former merchant's house now used as offices, the structure was as dark as the night. Viktor, rubbing his smooth head, opened his door, headed directly to the large gates, unfastened a lock, and slipped inside. He reappeared within seconds and signaled.

"Thanks for the lift, Yuri," said Stevens to the driver. "Come on, Volodya. The Chevrolet's in there."

"And then to the embassy?"

Stevens smiled. "Well, you might not make the party, but . . ."

As the two men climbed out and walked to the partially opened gate, Richard Stevens sensed his pulse quickening. The most difficult part was over. He looked forward to the rest being simple, even pleasant.

Motioning Volodya through first, Stevens said, "After you, *droog nash.*" Our friend.

He followed Volodya through the gate and there, where troikas had once stood, was the Chevrolet Blazer. White with red stripes, the enormous vehicle sparkled in the dull night. Volodya's eyes brightened as if he had just set foot in Manhattan, and Stevens saw his chance.

Volodya cried out, "Oi, it's beauti—"

The notched wire arced like a jump rope as Richard Stevens threw it over Volodya's head. In the same movement, he jabbed his knee into the back of the down coat, then jerked on the wire with enough force to rein in a wild horse. The tiny teeth slit silently through the outer skin, then lodged in the gristle of Volodya's neck. Stevens, all his weight pulling the Russian against his knee, jerked his hands back and forth, and the wire sawed cleanly to the neck bone.

Volodya's interrupted words were followed by a rush of escaping air and, as if from a garden hose, a spray of blood. His body tensed, jerked, quivered with a million misfired nervous impulses, and his nearly decapitated head toppled back.

Stevens jumped aside and let gravity suck the body to the earth. Once the body was still and the blood had slowed, he bent over the red tangle of meat and muscle and gingerly inched the wire back and forth. By the time it was free and he had wiped it clean on the down coat, Viktor Petrov had returned with Yuri, the driver. Suspended between them was a large trunk, crude holes punched in its top and bottom.

The two Russian men, working as fast as Siberian fur trappers, opened the trunk and lifted the corpse into it. Once they had sealed the latches, they carried the container to the waiting Volga. Stevens kicked dirt over the bloody soil, then stepped through the crack in the gate.

As he closed the car's trunk, Viktor said, "Don't worry, it won't float and it won't be seen. The Moscow River is very muddy."

Stevens gave the KGB major a friendly pat on the shoulder and watched as the two Russians sped away in the Volga. Once the taillights had disappeared and all was quiet, he swung open the gates. He climbed into the driver's seat, started up the Blazer's engine, shifted into reverse, and pulled out.

As Richard Stevens drove off into the cool Russian night, he took a deep breath, then exhaled. It had been as close as he cared to come. They had apprehended the cryptologist just as he was about to defect and reveal the Soviet agent's name. But her identity was safe now that Volodya, the one unexpected development, had been eliminated.

The next step, of course, was for Viktor to proceed to Leningrad, where he would oversee the end of the first phase. The fabricated life story—her legend—that had taken years to develop, was almost complete; one of almost 300,000 Soviet Jews to leave the U.S.S.R., one of over 100,000 to head for America, she would be a mere drop in this third wave of emigration. The KGB had made certain, too, that she had been put through each painful step of emigration so that she'd personally experience the difficulties and anxieties of leaving. That would ensure that she would be beyond suspicion because she would appear nothing less than a young Jewish woman—with a background in computers—fleeing persecution.

There was just one last detail, complex but relatively simple to achieve: they had to make her want to spit upon Mother Russia. That's why her young son had become so important. Once they had forced her to leave without him, Stevens was confident Vera would loathe the country she would serve.

At that point her cover would be complete.

# Chapter 2

## Minneapolis

"Let me get this straight," he said, his voice already flat with acceptance. "You want me to spy on them."

A few years ago Nick Miller would have bristled with disgust and shot back an immediate no. He'd worked in the Soviet Union since then—as a guide for an American exhibition—and his life had nearly fallen apart there. The KGB had arrested and charged him with murdering the Russian woman he'd been dating.

"Yes, Mr. Miller," answered Theodore Hughes. "We would."

Nick ran his hand through his light brown hair. It was a habit similar to his inability to hide what he was thinking. Now his expressive, angular face was frowning.

"We?"

The FBI. That's who they were. And Nick was now exposed enough to the realities of the political world to know that this grandfatherly-looking man with the white hair and ruddy face had a file on him that was every bit as thick as the KGB's.

So when Hughes had telephoned several days before and asked to see him, Nick knew immediately that it was in regard to his present work. To satisfy his curiosity, he'd finally agreed to meet Hughes, and now they sat in a small room on the twentieth floor of the Government Center. The room, which had two chairs, a plain desk, and no windows, belonged to no one.

Theodore Hughes clasped his hands together, set them on the desk, and leaned forward. He had a disarming smile, one that left people grinning in his wake.

"Mr. Miller," he said. "We have a very serious problem. I came from Washington specifically to talk to you."

Nick, mad at himself for coming, said, "So talk."

"Very well. But this matter is quite confidential. I have to ask that you repeat our conversation to no one."

He looked away. "All right."

"We had a stringer in Moscow who was very helpful to us. His name was Volodya. He was a cryptologist at one of the ministries. A very smart young man who spoke English quite well. He approached one of our embassy personnel four months ago and delivered a complete list of American high-tech items the Soviets had stolen in the last year. Complete, dated, and, as far as we've been able to discern, accurate."

Nick looked at the floor. "Actually, I'm not sure I want to hear this. I had enough of this stuff in the *Soyuz.*" He used the slang term—Union—for the U.S.S.R.

"Please, just listen. Last month Volodya contacted us again. He spoke to the same person at the embassy and delivered another list. He said he'd also heard that plans were being made to obtain the documentation of, well ..." Hughes paused. "Let's just say something terribly advanced. Volodya also said that one of the new emigrants was an agent of the KGB. One of the Jewish emigrants coming to America this summer."

Nick looked up. "You mean here, don't you? Here, in Minneapolis? Shit, so that's what all this is about."

Nodding, the older man said, "It does make sense. This is the fourth, maybe third, largest concentration of technology in the country. The East and West coasts have had their run-ins with industrial espionage—they're a bit more protective now—but Minneapolis and St. Paul are, you might say, virgin territory."

"Yeah, pure and untouched," Nick said coldly.

Hughes continued. "Volodya, however, held on to a good deal of information. He thought the KGB was on to him, and he wanted to defect. He said he'd only tell us everything after we got him out of the U.S.S.R. Unfortunately, we didn't act soon enough. We have reason to believe that Volodya was on his way to the embassy when the KGB picked him up." Hughes shrugged and added, "A woman at the embassy saw a man answering Volodya's description being pulled into a car. So either Volodya is in jail or—"

"But you don't understand," interrupted Nick, his throat dry and his mind racing. "They're my clients, my friends too. You want me to . . . to watch them?"

"That's right. You're the only resettlement counselor at the Jewish Family Service who speaks Russian." Mr. Hughes stroked the other side of his mustache. "Not to mention the security clearance you received for the National Security Agency."

After he returned from the Soviet Union, Nick didn't know where to go, what to do, so he applied for the only job he could find requiring Russian. It was at the NSA writing reports on political articles in *Pravda*. He was offered the position immediately and was due to start as soon as he received security clearance. Then he'd heard about the job working with Soviet Jewish immigrants in Minneapolis and accepted that instead. Anything, he figured, was better than sitting in a cubicle on an American military base reading Soviet newspapers.

Nick slowly shook his head. "I don't like what I'm hearing. You see, I'm working for them, helping them get settled, not—"

"I want to emphasize that the theft of American technology is no small problem. Without doing any of the research and at a minimal expense, the Soviet Union is literally harvesting our computers, our microchips, our lasers . . ." He lowered his voice and it became more gentle than ever. "You're an intelligent young man. All we're asking is that you be our local eyes."

Nick was at a loss. He was bitter about the Soviet Union—as much for the false murder charges against him as for reducing their people to the lowest common denominator and then proclaiming Utopia. But wouldn't spying on Russian immigrants here mean that he had gone full circle?

"I . . . I don't get what this is all about. I mean, what's at stake? Video games or . . . or artificial hearts or . . . ?"

Hughes sat in silence, two fingers resting on his lips. Moments passed before he shifted in his chair.

"All right, I'll tell you, but again this is highly confidential and I must ask that you repeat this to no one."

Nick knew Hughes would have to tell him eventually. "What's going on?"

"This is confidential."

"Yeah, sure." All part of the game, Nick thought.

Hughes studied Nick's face, then said, "We have strong reason to believe the Soviet Union is after a new and extremely fast computer—the fastest ever built. It's called the GALA-1 and is to be the nervous system behind the space-weapons program. It's the first all-gallium arsenide supercomputer."

"What in the hell's gallium arsenide?"

"Silicon overheats and simply evaporates at the speed the Defense Department needs in a computer, but gallium arsenide doesn't. It's the basis for a new chip, six to eight times faster than silicon will ever be able to go."

"Wait a minute," said Nick, "I thought the space-weapons program was on hold or—"

"Everything's in negotiations with the Russians, and not even the President knows the final status. We're going ahead with the research, however, just to make sure we have the basic technology in place. You can't have a space-weapons program without something as fast as the GALA-1 to calculate missile trajectories. And six years ago the Defense Department awarded a secret contract to develop such a computer to Thomas Lichton, head and senior designer of DataResearch. A Minneapolis company."

Wishing he were anywhere but here, Nick said, "I don't like this. This really isn't my kind of—"

Hughes reached into his pocket. "Here's my card. Just think about it overnight. Then call me. You wouldn't have to do much. We just want to know about any odd behavior by immigrants—too much money, odd work habits, and so on."

Grabbing the card, Nick saw that there was no name on it, only a seven-digit telephone number. He shook his head, slid back his chair, and started for the door.

"We need your decision as soon as possible," said Hughes. "Will you call tomorrow?"

"I suppose."

"You realize, don't you, that we'll reimburse you?"

Nick froze with his hand only inches from the doorknob. "Excuse me?"

"We'll pay you for your time."

Dragging one hand through his hair, he swung open the door. "Oh no you won't. If I do it—and I wouldn't put your rubles on it—I'm not taking any money. The last thing I want to be is a paid informant of the FBI. You can give me an apple pie, perhaps, but *kapoosti—nyet.*" No cabbage.

# Chapter 3

## Leningrad

Vera Karansky wasn't surprised when the KGB began ruining her life, because she'd been thoroughly briefed. As soon as she applied to emigrate with her son and mother, she had expected the denunciation that took place at work and at home. She arranged to have extra money, too, because she'd been told she would lose her job as a computer systems analyst. Anticipating that she would also lose their small apartment, Vera found a room in a communal building. By the time they were forced to move, she had sold everything except what they could carry in four suitcases.

Vera, however, hadn't expected the pain to bite so deeply. She thought she knew the steps as well as any actress knew her role, thought she had rehearsed the scenes enough to know how they would end. Still she was shocked when friends refused to speak to her, was appalled at the bribes the customs officials demanded. And she had by no means anticipated the humiliation and depression, even though she guessed that, too, was exactly what the KGB wanted. In the end, she repeated like a chant, it would be worth all this.

Now, three lives were reduced to a few heaps in a room without furniture. Vera sat on the floor with her six-year-old son's head in her lap. It was almost time. Their luggage had already been taken to customs at the airport. After so many years of waiting they were about to leave for America. She had been told these last few hours were the most difficult. And they were.

Vladik yawned and rolled over, and Vera proudly admired his smooth round cheeks and shiny brown hair. She was doing this all for him, just as she had gladly divorced her husband for the boy's sake. Leaving was the most difficult decision she had ever faced, particularly since Luba, her mother who knew so little, would be so affected. Like most Soviet parents, however, Vera did not hesitate to sacrifice for her son. He was her future, the part of her that would live beyond, and he would have all that she could not.

Clutching the small yellow plastic ball in her hand to hide it from her mother, Vera rose and stepped over to the window. Outside, only the tops of the buildings were covered with the first of the spring sunshine; the streets below had yet to shake off the chill of the dark night.

"The taxi will be here any minute," said Vera, searching the street.

As she swung open the bare window, she caught sight of her reflection and quickly looked away. People used to think her slim face pretty. But in these last few months her dark complexion had lost its healthy glow, and her once rich brown hair had grown dry and dull. She had aged, too, new lines cutting across her face and causing her to appear much older than thirty-one. Most recently, her ulcer had flared up, which was why she had lost so many kilos.

Luba Volshevetz, Vera's mother, stood in the middle of the room, staring at nothing.

"My mother and I stayed right here in Leningrad when the Germans blockaded the city," mumbled the older woman. "Nine hundred days. Maria Tiponova and her little girl—they lived in the room right across the hall—starved to death. So did old Arkady next door. All the people in the building across the street were killed one spring night by a Fascist bomb. . . ."

She was a handsome woman, a bit shorter than her daughter, with a round face that had settled softly with age. Usually quick and bright, eager to please, she had recently grown withdrawn. She could not make sense of what was happening around her. Everything was crumbling. Four years ago her husband had died. Then, the month after Vera was fired, Luba lost her job as a chemical engineer. Two weeks ago she had lost the apartment where she had lived all of her married life and where she had raised her family. And today she was losing even this anonymous little room, her last foothold in her native city.

"Mama, please." Vera, concealing the plastic ball in her tight grip, went over and kissed her mother's cheek. Vera spoke of her older brother and his wife, who had left two years earlier. "Anatoly and Larissa are there, Mama. Think of them." She glanced down at her sleeping son. "Think of why we are going."

"You're right," said Luba, forcing a smile.

Vera started for the door. "Mama, I'll be right back."

She had to take care of the plastic ball—load its hollow core with the precious cargo, then hide it where no one could find it. The ball was the one thing she had not mentioned to anyone. Ignoring the strictest orders, Vera was determined to take it, despite the risks.

"I'm just going to the bathroom. Will you get Vladik up?"

"Yes. Of course. Vladik—my little hope."

As Vera hurried out and made for the common bathroom, someone dropped an iron pan on the stove. Vera, unaware that anyone else was up yet, nearly crushed the toy in her hand. A moment later a *babushka* poked her head out of the communal kitchen. When the grandmotherly woman saw Vera standing in the hall, she scowled and retreated. Vera continued on her way, stepping into the bathroom moments later.

Vera pulled the door shut behind her and was immediately filled with a sense of relief. She stood motionless for a moment, her hand on a towel rack, and when she was certain that all was quiet, she locked the door with its small metal hook. Only then did Vera open her hand. The yellow ball, several centimeters in diameter, sat in the middle of her palm, beads of sweat on its shiny surface. She turned and placed it carefully on the edge of the sink.

Vera tucked her thick dark hair over each ear and took a deep breath. There was very little time. She closed the curtains, then slipped off her shoes, lifted her beige skirt, and stepped into the large bathtub. She knelt by the drain and leaned over the edge. There was an open corner between the free-standing tub and the wall, and she reached into it. Blindly feeling the floor, she located the crack and jammed in her fingers. The board came loose at once and she pushed the wood aside.

A smile appeared on Vera's narrow face as her fingers reached into the hole. Wrapped in a sheet of *Pravda*, the package was there. She carefully lifted it out of the hiding place and climbed out of the tub. Her hands trembling, she peeled away layer after layer until she came to a core of tissue paper. She ripped that apart until she exposed the package's heart: a diamond ring.

Vera struck the diamond ring on the edge of the sink and the tiny sound rang in her ears. She froze. There didn't seem to be anyone in the hall. She struck the ring again. The diamond, which Vera had loosened weeks ago with pliers, came free from its setting. She placed the gem, quite generous in size, on the sink next to the ball.

Vera was tempted by the gold ring which had held the diamond. She admired it only for a moment, though, before climbing back into the tub and cramming it into the hole. Anything metal was simply too dangerous. Wondering if anyone would ever find the ring, she replaced the floorboards. Then she grabbed the newspaper, wadded it up, and jammed it behind some pipes.

She returned to the sink and snapped open the plastic ball. Not wasting any time, Vera dropped the diamond inside. She put the top half back on, and it shut with a reassuring click. Then she reached for the *Vazeleen*, still in the medicine cabinet where she had left it the night before. She opened the jar, dipped into it, and smeared the yellow ball with the petroleum jelly. When the container was covered, Vera hesitated only for a moment. She stared at the ball, then opened her mouth. She winced as she shoved it past her teeth and though the plastic was greasy and cold on the back of her tongue, Vera realized that it might be easier than expected.

The young woman took a deep breath, closed her eyes. She tried to swallow, but gagged slightly. Undaunted, she was about to try again when she heard heavy footsteps in the hall. She lunged for the faucet and turned the cold water on full blast. Leaning her head back, she inhaled and, every bit of conscious energy concentrated on the rear of her mouth and the top of her throat, she swallowed. The ball, pulled by her muscles, moved backward. The lubricant helped, and the container carrying the diamond slipped downward.

Suddenly, someone angrily jiggled the door handle, and Vera grabbed her throat and stroked it. Bit by bit the ball moved deeper and deeper—like a dead mouse being sucked into a snake's long body.

The stranger pounded at the door. Was it the *militsiya?* The KGB?

Unable to speak, Vera threw herself forward and filled her mouth with cold water. She drank and swallowed and drank. Grinning, she touched her throat and felt the ball proceed to shoulder level. A moment later, she sensed it at the top of her chest. Her throat churning and pulling, the next instant the container was gone. She had swallowed the diamond; her body had accepted it.

The pounding on the door continued. A thick fist beat against it in hard, steady movements. The door and hinges rattled under the force.

Vera turned and stared at the jiggling knob. It was the KGB. They'd found out. Panicking, she threw open the door. Outside, however, was not a battery of officials, but the old woman from the kitchen.

"Let me in," she shouted. "I have a bladder problem." Shoving Vera aside, the old woman barged through and headed directly toward the toilet. Pulling her dress up over her fat thighs, she scowled and said, "All three of you are Jews, aren't you? And you're leaving, aren't you, just like a pack of dirty traitors?"

"I . . . I—"

Something so sharp burned in Vera's stomach that a hot spasm shot all the way up her spine. A white flash burst in her eyes. She doubled over, wrapped her arms around her stomach. Then, biting her lip, she groped for the wall and forced herself up.

She had to get back to her son. She was doing this all for him.

## Chapter 4

*Minneapolis*

In his office at the Jewish Family Service, Nick tilted his chair back and crossed his feet on the metal desk. It was time to call Hughes and tell him what he'd decided.

He hadn't been able to clear his mind, to think of anything else since the meeting yesterday. How could he ask for the trust of these Russian immigrants—so confused, so lost—only to abuse that trust by informing on them? And what would happen in the office if they learned what he, the only non-Jew working there, was doing?

But his mind as clear and sharp as a Minnesota January sky, he said, "Damn it!" He was going to do it.

The FBI was going to poke around no matter what Nick did. With the computer behind the Star Wars system at stake, they were certain to capture the Soviet agent—if, indeed, he really existed. At what expense, though? He kept wondering what damage this would do to the immigrant community. All too easily he imagined the FBI trapping one of the city's most successful immigrants, arresting him, putting him on trial. With only two million people in the Twin Cities, the media exposure would probably rival the hoopla accorded Hubert Humphrey or Walter Mondale or temperatures lower than forty below. It'd be top news. And even though there were more high-tech companies around here than there were lakes, how many doors would be closed to the Russian immigrants if this scandal erupted?

It was the right thing to do, his love/hate relationship with the Soviet Union aside. He'd be, so to speak, the Russian community's rep. He'd steer the FBI away from clearly innocent immigrants and, if he had enough hard information, point out those who were suspicious. With his link, his daily contact with the Russian community, perhaps he could even get there first. Just maybe he could discover who the KGB had sent to steal the specs of the GALA-1 supercomputer. That might help diffuse the whole thing, keep it out of the papers. . . .

Abruptly, Nick's office door was thrown open. He bolted upright, spun around. In the doorway stood Nancy Adelman, another of the resettlement counselors. Her face was struck with panic.

"Nick, Roza Rozen's on line two. I can't understand a damn thing. She's just screaming in Russian!"

Aware that the excitement could mean anything from a broken toaster to a suicide attempt, he said, "Okay, I got it." He'd call Hughes in a few minutes.

"Line two. Hurry!" cried Nancy, hovering behind him.

He picked up the phone, punched a button, and, in Russian, said, "Hello, Roza, it's me. Nick. What's the matter?"

"Oi, Nick, oi! I . . . I, oh, no!" screamed the voice from the other end. "My little brother's a very good mechanical engineer. Very, very good. But no one in America knows this. So he works driving a school bus. A good engineer and thirty-eight years old and he's driving a bus. Oh, *Bozhe moi!*" My God. *"Bozhe moi!* My dear Misha!"

"Roza, what is it? What's happened to Misha? Is your husband there? Let me talk to him."

Through the tears, she mumbled, "Pavel's working." Then she screamed as if she'd been struck.

"Roza, are you there? Speak to me!" demanded Nick.

To his side, Nancy asked, "What is it? What happened?"

"I don't know. She won't stop crying." In Russian, he firmly said, "Roza, what's the problem? Tell me what's the matter."

"He was supposed to get medical insurance! He was supposed to get it . . . next week. Just next week. He came over without his family. They were supposed to come later. You see, they forced him to leave by himself. That's why they were divorced."

"Roza," begged Nick, "what happened?"

"His wife and two children are still there. But his wife lost her job because he left. Fired, kicked out all because of him! So all of us—Misha, my husband, and me—sent all our money to his family. Everything!" She broke down sobbing.

"What?" It didn't make any sense. There was no way to send money to the Soviet Union. "You sent money?"

"Yes, everything. She lost her job because he left and she has two little children. So we sent every last dollar! Oi, no, my Misha! My baby brother!" she wailed.

"Roza! Roza, stop crying and tell me what happened. I want to help, but I must know the problem."

"Last . . . last night," she said, her voice torn and quick, "was the first one. He had the first attack about midnight."

Oh, shit, thought Nick. "Attack?"

"Yes, about midnight. But he said he was all right. You know, doctors are so expensive here. So . . . so much money! And we just sent all our money to his family. We . . . oi, my poor Misha!"

Nick turned to Nancy, who was hovering over him. "Her brother had some sort of attack!"

"Oh, my God." Nancy put her hand to her forehead and started out of the room. "He had a heart murmur. I'm calling an ambulance." She ran to a phone at the front desk.

"Roza, Roza, are you there?" he pleaded to the crying woman. "Please, talk to me."

"Misha said not to take him to the hospital because hospitals are so expensive in America! Oi, this would never have happened back home. Medicine is free in Russia!" She paused, her breathing heavy and erratic. "My husband and I made him lie right on the couch. I stayed awake all night. And then he was fine when my husband went to work this morning." She screamed with grief. "I stayed awake until nine this morning . . . and I fell asleep. Nick, where's my husband? You must find Pavel!" Her wailing became so loud that Nick had to hold the receiver away from his ear. "I just woke up. And my brother—dear God, he had another attack! And . . . and . . ."

Nancy rushed back into the room and grabbed Nick by the arm. "What's going on? Did he have a heart attack?"

Nick pushed Nancy away. All his attention was focused on Roza and what she was trying to say. And then he heard it all. He dropped his arm, receiver in hand. He rubbed his eyes, unable to believe it.

"Jesus Christ," he moaned. "It's too late for an ambulance. Roza Rozen's brother had two heart attacks. The first one, about midnight, didn't kill him. The second one, sometime this morning, did. They didn't go to the goddamned hospital because they were broke. She said they sent all their money to Misha's family in the Soviet Union. How the hell did they do that and why in hell didn't they just go to a hospital, money or not? Shit, shit, shit! Roza's sitting on the couch, latched on to her dead brother."

Shocked and disgusted, Nick spun his chair to the side and stared out the window. A man's life had been wasted simply because his family had passed from one enemy to the other, from communist to capitalist. The Rozen family had discovered, too, what Americans couldn't comprehend or just didn't want to hear: life in the United States wasn't necessarily the best in the world.

Well, thought Nick, he for one was going to make sure it wasn't any harder for the immigrants than it had to be. He was going to find the single rotten potato in the bunch.

# Chapter 5

## Leningrad

Leaning against the cold stone wall, Gennady felt the morning chill seep into his back. He was glad for it because the cold made his large body shiver, and the shivering kept him awake. He hadn't slept all night, nor the night before, and a stubbly beard covered his round cheeks. He sucked on the *papirosa*, its bitter smoke the only thing that had nourished him for days.

The dull sound of an engine filled his ears. The sound grew louder and ricocheted up and down the treeless streets. His dark brown eyes searched from side to side. Then, from around the corner of the building, came the splash of a car racing through a puddle.

His foot propped up against the stone building, Gennady pushed himself forward. He threw his cigarette to the ground, stuffed his hands in his wool coat, and knew that the moment had finally come.

Gennady felt far older than his thirty-six years. His body ached as he took two quick steps and reached the corner of the building. To his right and down the street, he watched a light green taxi stop in front of the apartment building. Now, every bit of Gennady's concentration was focused on who would come out of that building. He cursed himself for not having a camera, then bit his lower lip, determined to make a mental tattoo of what he was about to see.

Gennady stood there staring down the faintly lit street. To his shock, he could plainly see that no one was coming out of the building. The taxi, exhaust sputtering into the damp air, honked. Still no one came. Gennady tensed. Had the plans changed?

Suddenly, the building's door opened. The figures of two women and a small boy burst out, faint and blurry from this distance. Their movements frantic, they rushed down the three steps to the waiting taxi. The younger woman threw open the car door and shoved the child into the back seat. The woman swung several bags next to the boy, climbed in herself, then reached out for her mother. Her movements fast yet stiff, the older woman stepped in. Before her door was even shut, the taxi was off. Going not quite fast enough to make the tires squeal, the sedan disappeared around the first corner.

Gennady took a step forward, reached out after the rapidly fading sound of the taxi. Tears in his eyes, he called out after the most precious thing in his life.

*"Ceenok moi."* My little son.

Gennady didn't know how long he stumbled along and he didn't care. Weaving his way down the stark streets, along the banks of the Neva, over the Palace Bridge, across the windswept Palace Square, along the Moika Canal, all he could think of was Vladik. Gennady had done everything he could, yet still he had lost him, still she had taken him. He hated Vera in a way he never thought possible.

What seemed like hours later, he found himself back on Nevsky Prospekt. People on their way to work filled the buses and trolleys to capacity, then spilled out onto the sidewalk. Using the last of his energy, he pushed through the crowds and cut down a series of side streets. Soon he found himself standing in front of his apartment building.

Making his way inside, he was overwhelmed by exhaustion. When he was a child, after holding and holding it, he had wet his pants just as he reached the bathroom door. And now, so close to sleep, he didn't know if he had the strength to climb the three flights of stairs. How many hours since he had last closed his eyes? Forty-eight? Fifty? Sixty? His legs were suddenly too tired to move, and hanging on to the banister, he pulled himself up one step at a time. By the time he reached the top, beads of sweat were popping up all over his brow and everything in his vision seemed to float from left to right, from right to left.

To reach his small room, he had to walk the long hall and cut through the kitchen. He passed the refrigerator, then, his eyes on the floor, bumped into a girl heating water for tea. When he entered the narrow corridor which led to his room, he raised his head and saw that his door was open. A lamp was on. Glinting in the light was a shiny leather boot, just the tip of it visible.

He grinned and pushed open the door. He thought they wouldn't come.

"What's your name, Comrade KGB?" asked Gennady.

The man, dressed in a long leather coat, sat on the wooden chair.

"Major Viktor Petrov," said the handsome, balding man as he rose.

Gennady leaned against the door frame, exhausted but victorious. "Is this in regard to . . . ?"

"Your son, Vladik, of course. You didn't think we heard that you were opposed to letting the boy leave, did you?"

Gennady tried to think, tried to speak. "No, I—I didn't."

"Well, we did and we're on your side. And we intend to do something about it."

Major Petrov crossed the room in two swift steps and gently took Gennady by the arm.

Unable to hide his concern, the major said, "Comrade, when did you last sleep?"

"I . . . I . . ." said Gennady, unable to make any sense.

"Don't worry. Just relax, I have everything under control. You'll have your son back just as you wished." The KGB major shoved up his coat sleeve and showed Gennady his smoothly ticking Swiss watch. "You see, their plane hasn't left yet."

# Chapter 6

Leaving the outskirts of Leningrad behind, Vera focused on the red sign plastered on the side of the bridge: GLORY TO THE DECISION OF THE COMMMUNIST PARTY! The taxi whizzed beneath, and Vera turned around. The sign on the other side read: GLORY TO LENIN!

Let us be gone, thought Vera. Let us be out of here. There was so much ahead waiting to be done.

She wrapped her arm around Vladik, and the boy snuggled up to her. On the other side of her son, Luba sat engulfed in her winter coat with the fur collar because it could not be crammed into the one carry-on.

Breaking the silence, the taxi driver glanced in the mirror and said, "Kike faces. All three of you got 'em."

Vera gently slid her hands over her son's ears.

"That's what you are, huh? Kikes. A bunch of kikes going to America?"

Something burned in her stomach. She clutched her waist.

"Well, you're going to America, aren't you?" said the driver, a curious grin on his face. "Leaving the Motherland and going to America?"

"No." She clung to the story she was told to repeat no matter what happened. "We have family in Israel. First-degree relatives in Jerusalem. We are going there to be reunited with them and with our natural Jewish homeland: Israel."

"Ah, fuck your mother!" The driver laughed.

She let her eyes fall shut. Focus on the pain in your stomach, she told herself. That man is not KGB. He is a simple man. He has to be. And he's not interfering. He's just voicing his simple mind.

When she opened her eyes again, the taxi was pulling up to the second level of the airport terminal. The driver stopped in front of the Intourist office, the Soviet organization that oversaw foreign visitors and foreign travel.

"Mama," said six-year-old Vladik, sitting up, "are we going on the plane now?"

"We're at the airport, but we're not going on the plane for a few more hours." They had to be there four hours before the ten o'clock flight. "Soon, dear, soon." Vera kissed him on the forehead.

Luba opened the door and climbed out. Wordless, she stood on the curb in her winter coat, the warm morning sun on her back.

"You go to Baba Luba, dear, while I pay the driver."

Vladik crawled across the seat and got out, taking his grandmother's hand and huddling against her.

The taxi driver turned around and, with a sly grin, said, "Oh, silly me. I forgot to turn on the meter."

"You what?" Vera lurched forward. The meter was blank.

"I forgot to turn on the meter. But we can settle this nice and friendly," he said, as if he had planned it all along. "We don't want to cause a problem, do we? There's no need for the police. Let's see, why don't we just call it . . ."

Her eyes met his as if they were in a bread store about to choose the same loaf. At once, the cab driver lowered his head and shook it.

"Ah, forget it," he said, ashamed of himself. "Just go and be happy."

"You . . . you mean . . ."

"There's no charge." An idea came to him and he looked up. "Wait, yes there is. You can repay me by . . . by telling everyone in the West that we don't want war. We want peace. We are not a country of warmongering capitalists. All we want to do is live in peace." He turned around and, raising a finger, said, "But we will fight back."

"Yes, yes, I'll tell everyone."

Quickly, before the man changed his mind, Vera grabbed her purse and carry-on bag and made her way out of the taxi. What people said was true. Russia was a country that made good people better and bad people worse.

As the taxi drove off, Vera, her son, and her mother headed into the terminal. Bowing her head for an instant, Vera wondered how Jews prayed.

Over three hours later they were still seated on a vinyl couch in the Intourist waiting area when a group of Italians—loaded down with balalaikas, samovars, and other souvenirs from the hard-currency store—burst in like a gust of air. The foreigners, given special treatment as always, were whisked through customs and onto the plane.

The very sight of them, though, filled Vera with fear. This wasn't right, she thought. Emigrants had to be there so early because they were supposed to go through customs before the foreigners. That way the foreigners were inconvenienced as little as possible; they could arrive, proceed directly through customs, and then board the plane. The emigrants, along with the rest of the country, waited on for-

## THE RED ENCOUNTER

eigners. Not the other way around. This was wrong. The Italians were now on the plane, ready to take off for the West, yet she and Vladik and Luba hadn't even gone through customs.

Vera glanced at her hands, which glistened with sweat. Turning to her mother, she said, "We'll go any minute, any minute now. I'm sure that—" Sharp pain. She leaned forward and grabbed her stomach.

Luba's eyes opened wide. "What is it? Are you all right?"

Vera forced herself to sit up. "Y—yes. I'm . . . I'm fine. It's just my ulcer, Mama. I'm fine."

"You're too thin. You need to eat," said Luba, glancing about nervously. "I'll go get some food."

"No, I'm fine. We must stay together."

Suddenly there was a pair of high leather boots right in front of her. Vera looked up. A tall border patrol soldier stood before her.

"Soviet planes do not wait for Jews," said the lieutenant.

Vera gasped. She knew this man. She had gone—yes, that was it—they had been in school together. They had only been fourteen or fifteen, but she recognized him. He was the one who always received top grades. What was his name?

"I . . . I . . ."

"Everyone is on board except you," said the rugged, blond man.

Vera was paralyzed with confusion. He recognized her; she could tell by his laughing blue eyes. So what was the KGB trying to do? What game were they playing? And why now, after so many months of careful planning?

She stared up at him and it came to her. "Sergei . . ." Yes, that was his name.

For a moment he seemed fifteen again. Young, idealistic, an overachiever, and naïve, just as she had been. That passed quickly, however, unlike the years since he and Vera had been in school together.

At the sound of his name, the soldier stepped aside, smiling as if he knew exactly what lay ahead.

Waving them on, he said, "Your luggage is already aboard the plane. You may proceed to customs. Have a nice trip."

Full of distrust, Vera rose slowly. This was not going as smoothly as it should, and all the horror stories flooded her mind. X rays, body searches, arrests, Siberia—was this what they had planned for her as well? No, it couldn't be. The KGB was just trying to frighten her, show her what they could do, impart what it meant to leave the Soviet Union.

Still, she couldn't be certain. She stood and took Vladik's hand as tightly as if she were holding him above an abyss. They must not be separated.

"Come along, Mama. Put your coat on. We're going to Vienna."

Leaving the soldier, who laughed aloud, Vera led the way into the next room. She towed Vladik by his hand, and Luba scurried after them.

"Mama, that hurts!" said Vladik, trying to loosen his mother's grip.

Vera glanced up at the clock. It was 9:45.

*"Nado spesheet."* We have to hurry.

They entered the customs area, a stark and poorly lit room, and proceeded directly to one of the low tables. A stout, orange-haired woman stood gossiping with the young soldier at the passport desk.

"Comrades!" shouted Vera. "We have a plane to catch!"

The woman glanced over at Vera, eyed her in disbelief, then turned back to the young soldier and whispered in his ear. They burst out laughing. A moment later the woman approached Vera.

"A plane to catch, eh?" she said, picking at her teeth with a bright red fingernail.

The customs woman took the carry-on bag and set it on the scales. When the weights had settled, she shook her head and frowned.

"Now, isn't that a shame!" This was how the woman afforded a car and a color television. "Sorry, but it's a half-kilo over."

Vera glanced at the clock: 9:47. Thirteen minutes until the flight left. She had to do something to make the woman hurry. Then she spotted her mother's coat.

"Mama, turn around."

Luba, her face red and beaded with perspiration, put her fingers to her mouth. "Wh—what?"

"I'm sorry, Mama. . . ."

Vera grasped her mother and forced her around. She then tugged at the coat's fur collar. Nothing. She pulled again. Stitches popped. Then she pushed on Luba's back with one hand and pulled on the fur collar with the other. Finally the collar came free of the coat.

Luba bent forward and buried her face in her hands. *"Bozhe moi!"*

Vera threw the hide at the customs woman. "There, take it, it's yours. A half-kilo doesn't make any difference and you know it."

The woman picked up the fur and examined it as if it were a dirty sock. She shrugged and tossed it under her table.

"All right, the weight's not so bad, but I have to still see what's inside." To Luba, she motioned with her head toward a side door. "You can go in there."

Vera knew what the room was for. "It's okay, Mama. They're going to search you, but we'll make the plane. Just hurry, okay?"

Luba didn't move. Sweat drenched her face, plastering silvery curls of hair to her temples. She stroked the place on her torn coat where the fox collar had been.

Vera glanced at the clock: 9:50. "Mama, go!"

When she saw her mother enter the room, Vera dumped the carry-on bag on the metal table. She spread the contents out in plain view.

"Everything's all right," said Vera, growing frantic. "We are taking nothing illegal." She searched the room for someone to whom she could report this woman.

The woman pawed through it. "What about this book? If it was printed before the war, you can't take it."

"Nineteen forty-eight," snapped Vera.

"How many cameras? Only two per family."

"We have one. Just one." Vera shoved her hand out. On one finger was her thin wedding ring, which she planned to sell in the West. "And this is the only piece of gold we have.

I'm allowed to take two hundred and fifty rubles' worth of gold, but this cost only a hundred."

Suddenly peal after peal of robust laughter filled the entire area. Vera, recognizing it, covered her mouth.

"Mama!" she muttered.

Uncontrolled and as loud as could be, Luba's hysterical laugh rang out from the small side room.

Vera slipped the ring off her finger and threw it at the woman.

"It's yours!" She turned to her son. "Help me, Vladik. Quickly."

The woman caught the ring, slipped it into her pocket, then sauntered back to the young soldier at the passport desk.

Vera and Vladik snatched up their belongings. They crammed the camera, the book, wallet, and loaf of black bread into the carry-on bag as Luba's howls filled their ears. When they finished loading the bag it was 9:53.

"Come on!"

Vera grabbed the carryon and took Vladik by the hand. They ran to the side room, Vera terrified of what she would find. They reached the room and she threw open the door.

"Oh, God!"

Luba, shaking with shrieks of laughter, sat on a chair. Her undergarments were rolled down to her knees and her dress was hiked up to her waist. Her legs were spread wide, and a female doctor in a white robe had her right hand in Luba's vagina. Peering over the doctor's shoulder were two young soldiers and their superior.

Vera grabbed Vladik and shielded his eyes.

The doctor pulled her rubber-gloved hand out. "Nothing, Comrade colonel."

The officer turned to Vera. "Just checking for contraband."

Tears welled in Vera's eyes. "Our ... our plane. Please!"

He smiled. "How about you? Carrying anything? Or your son—what about him? X rays, metal detection, or, as you can see, a bodily search." He paused. "Any of that necessary?"

"No! No!" shouted Vera.

Luba fell silent. She looked down at herself in disbelief, then reached for her stockings.

"I saw you clutching your stomach," taunted the colonel. "Did you eat anything unusual? Some gold perhaps? We could run you through the metal detector or X-ray you."

Vera panicked. "No, no, I have an ulcer. An ulcer, and it's burning a hole through my stomach." She crudely wiped her eyes. "Why are you doing this? Why? Please, just let us go!"

The colonel turned to one of the soldiers. "Help the old woman to the plane." To Vera, he said, "Give your mother her Israeli visa and her plane ticket. The soldier here will help her. Don't worry, you'll join her. I'm afraid, though, we must check you first."

Trying to convince herself that she had nothing to worry about, Vera said, "Yes, of course."

Luba pulled up her undergarments, stood, and lowered her dress. Her face was pale, her look vacant, as she turned to Vera for guidance.

"Mama, go with the soldier. He'll help you to the plane." Vera handed her mother her ticket and documents. "Vladik and I will be right behind you. Get your coat."

Luba passively reached for her coat and started after the soldier. She took a few slow steps, then stopped in the doorway.

"*Vladichka, dorogoi,*" my dear, she said as if she would never see him again.

"It's all right," snapped Vera. "We're right behind you."

Luba silently turned and followed the soldier, disappearing around a corner.

The colonel said, "Won't you step in, please."

Vera led Vladik into the cool, white room. There were two chairs, a table, and a door on the other side of the room.

"Vera," said the colonel, pointing to a side wall, "please step over there. Leave the child here."

She grasped her son's hand more firmly. "But . . ."

"Step against the side wall, Vera," he demanded. He then motioned to the younger soldier. "This is a very fine member of the border guard and he's going to search you."

"But . . ." That would be the end, she was certain of it. "Must we use force?"

Accepting her powerlessness, she bent down to her son. "Vladik, dear, I'll just be right there, only a few meters from you." She began to loosen her grip. "You wait right here, with the carry-on bag, and then we'll go to the plane."

Vera embraced her son, smoothed his hair, and kissed him on the crown of his head. Terrified that they somehow knew what lay in her stomach, she could not tear herself away.

"To the wall!" demanded the soldier.

Holding her arms close to her sides and not taking her eyes off her son, Vera crossed the room. She began to shake. Luba, Vladik, and she were all now separated.

"Turn around!" ordered the guard. "Raise your hands and lean against the wall."

"I . . . I don't have anything. Honestly."

The guard took her by the arm and threw her up against the wall. His hands were thick and hard, and Vera felt them dig into her body as he forced her into position. Leaning forward, her palms were flat against the wall, her legs spread. Abruptly, the soldier began working his hands over her body. He rummaged through her hair, then, almost as if he were going to choke her, wrapped his fingers around her neck. He squeezed her shoulders until he felt a bone. Satisfied that it was not an implant of some sort, he moved on.

"Mama . . ." cried the young Vladik from behind.

Vera bit her lip, then spoke. "It's okay, Vladichka." If only she didn't have to be so strong. "It's okay." She began to turn.

The guard shoved her face back toward the wall. "Don't move! Don't turn around!"

As his hands moved lower they became more sensitive, more probing. First he quickly reached into her armpits. When he came to her small breasts, he cupped them and lingered. He was not much interested in her back, but found delight in her taut belly. His hands drifted lower and caressed her through her cotton dress. Moaning into her ear so that no one else could hear, he rubbed his hand up and down, then pressed his pelvis against her buttocks.

Her fingers turned to claws and she dragged them down the wall. She bit her lip, almost cutting through it, and she screamed over and over in her mind. She concentrated on the acid burning in her stomach and not on whether or not the soldier would rape her or whether they knew about the diamond.

"Mama . . . Mama . . ."

Something was wrong. She recognized it in her child's tight, high-pitched voice, and she tried to look over her shoulder.

"Don't turn around!" The soldier took her head in his hand and forced it back to the wall.

But her instinct was stronger. The minute the soldier loosened his grip, she twisted her head.

"No!" screamed Vera. "Leave him alone!"

The colonel had taken hold of her son and was pulling him out of the room.

"Mama!" cried the child, bursting into tears.

"Quiet!" ordered the soldier, grabbing Vera.

Vera kicked the soldier in the shin, then elbowed him in the stomach.

"What are you doing with my son? Bring him back!"

She spun around and tried to break away. The soldier grabbed her from behind, pinning her arms back. She jerked herself from side to side, kicked, and screamed.

Vladik followed his mother's example, and struggling, cried, "Mama, where's he taking me?"

"Vladik!"

Wrapping his arms around Vladik, the colonel picked him up and effortlessly tucked him under his arm. He headed toward the side door, and with each step the distance grew between mother and son.

"Mama!"

"Vladik, Vladik!" She shook her head, thrashed from side to side. "No! No, don't take my child!"

Her mouth opened in a single shrill cry, and she understood why the foreigners had been boarded first. That way there was no one to hear. No one except Soviets, and no Soviet would dare risk question or intervene in what the authorities were doing.

"Bring my baby back!"

The colonel turned to Vera. "You must not act so. I'm sorry for this, but it has been decided."

"What? What are you talking about? You can't do this!" But they were. They were taking her child away. "No!"

The next instant the Russian stepped through the rear door. First Vladik's head disappeared through the opening. Then his waist. And finally, kicking and squirming, his small legs.

Vera exploded. "No!"

And the last she heard was Vladik's muffled "Mama!"

The door swung shut. Her child was gone, ripped away from her.

"No!"

The border guard still had her pinned from behind. She heaved her head back, smashing it into the man's face. When his grip loosened, she twisted and broke loose.

"I want my child!"

Her knuckles pointed outward, she whipped her hand into the soldier's eyes.

"Bitch!" he muttered, trying to shield himself.

The soldier lunged for her, but just as he was about to grab her, the rear door opened once again. The colonel returned, escorted by two more soldiers, who moved directly toward Vera and calmly took her by each arm.

Not resisting, Vera said, "I want my child. I'm not leaving without him. I was told I could take him, they said I could—"

"Vera, you no longer belong to this country. You are an Israeli citizen. But the child is ours, a Soviet. He is staying behind."

"No, he's—"

"Comrade," said the officer with cool military precision, "the child is being reunited with his father."

"Wh—what? But the court gave me custody."

"I'm sorry, but evidently the father appealed and the court reversed its decision."

"Gennady did that? No! That's impossible!" She began to twist. "The bastard. I won't let him have Vladik, I won't give up my son!"

The colonel turned to the door and shouted, "Doctor!"

"No," pleaded Vera as she struggled. "Just give me back my son."

The doctor in the white robe returned, carrying her black bag. From the kit she pulled a sparkling clean syringe.

Vera knew what it was for. "I'll . . . I'll stay. I'll stay for my son. I won't go. Just give me back my little boy."

The officer no longer paid attention to Vera. He nodded to the soldiers, who flattened her against the wall and straightened out one of her arms.

"No, no!" said Vera, writhing as they forced up her sleeve. "Please, no!"

The senior soldier nodded to the doctor, who stepped forward in silence. She held the needle upward, a clear liquid beading from its pointed tip. The doctor swabbed Vera's arm, then brought the needle down and into Vera as if she were inserting a car key into an ignition.

Vera screamed. "No, you fascists! No!"

"Hold her still," demanded the doctor, "before she breaks the needle!"

"Comrade," said the colonel in a fatherly voice as he stepped toward her, "you already feel the effects of the drug. It will make you sleep. Don't worry, your belongings will be put on board the plane. Your mother is there, in a window seat. She has been given a sedative, too, and is already asleep. Just relax. These soldiers will put you comfortably on the plane. And don't worry about your son. He'll be all right. Trust me. I'm a grandfather. I will personally make sure the boy is promptly returned to his father."

Vera could no longer hold herself upright. Her bones were melting and a black fog was seeping through her mind.

"My . . . my little Vladik," said Vera, her head toppling forward. "I did . . . this all for . . ."

As she slipped away, she heard the colonel say, "Vera . . . Vera, listen to me. You will know your contact by these two words: American roulette."

# Chapter 7

## Minneapolis

After Theodore Hughes received security clearance at the front desk of DataResearch's Minnesota Valley lab, a guard wearing a striped rugby shirt, jeans, and running shoes led him through a door and to the lone elevator. The guard then pressed his right thumbprint on a magnetic pad, and the elevator, checking and clearing the fingerprint, eased open.

As they descended, the security guard said, "Tommy's lab is four stories below ground. No windows. Nothin'. It's easier to cool the computers that way, security's easier, and Tommy likes the quiet. That guy can't think if there's so much as a digital clock whirling. The bottom two floors are all his."

Hughes watched the numbers light up. "Interesting."

The elevator settled on the bottom floor and the doors opened. Hughes stepped into an empty ten-by-fifteen-foot room lit by an overhead panel of fluorescent tubes. Somewhere down here was the hermit-genius who was developing the world's fastest computer.

Behind him, from inside the lift, the guard said, "Have fun."

"Hey, wait a minute," said Hughes, spinning around. "Where's Mr. Lichton?"

As the elevator doors shut, the guard shouted, "Just press the button over by that door. Only, when you go in, don't leave the door open for more than fifteen seconds or the main alarm will go off."

Hughes shook his head. Yesterday he'd gone to Data-

# THE RED ENCOUNTER

Research's downtown headquarters to ask for their cooperation, but Lyle Johnson, the chief executive officer, said Tommy was the only one to give permission of that sort. Hughes hoped the trip would be worth it.

Just to the side of the door was a large plate-glass window which opened into a computer room. A small, rectangular machine sat in the center of the room, and what appeared to be a workman—in a plaid shirt and corduroys—stood by an open panel. Actually, the man, who looked to be in his early fifties, could have passed as easily for a plumber as he could for Tommy Lichton, airplane fanatic and creator of the GALA-1.

Hughes pushed the button and through the window saw the startled man jump and drop his wrench. Irritated, he stepped over to a table and pushed an intercom button.

"What is it?" came the voice over a speaker.

"My name is Theodore Hughes and I'm—"

The door buzzed and Hughes grabbed for the handle. He stepped quickly through the security door, pulling it shut behind him. It was a large space, cool and well lit. White panels covered the floor, the walls, the ceiling. Immediately in front of him was a row of magnetic tape drives, waist high and filling the entire corner. Along the other wall was a series of keyboards and black video display terminals. Filling the other end of the room were another twenty or so magnetic disk drives, behind which were a dozen IBM mainframe computers.

"Excuse me," said Hughes to the man, who had disappeared behind the computer. "But are you—"

"Just a minute," came the quick response.

"Yes, of course."

His hands folded behind his back, Hughes patiently made his way into the middle of the room and studied the small machine. About the size of a large aquarium, through several windows on its side Hughes could see a variety of indiscernible components fully submerged in a bubbling liquid.

On the far side of the machine, the workman had removed a portion of the flooring and was reaching to some wires beneath. He tapped away at something, and Hughes moved around and saw the man's corduroy-covered legs and stocking feet stretched out on the floor.

"Excuse me," said Hughes, "but I'm just looking for—"

"One second," he said.

The man pulled a wire free then hopped to his feet. He threaded the wire upward, then inched a book-size metal plate out of the machine.

"There. These cooling plates are a real pain." The man stepped around and handed it to Hughes. "Heavy, huh? Gallium arsenide chips don't put out as much heat as silicon, but cooling's still a problem. Hi, I'm Tommy."

Hughes accepted the microchip-covered copper plate with one hand and with the other reached out in a handshake.

"Uh, Theodore Hughes, FBI. Thank you for your time."

With a pleasant, boyish smile, Lichton said, "I don't know why Lyle sent you all the way out here—except to cover his ass. Sure, you can do whatever you want just so long as no one comes tromping down here."

This wasn't the type of person Hughes had pictured as the creator of the world's fastest and most capable computer. He had imagined someone much shorter, with a chalkish complexion and thick glasses. Here, instead, was a tall, fit man with dark wavy hair and a deep tan.

"But are you aware of everything it would entail? Did Mr. Johnson inform you of the details?"

Tommy reached for the cooling plate, nodded, and turned. Hughes followed him to a side table.

"Something was wrong with one of the chips on this plate," said Lichton, putting it down and reaching for another. "See, this is one of the gallium arsenide chips. Know anything about it?"

Hughes smiled and tried to look intelligent. "A bit."

"It's pretty interesting. Made from gallium and arsenic. It's not a metal, but it's not a nonmetal, either. That's what makes it a semiconductor, of course, and because of its atomic structure it's much faster than silicon. Won't heat up and evaporate like silicon, either."

"Yes, I see," said Hughes, peering at the small, fingernail-size chips attached to the copper plate. "Of course. And it just slips right into the computer, the GALA-1. That's it right there, eh?"

"You bet." As if he were recounting his own child's grades, he added, "It has a four-thousand-gate logic and is capable of doing twenty-five billion floating operations per second. The clock rate—the rate at which it accesses information—is two hundred picoseconds."

Hughes couldn't hide his confusion. "A . . . a picosecond?"

"You know, a trillionth of a second."

"Yes, of course." Smiling, he said, "I guess that's why they call this a supercomputer."

Yet he found it hard to believe that this box of a machine was to be both the brains and the reflex system behind the space-weapons system.

"It's so . . . so small," said Hughes, unable to hide his awe.

Tommy glanced over at the GALA-1. "Of course. The chips are packed in there as close as they can go. The tighter the fit, the less wire. The less wire, the less distance the electrical signals have to go. The result: a much faster computer."

Hughes' white eyebrows rose upward. "I . . . I see."

Tommy returned to the computer with the new cooling plate. He lifted aside some wires and carefully slid in the copper panel.

"These things are pretty useful, nuclear missiles aside," he added a bit defensively. "Weather forecasting has thousands of variables and you need something lightning fast like the GALA to run the calculations. Several oil companies are using them to analyze oil reserves too. They're just real handy when it comes to simulating complex natural phenomena."

"So I understand." Hughes shifted from one leg to the other. He had to get Lichton's concrete approval. "Mr. Johnson did tell you what we want to do?"

"Sure."

"And it's all right with you if we go ahead? He fully explained it all?"

Tommy stopped jiggling the plate and stared up at the ceiling.

"He told me someone's trying to get the specs for the GALA—the Russians supposedly. You want to use one of our computers as bait and secretly arrange for their agent to have access to it. As he tries to break into it, you film him and then arrest him. I guess, too, you want to make a big media splash—put the spy on trial and so on to show the country how the Russians are stealing our best technology." He shrugged. "Sounds fine to me."

Hughes opened his eyes wide. "Good. Very good."

"The only thing I told Lyle is that I don't want to be bothered with any of it. I've got a lot of work. He said our security guy—what do they call him?" He laughed and rubbed his forehead. "That's it. The director of corporate relations. I forget his name. He's a tall guy with curly hair."

"Yes, I've spoken with him and he's to handle everything from your end."

"Well, just as long as he takes care of it and as long as you use another computer. . . ."

"The one at your downtown software-research building has been suggested."

"There you go. Then it's all fine. Simple."

"Yes," said Hughes, forcing a hesitant smile. "And I thank you."

Tommy took out a pocket watch, glanced at it, and groaned.

"Now, if you'll excuse me, I have to get back to work so I can get out of here. I've almost finished building my new airplane. Only don't tell anyone that because Lyle and every DataResearch board member has a shit fit every time I go flying."

"I'm sure." And with good reason, thought Hughes as he extended his hand. If Tommy were to crash, the company probably would too. "Our thanks again."

They shook hands and Hughes, unable to hide his satisfaction, hurried out of Thomas Lichton's underground lab. Everything was going as well as could be expected. DataResearch's security man—or as they referred to him, the director of corporate relations—had been cooperating for some months already. A former CIA agent by the name of Richard Stevens, he had been instrumental in laying the operation's groundwork. With his help and now with Tommy Lichton's consent to use the GALA-1, there was no way in hell they weren't going to trap the Russian agent.

Standing in the lobby just outside the lab, Hughes laughed. A red-handed red commie. That's what he'd have. And soon. With a grin smeared across his face, he glanced to his left. On the other side of the plate-glass window, Tommy Lichton nodded his head and waved. Hughes' smile spread wider and he returned the gesture.

That man, thought Hughes, was nothing less than a national resource.

As he watched the FBI man disappear into the elevator, Tommy Lichton continued to smile. He had every reason to be pleased. Exactly on schedule, Theodore Hughes had arrived and asked the right questions. Enough people were convinced of the Soviet spy's existence.

The situation was proceeding as if it were being read word by word from an imaginary script.

# Chapter 8

## Vienna

Confident that no one suspected his meeting, Richard Stevens passed quickly through the Westbahnhof. He reached the train destined for Paris, climbed into the sleeping car, and turned down its narrow hall. He stopped at the third door, glanced up and down the corridor, and knocked twice. He paused, then knocked three times.

The door clicked open, and Stevens slipped in. He fastened the lock and turned to the Russian, who stood only inches from him. The sturdy figure in front of the drawn shade did not move.

"Viktor," said Stevens, and warmly extended his hand.

The Russian reached from the shadows and took the American's hand in both of his. It was the first time they had seen each other since the incident at the Moscow River.

"Richard."

They stood awkwardly facing each other until the KGB major backed away and sat down on the benchlike seat.

"Sit. Sit," said Viktor, rubbing his balding head with one hand and nodding toward the other seat. "Any problems?"

Stevens placed his suitcase on the floor and sat down opposite the Russian. Between them a small table projected out from the wall.

"None whatever. Actually, it's been rather a boring month. Just the regular old work in the States." He rubbed his hands together and looked up. "No problems in Moscow?"

"None at all. The Americans are wondering where their Volodya is . . . but, well, they'll just have to keep wondering." Laughing, Viktor said, "I don't think he'll ever surface."

"We make a good team."

"Yes." Viktor smiled, and added, "I couldn't have done it so smoothly and quickly without you." He reached down and patted a thick black briefcase, the final payment for the business computer prints Stevens had brought to Moscow. "The final half of your money is here—forty thousand dollars. Our engineers were most pleased. And I've been given approval for the full amount you requested for our next project—two hundred fifty thousand dollars."

Stevens heard voices in the corridor and glanced toward the door. He was silent until the people had passed.

"Good." By all accounts, Stevens knew the affair with the GALA-1 would be his most profitable venture. "What about your Leningrad agent?" he asked, wanting to make certain the Soviets were still on schedule.

"She's already out. In fact, she's in Rome now while her documents are being processed." Viktor smiled. "Don't worry. She'll do whatever you want her to. And we will do everything we promised."

The conductor called out, and seconds later the train jerked forward. Viktor rubbed his chin and leaned toward the window. Raising the shade slightly, he peered out into the bright day. The last of the platform slipped quickly behind.

## THE RED ENCOUNTER

Stevens leaned back and said, "It's all under way then. At last. That business with Volodya was a minor irritation, but that's all straightened out now."

Viktor let the shade drop back into place. He looked at the American, a stern expression on his face.

"Yes, it's all under way," he said. "And there's no stopping it. We are both professionals at this, Richard. Both of us. So as a colleague, let me warn you. My superiors will follow all the way through. Regardless. We are rather inflexible as a country. Not like you Americans who flip and flop. If by chance, Richard, you change your mind, my people would not tolerate it. They would expose you. I guarantee that. I could do nothing to stop them."

Stevens appeared not to be bothered. "Of course. Now what else do we have to talk about?"

"Scheduling. When she will arrive in the States, how long it will take, and when I'll be there."

"That can wait. Paris is a long way away."

Viktor nodded and smiled. "Yes, of course. Business can wait."

The Russian reached down to his briefcase, opened it, and pulled out a small bottle of pepper vodka and two small shot glasses. Setting the glassware on the table, he glanced back down at his briefcase, then at Stevens.

"Your money—now or . . . ?"

"Later," said Stevens automatically.

Grinning, Viktor twisted off the cap and poured them each a drink.

"A toast to our friendship," said Viktor, a nervous edge to his voice.

Stevens glanced toward the door to make certain it was locked.

"Yes, to two professionals who respect and admire each other's work," responded the American. "It's been three years."

Stevens would never forget when they had first met. It had been in a pub in England. Viktor was there to make a trade with an English scientist. Stevens was there to observe. And when by chance Viktor and Stevens had looked directly at one another, their eyes locked for a moment too long. In that extra second, they not only recognized each other as agents, they also recognized that shared secret.

Silently, the two men raised their glasses, clinked them together, and then tossed down the vodka.

His voice faint from the liquor lingering in his throat, Viktor said, "I missed you, Richard Stevens."

The American nodded, and the two men set down their shot glasses and silently rose. It made complete sense to both of them that they trusted each other. Each could ruin the other, yet they didn't because they both needed the same thing and had been unable, over the years, to find it. That they were from opposite ends of the political spectrum made no difference once they had concluded their work.

The American with the curly hair and the bald Russian stood only inches from each other. The last moment of shame and doubt passed, and Viktor reached out and put his hand on Stevens' waist.

"I wonder how many spies there've been like us."

"Hundreds." Laughing to himself, the American said, "I've always said secret sissies make the best secret agents. Operating undercover, so to speak, is natural for us."

Viktor grinned, and the two men embraced.

# Chapter 9

## Minneapolis

"Anatoly, you're full of shit."

Nick was good at his job because he didn't put up with any of the Russians' games. Anatoly Volshevetz, one of the most successful immigrants, was refusing to offer any financial assistance to his mother and sister.

"Nick, please," said Anatoly, in the front hall of his house. He was a sturdy man of thirty-five with a big face made that much larger by a receding hairline. "Why do you get so upset like this? There's no need."

It was almost 10:00 P.M., and for over an hour they had been seated at the dinette table in Anatoly's New Hope split-level home. They had been arguing about who was going to pay for Luba and Vera's apartment, food, and medical needs for the first four months. When Anatoly conceded that he would buy them a color television and nothing more, Nick got up to leave.

"What do you think—the Jewish Family Service is made out of money? Why can't you believe that it's donated money and there's just not that much?" Nick never hid his feelings from a Russian mostly because they never hid theirs from him. "You know, you Russians are a real pain in the ass. You don't know anything about putting back into the pot. You only know how to take."

"But I told you, Nick," said Anatoly, gesturing almost frantically, "I just started a new job. What happens if I lose it? How will I pay for my house? Believe me, I'll help them as soon as I can."

Of all the immigrants, Nick found Anatoly one of the most difficult. He and his bleached-blond wife, Larissa, had arrived two years ago with only three suitcases and a scant knowledge of English. Since then, though, they had passed completely through and then way beyond what Nick called the "rites of immigration": elation, designer jeans, driver's licenses, a big old Oldsmobile that broke down, depression, a minor auto accident, no American friends, unemployment, disdain for the lack of culture in America, nostalgia for Mother Russia, a $30,000-per-year job, a house in a treeless suburb.

Where most immigrants slowed down, however, Anatoly and Larissa sped up. One after the other, they owned six cars before settling on a Saab and a Honda Prelude. Anatoly, a computer analyst, had switched companies three times, increasing his salary by 30 percent. Larissa had attended beauty school, found a job in Edina, and then opened her own shop, The International House of Beauty, in Richfield.

But it was hopeless. Nick knew that tonight there wasn't any more ground to gain than a color television.

"Listen, your mother and sister are going to be here in a little less than a month. And if you don't help them—with money or English lessons or whatever—then we're not going to either. Clear?"

"Don't worry. English and money isn't going to be a problem for them," he said with confidence. "My sister speaks English very nicely, and my mother does okay. And they'll be working in no time. Vera knows computers like no one else and Mama was the best chemical engineer in Leningrad."

"Oh, brother," muttered Nick.

He turned away and leaned down the half-flight of stairs to the family room. In the far corner, Larissa sat glued to the large-screen TV.

"Good night."

"Bye, Nick," she called without turning around.

He opened the door and glanced out into the dark evening. His rusted-out Nova was parked behind their two shiny cars.

"You know, you should just sell some of this crap."

"Good night, Nick," said Anatoly, stifling a yawn as he checked his new prize, a Rolex watch. "Time for bed."

Nick nodded and stepped out. As he walked to his car, he guessed that their problem was that they had charged every cent they possibly could yet were barely able to pay the interest alone on their debts.

Nick's old Chevy, eaten away by time and road salt, hesitated before coming to life with a roar. Shifting into reverse, he considered mentioning Anatoly, along with his computer background and his spending habits, to the FBI. It would be Nick's first report since he had met with Hughes a month ago.

The idea, however, quickly left him. Anatoly's mother and sister were to arrive in a few weeks, and they deserved a clean start. Educated and with marketable professions, Vera and Luba were probably as ambitious and motivated as every other Russian immigrant. If Nick reported Anatoly to the FBI, they might also put the two women under surveillance and jeopardize their opportunities. Besides, Nick was certain a seasoned Soviet agent wouldn't be as obvious with his money as was Anatoly.

Nick accelerated and the car jerked forward. The engine sputtered, faded, came back with a surge of life. The car lunged forward. He backed off on the accelerator, but when he pushed it again, the engine faded, then quietly died.

"Ah, shit!"

He coasted over to the side of the road and brought the vehicle to a halt. He shut the lights off and turned the ignition. Nothing. He tried one more time. Again, the engine did not catch. Frustrated, Nick cranked the ignition and pumped the gas.

"Damnit!"

The engine was flooded. It happened once or twice a week, and he'd just have to sit it out. There was no real rush. Linda, the woman he was living with, had a job singing tonight with her jazz group. Like so many nights, all he had to go home to was an empty apartment. Even if she were home, they'd probably just have another fight; their short relationship had peaked the first month and been declining ever since.

He turned around and glanced toward Anatoly's, the fourth house down. At least he could use their phone if he couldn't get the damn jalopy started at all.

Then abruptly he saw their front light go out. The next moment, in the glow from the neighboring houses, Nick saw a large black car, its headlights off, move up the street. It glided to a silent halt in front of Anatoly's. Almost instantaneously, a figure emerged from the side of the house. Even in the dark, Nick could recognize Anatoly.

Nick sunk a bit lower in the vinyl seat and watched as the Russian climbed into the dark car. The sedan wasted not a moment in pulling a U-turn and heading off in the other direction.

"Like hell you're going to sleep, Anatoly."

Nick jammed the accelerator to the floor and twisted the key. Once again, the Nova came to life with a roar. Not questioning whether he should or shouldn't, Nick spun the car around and, without turning on the headlights, sped to catch up with the black sedan.

He came around a curve and spotted their glowing taillights just pulling out of the subdivision. Nick slowed to give them a lead before pulling up to the main road, turning on his lights, and heading left after them.

He had no trouble keeping both his distance and his eye on them on the open suburban road. They headed straight for a mile, past two more subdivisions, and turned right at a four-way stop. They disappeared around the wooded corner. Nick waited several seconds at the stop sign, and by the time he rounded the corner, he saw the end of the sedan pulling off to the left. As he drove past their turnoff, he saw the sign of a Lutheran church and there, in a corner of the parking lot, the black car pulled at an angle alongside a smaller vehicle.

Nick passed a clump of trees and, certain that he was out of sight, pulled over. Everything to this point had been to satisfy his own curiosity. But he wanted to know more. He wanted to know what was going on in the immigrant community. He wanted to know what Anatoly—the one who'd owned eight cars yet who was too broke to help his own sister and mother—was up to.

Screw Hughes. Nick wasn't going back for the FBI or for apple pie and national security. These were his Russians—they were up to something and he needed to know about it.

He darkened his car again, pulled around, and parked by a lone house. Proceeding on foot to the edge of the church property, Nick slipped behind a wilting elm tree.

A security light posted on the side of the church cast a faint glow, and Nick could clearly make out the figure of Anatoly and, on the hood of the car, a fat envelope. The driver of the car that had picked him up remained behind the steering wheel. Facing Anatoly, as if in confrontation, were two other men. Sovs. They had to be by the looks of their tight clothes and protruding bellies. Russian fat just looked different from American. It was all that lard they had eaten. Nick could identify a Sov body anywhere.

Voices in Russian rose in the night air. Typical. Even if

## THE RED ENCOUNTER

they were doing something illegal, they were arguing. No, haggling. Anatoly reached for the envelope but one of the other men, the shorter one, snatched it back. His partner nodded in agreement. Then in disgust the short one threw the envelope at Anatoly, who seized it and began counting its contents.

Headlights bathed Nick from behind, and he flattened himself against the bark of the tree and edged sideways. There was nowhere to go without exposing himself to Anatoly. If this were a car of more Russians pulling into the lot, they'd spot him for sure.

The headlights grew brighter and stronger until the car shot past. Nick sighed and peered back to the lot. Anatoly was throwing the envelope into the bushes; the other men were getting into their vehicle. Without further exchange, the two cars started and pulled out. Nick slipped around the tree as first one, then the other reached the main road and sped away.

Nick stepped into the deep grass, certain that whatever was being exchanged—dope, icons, hot stereos, or computer specifications—was the key to Anatoly's Saab, Prelude, and split-level home. Visa and Master Charge could not do it all. Nick knew it now. Anatoly was making bucks on the side.

The red dots of the cars' taillights finally disappeared, and Nick broke into a run. Gravel shot out from beneath his shoes, and there he was, in the same spot they had been. Cigarette butts were ground into the pavement but he didn't stop there, instead going directly to the bushes.

The envelope was torn, crumpled, and empty. He lifted it out of the leaves and flattened the paper over his knee. The back of it was plain, unmarked, offering not a clue. Then he turned it over.

There, in the upper left corner and printed in slick horizontal bands of ink, was the return address: DataResearch.

# Chapter 10

## Rome

Luba was sick. And Vera had to wait four hours at the HIAS office just to get an appointment to tell one of the resettlement counselors that her mother needed to see a doctor. The meeting with the counselor took no more than five minutes, during which Vera pleaded for an immediate doctor's appointment. It was pneumonia, insisted Vera, although she wasn't really sure. All she knew was that her mother wasn't able to get out of bed. Having lived all her life in the Soviet Union, Vera was prepared to shout and scream in order to get what she wanted. But it wasn't necessary. The counselor gladly set up an appointment for the next morning.

Pushing open the door, Vera stepped into the main waiting room and the stale odors of sweat, garlic, onions, pickles, flowery perfume, and pungent *papirosa* cigarettes swirled about her. Vera noticed this scent of Russian immigrants immediately and was surprised. After spending three days in Vienna, they'd been in Rome just one month. Already a complex smell that had surrounded her and warmed her insides all her life without ever being noticed now seemed foreign.

Upset, she pushed past a handful of men from Odessa.

With his index finger, one of the men poked another with each syllable, proclaiming, "I'm going to Atlanta! It's good. Perfect. The best."

The other took a long drag on a cigarette and poked back. "No. You're wrong. Too many blacks. My friend Pasha says

Lincoln, Nebraska, is the best place to live in the United States."

"Lincoln was the greatest President, you fool, not a city!"

Vera ran past them and through the door. Quickly making her way down the narrow staircase, she didn't care how many different nail polishes one could find here or that jeans were as plentiful as black bread in Moscow.

At the bottom, she shoved open the door and half ran onto the sidewalk. The trees were full of fresh leaves, the air was pleasant and brisk. She took a deep breath, and suddenly the sidewalk seemed to rise and fall. Knowing that she simply needed to eat, Vera closed her eyes in an attempt to stem the dizziness. All she'd had today was a glass of tea, a piece of bread, and some cheese. Rome was full of beautiful fruits and vegetables and meats, and there weren't any lines, either. She'd hardly tasted any of them, though. How could she?

To her right, a young group of emigrants sat in orange plastic chairs at a sidewalk café.

"Hey, friend!" called out a smiling man in Russian. "I've seen you around. What city are you from?"

Vera tried to speak but nothing came out. She cleared her throat and tried again.

"Leningrad," she said faintly.

Pointing to the other members of the group, the jovial Russian said, "Moscow, Moscow, Minsk, Kiev, Kiev, and Tallinn." He paused, pleased with himself, as if he had just introduced his new friends at camp. "Come and join us for some cognac!"

Vera reflexively pulled her purse close in and then tightened her beige raincoat around her waist.

At the table, a woman who had discovered red lipstick and blond hair coloring, stared at Vera.

*"Devushka."* Young girl. "Are you all right?"

It took a moment for Vera to comprehend that the woman was talking to her. Realizing they were all staring at her, she brushed back her flat, oily hair, then turned away to hide the puffy pockets of flesh that swelled beneath her eyes.

"I'm fine," said Vera. "But my mother is ill and I . . . I have to go."

She started off at a half-trot down the curving, tree-lined

street. She couldn't have joined them. She wouldn't let herself, just like she couldn't indulge in any of the delights of Rome. How could she when little Vladik was back there, eating nothing but cabbage and potatoes?

Still, a half block later when she heard the little party of émigrés roaring with laughter, she stopped and turned around. The group was talking, drinking, and dreaming aloud of their rich futures. There was no one else on the sidewalk except a man in a long coat who, walking toward her, suddenly lowered his head.

Vera smiled faintly. For an instant, she wanted to go back and join the group of young people. She wanted to run to them, laugh hysterically, then break her oath of silence.

Instead, Vera ran on, wanting to be as far away as possible from the émigrés and her future.

She had never imagined life beyond the Soviet Union could be so horrible. When they arrived in Vienna, the drug was just wearing off. As soon as they had set foot in the dazzling airport, they were met by Israeli immigration agents, who welcomed them on their first stop to the Jewish homeland. As the Israelis whisked Vera and Luba to a tiny, cockroach-filled hotel, the agents expressed horror and disgust when Vera mumbled that they were going to America.

The Israeli agents returned the next day, and the next. They insisted each day that Vera and Luba go to Israel. That was, after all, why they got out of the Soviet Union. And they were Jews. And the country of their ancestors needed them desperately. And the United States was, in fact, an awful place. One of the agents herself had been there and found it disgusting.

As the Israelis pushed and intimidated and insulted, the last of Vera's defenses broke. That very afternoon Vera and Luba were given over to the Hebrew Immigration Aid Society and the next morning they were put on the first train to Rome.

Vera turned a corner, automatically looking behind. Her eyebrows coming together in worry, she noticed that same man. She continued and a half block later stole another look over her shoulder.

There he was again. A muscular, balding man following

her. Vera froze, planting her feet on the sidewalk, and stared at him. He stared at her and then unexpectedly burst forward. Vera stood paralyzed. She couldn't believe it, didn't want to believe it, but this man was charging her.

Vera's shoes cut into her skin as she broke into a run. They were stupid shoes, with low heels and a thick band at the front. Slowing her down even more was the large black purse slapping against her side.

The purse, thought Vera, as she ran. She had carried bread and cheese in that purse just last week. She and Luba had eaten lunch near the American market and had cut the food with a sharp kitchen knife. She jammed a hand into the huge, deep purse, pawing for that pointed knife.

Hearing the man's pounding steps growing closer, she searched the yellow-stuccoed buildings that lined the empty street. She scanned the windows but they were all covered with peeling wooden shutters. Vera saw no one and knew it was hopeless. He'd catch her in seconds. What did he want? Money? Her body? God, she wanted to be home. Leningrad was safe.

Just up ahead she spotted a black opening on the right and ducked in. It was a passway, dark like a sewer, some five meters long, with an iron gate at the other end. Fumbling for the knife in the purse—dear God, was it even in there?—she ran to the gate and pulled it open. She slipped through, closed the gate behind her, and threw herself back against the stone wall.

With both hands digging in her purse, she looked up and realized she was in a large, covered courtyard. There were two doors on the other side and windows above that glowed with blackness.

One instant the sharp metal sliced into her finger and the next she heard the man's steps slow. He paused, then entered the passway.

Vera grasped the knife and withdrew it from her purse. The man would soon pull open that gate, step through, and she would be upon him, plunging her raised knife into him.

The man stopped.

Vera heard the scratchy grit between his shoe and the cobblestone as he turned from side to side. Another step forward. Another. He was searching her out, carefully, meticulously. He knew he had her cornered.

Suddenly, his hairy hand appeared around the edge of the iron gate and Vera bit her lip. It was only a half-meter from her. But the hand did not move. Nor did Vera. The man seemed to possess infinite patience as he stood motionless, stalking her. Vera refused to betray herself, though, and her whole body remained fixed on that hand as she focused on its thick blue vein. Then a beam of light with a black hole appeared between the bars. A gun with a silvery barrel.

Minutes later, the gate and the hand seemed to quiver and float away. Vera closed her eyes against a teetering dizziness. When she opened her eyes again and saw the gate being pulled silently back, she wasn't really sure if it was moving until she heard the rusty squeak.

She saw her chance and jabbed the knife at the hand and hurled her body against the gate.

"Ahhh!" she screamed as if she were the one being stabbed. "Ahhh! Ahhh!"

The man cried out as the knife sliced through the back of his hand. The iron gate flew into him. He lost his balance, caught his foot on a loose cobblestone, and fell backward. He dropped to the ground, the gun spilling from his hand. Filled with manic power, Vera shoved and screamed without stopping.

"Ahh! Ahh!"

In her mind she saw the last of her son's kicking legs disappearing through the door and she saw that needle of drugs jabbed into her arm. She pushed and shoved on the gate and sliced the knife through empty air. Then, as the man rolled back against the wall, she smashed the gate right up against him, grabbed a chain hooked to the wall, and tied the metal links to the gate. In a matter of moments, she had him pinned behind the iron bars.

Vera stepped back, air heaving in and out of her body. Her eyes fell shut and she clutched at her chest with her left hand. Her blood, dripping from the slice in her hand, trickled onto the blade of the knife and mixed with his. She opened her eyes and looked at the man, who lay there, trapped like a defeated dog.

She recognized him.

"You're Russian." Her voice, torn by the screams, was deep and coarse.

His silence was her confirmation.

"KGB?"

When he still did not answer, she dropped to her knees. Vera raised the knife toward his throat, then abruptly moved it in the other direction. When the knife was midway down his body, she pressed the point of the blade into his crotch. She felt his clothing and genitals squirm beneath the blade.

"KGB?" she repeated. "Speak or I'll cut your balls off."

The man looked down and knew that the knife was sharp enough to cut him and dull enough to do it crudely. He raised his eyes to hers.

As if he were proclaiming checkmate, he said, "Yes. My name is Major Viktor Petrov, and I'm told you like to play . . . American roulette."

Rage flooded out of her and she jabbed the knife deeper. He flinched, caught his breath.

Confident, though, Petrov said, "Hurt me and in the end you'll hurt yourself ten times as much. Now let me up."

Vera knew she was beaten. The knife fell from her hand and clattered on the cobblestones.

"Of course, Comrade Major," she said, "I just wasn't expecting you so soon."

# Chapter 11

## Moscow

The morning after his return from Rome, Major Petrov was summoned to the Lubianka, the massive KGB headquarters in the center of Moscow. Wondering if his superior had even read his report yet, Petrov made his way to the offices of the special directorate established to obtain Western technology.

"Come in, come in, Comrade Major," said Colonel Orlov, who stood by a large window.

The office filled a corner of the building and had expansive windows overlooking the square below. Befitting Orlov, a hero of the Great Fatherland War, the room had a shiny parquet floor and a collection of heavy dark wood furniture.

Orlov crossed behind his expansive desk, on which sat three telephones and a silver-framed photograph of Lenin.

"Please have a seat," he said with a generous wave of his arm.

Colonel Orlov was a rugged-looking man whose features—a smooth head, thick jaw, broad shoulders—were clean and square. In his late fifties, he was one of Petrov's younger superiors.

As the colonel seated himself, he asked with a slight smile, "Anything further to report on your relationship with this American?"

Petrov looked up sharply. Had he been spied upon and found out? His mind raced over the time he had spent with Richard. It must have been the hotel in Paris. Viktor knew it was risky meeting there.

Orlov's look of amusement sunk into a frown. "Comrade Petrov, what is it? You look as if you were about to be shot."

"I . . . I . . ."

The conversation ceased as Orlov's aide knocked once and stepped in. The young man carried a tray with a pot of tea, two glasses in silver holders, and a bowl of sugar. The aide set the tray on the desk.

"That will be all," said Orlov, waving the man away with the back of his hand. "No interruptions, please."

Orlov's eyebrows seemed to twitch as he poured tea into each of the clear glasses. The older man was definitely disturbed about something.

Orlov caught Viktor by the eye. "Once or twice?"

Viktor was unable to speak. Was he asking how many times he had slept with the American this trip?

Orlov started to laugh. "Dear Comrade, what's the matter with you? Didn't you get any sleep?" He tapped the bowl of sugar with the spoon. "The sugar—once or twice?"

Viktor laughed and covered his eyes. "Twice." He cleared his throat. "And, no, there's nothing further to report on Stevens. Everything's in my report."

He wished that, like Richard, he had the opportunity to withdraw from government service and work in the private sector. It was just his fate that there was no private business in the Soviet Union, leaving him stuck in the KGB unless he wanted to defect.

Orlov placed the sugar in Viktor's glass, then three spoonfuls in his own. He handed Viktor his glass, took his own, and settled into his deep chair.

Casually stirring his tea, Orlov shook his head and said, "These capitalists! They have no beliefs and are so easily bought and sold. Tell me, even though your Mr. Stevens is now employed by DataResearch, can we be certain that he's no longer working for the CIA?"

"Yes, I'm fairly sure we can. Especially in our case. As you say, he has a lust for money."

Orlov thumbed through some papers on his desk. "And you're confident about his ability to help us with the GALA-1?"

"Absolutely. For two hundred fifty thousand dollars he'll be most cooperative."

"Good." Orlov turned away and shook his head in disgust. "Damn the Americans. They're about to escalate the arms race for the next century. We have no other choice!"

It was true. Viktor knew it. "But once we obtain the specifications of the GALA-1, we'll be able to construct our own system. The Americans will gain nothing."

"If that is necessary, then let us hope we can," said Orlov. "Now, Comrade Major, you know that obtaining the GALA-1 documentation is of the utmost importance to our entire nation."

"Of course."

"It's a grave matter of national security. But something

else has come up, which is why I've called you here. It has to do with someone you've mentioned several times in your reports. And that's the person who's been advising Stevens on what to sell us."

"That's right. His information source," said Viktor. "Stevens' technical background is not that broad. He's told me several times that he has sought the counsel of a scientist."

"Exactly." Orlov leaned over his desk, his eyes wide with hope. "Find out who that is. Discover who this source of Richard Stevens' is. I want that, need that."

"Yes, Comrade Colonel."

Orlov sighed, leaned forward, and poured himself more tea. He added two more spoonfuls of sugar to his cup, then gazed directly at Petrov.

"Stevens' source, this scientist friend, is very important. We have so few contacts there in . . ." He searched his papers. "There in these Middle Western cities of . . . ah . . . of Minneapolis and St. Paul." He raised his head again. "Out in the provinces, I'm told, but they're doing some remarkable things. One of the largest centers of technology in the country. Some culture there, too, if there is such a thing in America. My reports say this place is the capital of these supercomputers, medical technology, and . . . inflatable penile implants!"

A laugh burst from Viktor's throat, and he asked, "And which is of interest to our great leaders?"

"Now, now, Comrade Major." Smiling, Orlov raised his hand. "Let's not be cruel."

Viktor quickly contained himself.

"As you are well aware," continued the colonel, "our embassy in Washington and our consulates in New York and San Francisco have enabled us to establish quite a broad network."

From the Silicon Valley to the science institutes of Washington, Viktor knew that the KGB's theft of American technology was causing a virtual hemorrhage of U.S. scientific data. It was completely necessary too. While the Americans could afford both guns and butter, for the Soviets it was a choice of one or the other.

"One of the KGB's greatest successes," said Viktor.

"Absolutely. So find this source of your Richard Stevens." Orlov grinned. "After all, America is nothing less than the Soviet Union's most productive industry, and it's our job to keep it that way."

## Chapter 12

*Minneapolis*

Nick pulled the sheet over his crotch as his girl friend, Linda, muttered something and rolled to the far side of the bed. He looked around the small bedroom, which was flooded with morning sunlight. Four empty walls, a mirror, pressboard dresser, and the hard futon bed they lay on filled his vision.

Some things just don't work, thought Nick, and he and Linda were obviously one of them. He had moved into her place five months ago, but their relationship was coming to an end. Time to start looking for a place of his own. Maybe he could find something for the first of September. Over two months away—that should be plenty of time.

At first things had been good between them, even fun. Mostly sex, but otherwise too. As they got to know one another, however, the situation worsened. She quickly tired of his Russian immigrants and their constant phone calls, while he anguished over her jazz band's frequent rehearsals and late-night performances. This was the first time he'd been in a relationship and lonely at the same time. It stunk.

He glanced over at Linda, whose long blond hair lay gently on the sheets. They just about always had sex in the morning because Linda usually returned late at night when he was asleep or she was too tired. Most important, though, in the morning neither of them had yet to get mad at the other and so they tended to be more relaxed.

This morning, however, was too typical of their recent intimate moments. Sex definitely wasn't fun; it was a chore. For Nick, it was a matter of digging his knees into the bed and thrusting as hard as he could. For Linda, it was a matter of his weight on top of her, of feeling invaded. Just minutes ago, with no sense of pleasure and seemingly hours away from any hope of climax, they called it quits. As they rolled to opposite sides of the bed, Nick realized it was the first thing they had agreed on in days.

"Do you know why the Japanese are so small?" he asked. "Because they sleep on these rock-hard futons and it stunts their growth." He sat up stiffly. "Do you have any lotion?"

She shot him a disgusted look over her shoulder. "Oh, gross, Nick. If you're going to do it to yourself, I'm going to leave."

"Linda, you're such a prude." He reached down to his legs, lifted aside the covers, and pointed to his red knees. "Burn marks from the sheets. That's what I want the lotion for."

Her back still to him, Linda reached to the bedside table and poked around for the plastic bottle of lotion. She found it and tossed it over her shoulder.

As he picked the bottle off the bed, Nick spotted the clock.

"Man, I got to get going. I'm late already."

His new clients, Anatoly Volshevetz' sister and mother, were due to arrive at the airport in little over an hour.

"Nick," said Linda, soberly, her back still to him, "I don't want to live together anymore."

Nick froze, a forced smile on his face. "That's the second thing we've agreed on in ten minutes. A record. Linda, maybe there's hope for us after all."

As soon as the words left his mouth, however, he knew there was no choice. He had to move, even though he hated the thought of living by himself.

"Yeah, I was thinking about looking for a place for the first of September." He flipped open the lid of the lotion. "Maybe I should change that to the first of August."

"No. I mean, I don't want you here from now on. I want you to leave today. Now. This morning."

# Chapter 13

## New York

At JFK Airport, Richard Stevens exited the 747 jet from Paris and calmly made his way through the terminal to the main building. At the end of the broad hall he came to a narrow, open staircase, which he climbed. At the top, overlooking the corridor below, were a series of doors. He proceeded to the last room, where his American contact was waiting, and knocked.

The door was quickly opened by an older man with a white mustache and white hair which rimmed a bald head. His smile really is persistent, noted Stevens of the veteran FBI man.

"Oh, good, you're here," said Theodore Hughes. "Pretty much on time too. I hope you had a pleasant flight. Mine was. Just flew in from D.C. about ten minutes ago."

Hughes ushered Stevens into the small conference room. Two cans of beer, plastic glasses next to them, awaited on a round table.

"The flight was just fine." Stevens eyed the room. It was exceptionally plain, filled only with the table, four chairs, a lamp, two ashtrays, and a wastebasket. "Is it safe?"

Hughes pulled out one of the chairs, exposing an ordinary briefcase. He flicked open the latches and opened it. Inside, occupying every available inch, was an array of electronic sensors, recorders, and detectors.

"The very latest," said Hughes. "Whatever that means.

You just flip on a switch, wave this wand, and it tells you if anyone's listening. And, apparently, no one is. There's another sensor that's on now too. So please, sit down. Have a beer, and tell me everything."

Stevens sat down and placed his briefcase on the empty fourth chair. He wrapped his hand around the cool, sweaty can of beer, opened it, and filled his plastic glass. "They liked it very much." He took a sip, the frothy coolness filling his mouth, and eyed Hughes. "The business computer was a very good choice." At the very start, Stevens had gone to the FBI, who had carefully orchestrated each of his contacts with the Soviets. "Viktor said they were most eager in regard to the upcoming project."

Hughes took a slow drink. "Always Viktor?" A trace of yellowish beer was left glistening on his white mustache.

"Always. In Moscow too. There were others, but Viktor was always there." Even at the river, he thought. Even there.

"Well, he's obviously the one running you."

"And he had the money. The final forty thousand dollars, as agreed. It's on deposit now in my account over there," he said, motioning with his head as if toward the Continent. "Evidently they're convinced of my abilities and my greed. Viktor brought word that they're quite willing to pay what I asked—two hundred fifty thousand dollars for the specs and lab reports on the GALA-1."

"We've got them now. Terrific!" Hughes laughed and reached for his beer. "I thank you for coming to us, as does our government. You've been wonderfully helpful." He took a drink. "You left the CIA to go into private practice, but I bet you never expected to make that much."

"No, sir." Stevens tried to smooth his curly hair with one hand. Actually, that had been precisely his intent. "So the Soviets think that because I'm DataResearch's security man, I'll be able to provide their agent with access to the GALA-1. . . ."

"Oh, yes. Not to worry," said Hughes, waving a hand. "I've been to Minneapolis several times this month—in fact, I'll be in Washington only a few more days before returning—and I've spoken with DataResearch. I met with the

## THE RED ENCOUNTER

chief executive officer and Tommy Lichton, too, and as long as we're overseeing this, they'll gladly provide all the documentation. They speak highly of you. And they both agree that it's well worth the risk not only to catch the Soviets in the act, but to identify their agent in the Midwest."

Richard Stevens frowned, and said, "I trust that not many people know about this."

"Just the CEO and Lichton." Hughes smiled. "Don't worry. You've been extremely helpful to us. We won't let the Soviets find out you've been helping us. It's just a shame we've had to go to all this trouble. If only we'd been able to get hold of that cryptologist I mentioned—Volodya. He knew the name of the Soviet agent and he knew what they were up to. I guess that's a lost hope."

Stevens stared into his slightly bubbling glass of beer. "Evidently." Really, it was a sunken hope. "But Viktor did say they would provide help and he told me—"

Hughes cut him off, unable to contain his excitement. "At last he gave you the name? Bravo! Now we're really getting somewhere. And better than just watching this agent, we'll make a showcase of this whole thing. We'll let the media in on this—make a big splash in the papers, you know—and catch him right in the act."

Shaking his head, Stevens said, "Not him. *Her.*"

"What?"

"She's a young woman and, as you suspected, an immigrant. In fact, she's just arriving."

"Seriously?" asked Hughes, his eyes wide. "Well, what's her name?" he demanded.

Richard Stevens cleared his throat and looked directly at Theodore Hughes.

"Vera Karansky," he said, and then proceeded to spell it.

## Chapter 14

*Minneapolis*

Nick didn't know what to do, where to go, so he took a shower and tried to postpone making a decision. Then he pleaded that he was late for the airport and that they would talk later. He practically ignored Linda as he dressed. Well, he told her, what in hell was he supposed to do, find a place in five minutes? As soon as he tied his shoes though, she shoved him out the door with an armful of his clothes.

"Just take your shit and get out of here!" she had yelled.

In the end, he convinced her to let him come back after work to gather his belongings. He was really late, he insisted, as he hurried off to the airport.

Now, as he trotted down the broad corridor of the Minneapolis-St. Paul International Airport, he couldn't imagine what he was going to do once he moved out. He had a standing invitation at over fifty Russian households for blini and vodka, but where was he going to sleep tonight? A motel?

As he often said, he suffered from advanced mobility. Moving, leaving. His life had been a series of departures, and he was sick of it. That was what he hated about his own country: the terrifying sense that things didn't last. No one made any commitments. That, however, was what made Minnesota a bit different. If you didn't like it, you left quickly because January weather was reason enough to flee. If you did like it—and boasted like a propaganda slogan that you'd been bitten by the Minnesota mystique—you endured the winters and tried to justify your decision. And Nick was going to stay. With more mosquitoes and theater

## THE RED ENCOUNTER

seats per capita than anywhere in the country, this was home now.

As he neared the last gate, he cut through a swarm of people going in the opposite direction. He cursed himself for being late. He hoped at least that Anatoly was on time, that his mother and sister hadn't arrived with no one to greet them.

Nick strained to see over the crowd. There was no sight of Anatoly, Larissa, or any other Russians. He glanced to the side, opposite the gate, and spotted a row of telephone booths. Standing next to one of the phones was a large man taking a picture. Reflexively, Nick's eyes followed the direction of the camera. And there they were, the four of them, huddled, hugging, sobbing.

Nick slowed, unable to keep his own emotions from swelling as he watched the reunited family kissing and embracing.

The mother, wearing a baggy blue dress with flowers all over it, cried and laughed with the realization that she had finally set foot on American soil. The younger woman, obviously Vera, wore a dark brown skirt and a worn beige blouse. Her face was simple, pure, beautiful—yet torn as if she already realized how much she had lost and how difficult it would be to start over again.

Then Anatoly spotted Nick and called him over. "This is Nick. He speaks Russian."

"It's a pleasure to . . ."

Nick's voice faded away as Anatoly possessively embraced him like his best friend. Oddly, all five of them stood in silence. No one moved. No one spoke. Nick stared at Vera for as long as he dared.

"Welcome to the United States," Nick finally said.

Luba laughed aloud and ran up and hugged him as if she'd been looking for him all her life. "Our very first American!"

The young woman stepped forward, a forced but friendly smile on her face. "I'm Vera."

Luba moved aside and Nick, looking directly into the young woman's eyes, slowly extended his hand.

Vera's soft, warm hand met his, and he said, "I'm happy." He quickly shook his head. "I mean, I'm Nick and I'm happy to meet you."

A faint smile appeared and, just as fast, faded on Vera's face, and then Larissa reached over and jabbed an expensive Japanese camera into Nick's stomach.

"A picture!" said the blonde, the big smile on her mascara-streaked face exposing three gold teeth.

*"Da, da!"* echoed Anatoly.

Nick took the camera and backed away. "Okay, everyone line up. I'm going to take a family portrait, you know, so that in a hundred years your great-grandchildren can look at it and say, 'Those are my ancestors, they came over by jet!' "

Vera, Luba, Anatoly, and Larissa lined up. Nick took off the lens cap, but as he focused on them, he saw something else. That man. The large man who had stood by the telephone booth taking a picture. Again the stranger stood off in the distance and again he had the camera to his eye, the equipment covering his face. All that Nick could see was a long, deep scar on his lower right cheek. Squinting through the lens of his own camera, Nick watched, in shock, as the man photographed him.

"Go on, Nick, take it!" shouted Anatoly.

Nick lowered the camera. The stranger was gone. He had melted into the crowd. Had he really photographed Nick?

"Nick, what is it?" asked Larissa, a silly grin on her face.

"I . . . I don't know. I . . ." He could no longer hold back the question he'd been wanting to ask ever since that night in the parking lot. "Anatoly, where are you working now?"

Anatoly's face wrinkled in confusion. "What? Where am I what?"

"Working?" repeated Larissa. "DataResearch, of course. Now, come on, Nick. Take the picture!"

*"Ulibka,* everyone!" Smile, said Vera.

Luba, together again with her two children, embraced them, laughed, and said, "Yes, everyone say *izyoom!"* Raisin.

Nick lifted the camera to his eye, focused, and offered the counterpart. "Luba, over here we say *cheese."*

Russian or American? Which, he wondered as he snapped the picture, was that man with the scar?

# Chapter 15

Nick Miller stopped by only briefly and left after setting up an appointment. Anatoly and Larissa remained for hours at the St. Louis Park apartment before hurrying home to finish cooking the celebratory dinner. After making a business stop, Anatoly said he'd be back to pick them up, which left Vera and Luba a little over an hour to wash and change.

Vera, her mother right behind her, gently shut the door of their new one-bedroom apartment. All afternoon, the conversation had flown from one topic to the next.

As if in a trance, Vera moved away from the door and into the living room. Her limbs, heavy with exhaustion, ached for sleep. She ran her hand over the back of the stuffed chair, which the Jewish Family Service had given them along with a matching couch, dinette set, twin beds, and dishes.

Her voice strained, Vera said, "It's a nice place."

Luba nodded. "Oh, yes. It's a wonderful apartment. And look at the beautiful color TV Anatoly and Larissa gave us."

Vera, her eyebrows pinched together, turned to her mother. "Wh—what? What did you say?"

Luba, walking across the living room, said, "The TV—it's quite nice."

"Yes," she said, staring down at nothing.

"Verichka, look."

Her mother, younger and more lively than Vera had seen her in months, had sunk to her knees and was feeling the flooring.

"What did Larissa call this?" asked Luba, running her fingers through the acrylic, hairlike substance.

Vera put her hand to her head. "Something ... something like ... like *shog karpetink.*"

"It certainly is strange." Luba forced a laugh, hung on to the couch, and pulled herself up. "She said it was everywhere in America. I've never seen anything like it before. Don't they have wood floors here?"

"I don't know, Mama."

Luba paced nervously, trying to postpone the inevitable.

"Yes, this is a nice apartment. That dial over there automatically controls the heat." Luba spun in the other direction. "And that box—the air conditioner—for when we get hot."

A dense fog seemed to creep into Vera, seep into her bones. Everything stopped and became silent when something abruptly clasped her arm.

"Come, let's look at that funny kitchen sink." Luba, her joy forced, grasped her daughter's wrist. "America—so many things!"

Vera let herself be pulled into the kitchen, where Luba flicked on a wall switch. At once the machine inside the kitchen drain burst on in a smooth whirl. Curiosity caught Vera, and she leaned over the sink.

Luba held back her grayish hair with one hand and bent over. "This is where we put our garbage, eh? In that little hole?"

"I ... I think so."

The sound was captivating, and Vera reached into her skirt pocket and found a paper napkin from the airplane. She unwadded it and dropped it into the disposal. Luba stuck out her hand and started to push it in.

"No, Mama." Vera caught her mother's hand and pulled it back. "Anatoly said to turn on the water."

But Vera wasn't quite sure how to activate the strange device. There weren't two regular faucets, only one lever. Vera pushed it from side to side. Nothing happened. Then, by accident, she lifted up on it. Water shot out, pushing the napkin into the hole.

"There it goes," said Luba, shaking her head in disbelief. "This is a great country."

## THE RED ENCOUNTER

The two women peered in and watched as the napkin was chopped into shreds and washed away. Luba spotted an empty can of Coke that Anatoly had left.

"Let's try the can!" she said, childlike.

"We'd better wait," said Vera. "I think only food is supposed to go in there."

"Well, it wouldn't fit anyway."

Vera shut off the water and the disposal, walked over to the window, and parted the thin curtains. Outside, she could see a whole street of brick, two-story walk-up apartment buildings just like hers. Anatoly had told her how a majority of the thousand Soviet immigrants in Minneapolis had been settled right here on Virginia Avenue.

Out of nowhere Luba's hands gently descended on Vera's neck. Vera tensed, catching her breath as if she were about to be struck. But as her mother's fingers began to work gently on her knotty muscles, Vera let out a long sigh.

"That's it, dear. Just relax. Everything's going to be fine." Luba, though, could not contain her curiosity about her new country, and in a hushed voice asked, "How come there aren't any people on the streets in America?"

"Because everyone goes by car." Vera closed her eyes. "Did you notice the Americans at the airport? Everyone seemed to be smiling so much."

"That means they must like it here. Shh! That's right. Just relax, dear." Luba walked her fingers up and down her daughter's neck. "I thought Minneapolis was a big city. It looks like the country to me."

Vera, her head falling forward, thought how everything was new, even the kitchen faucet. In the Soviet Union and, it seemed, in Rome and Vienna everyone wanted to live in the center of the city. That's where all the culture and beauty were.

"This is a suburb," explained Vera. "American cities are different. Remember, Anatoly wrote and said most Americans live outside the city."

"That's strange. I mean, what's a city without people in its heart?" Luba kneaded Vera's shoulders.

Vera rolled her head from side to side. "Well, we'll see

the center of Minneapolis—they call it *downtown*—day after tomorrow when we have our appointment with Nick." He had set up a meeting in the morning.

"He's a nice man. You know, my birthday's in two weeks. We'll have a big dinner at Anatoly's and I'll invite him." She paused. "Fifty-three. I'll be fifty-three years old."

At the mention of the American, Vera broke away. She stepped over to the next window, taking a clump of the white curtain in her fingers.

Her back still to Luba, Vera said, "I'm sorry. I'm just a little tense still. Why don't you go wash up? Anatoly will be back soon and then it'll be time to see his house."

"But are you . . ."

"I'm fine. I'll use the bathroom after you."

"Okay. Just sit down and relax." As Luba headed toward the bathroom, she muttered, "Imagine—Anatoly has work to do now, so late in the afternoon. Larissa has her own business too. No wonder they're rich and have so many things."

Only when her mother had disappeared down the hall did Vera look around. They didn't have much to make it feel like home—only the two suitcases and a carry-on bag—but it was a nice apartment. She couldn't believe that some organization had provided all this and that there would be others—Nick had called them *volunteers*—to help them in the future. Her eyes drifted from the white walls to the furry flooring to the kitchen. . . .

She began to cry. All these months she had held back, but the last of her energy evaporated and she felt weaker than she could ever remember. She stumbled to the couch and collapsed on it, burying her face in a cushion. Her body quivered in convulsions.

Finally, she wailed, "Oh, God!"

Footsteps across the floor and once again Vera sensed her mother hovering over her. An arm, two arms, then a body reached down and pressed close to her in a motherly hug. Luba began to stroke her daughter's hair.

"I . . . I miss Vladik too," said the older woman. "A piece of my heart went with that child."

## THE RED ENCOUNTER

"Mama, I ..." It burst out of her. "I hate the Soviet Union! With all my heart, I hate it!"

"You mustn't talk like that. There's already too much hate in the world. Russians are good people. You know that. They want to be liked, accepted, but they're so afraid. They don't know what to do with their fear so they've put up a big wall to protect themselves." Luba wrapped her arms around her daughter and rocked her. "If only ..."

Vera stopped. "Mama, don't. Please don't start that." Vera propped herself up with one arm and looked around. "My purse? My handkerchief is in my purse."

Luba reached for the handbag at the end of the couch and gave it to her daughter.

"Thank you," said Vera, once again trying to hold back the tears.

She stuck her hand into her purse and blindly felt for the handkerchief. She pushed aside some papers, a pen, lipstick. Instead of the soft folds of the material, though, she felt something small and cold and hard. Plastic. The plastic of the small yellow ball which held the diamond. Miraculously, she had transported it across the borders of Russia, Poland, Austria, Italy, and the United States. And no one, not even her mother, knew she had it.

She found the handkerchief and pulled it out.

"Don't worry, Mama. We'll work things out." Vera wiped her eyes and forced a smile. "I'll do what I have to and everything will be fine."

# Chapter 16

Richard Stevens heard the buzz in the sky before he spotted its source. The noise was like a lawn mower, and he pulled his BMW to the side of the dirt road. Squinting, he searched the cloudless blue sky. Suddenly, the craft, looking like a lawn chair with wings, whooshed over a stand of birches.

Stevens waved and the ultralight aircraft tipped its wings in response. That meant that from the sky the pilot had checked the desolate road and was certain no one had followed the BMW.

Loosening his collar in the warm summer air, Stevens continued down the road for another mile. Although he lost sight of the plane, he could still hear it as he turned into a field and parked behind a deserted farmhouse. He shut off the engine, patted down his curly hair, and started across the meadow. As he stomped through the tall grass toward the forest, he stopped and listened. The droning engine of the plane now sounded like a herd of the area's monster mosquitoes.

His superior was paranoid about security in the way some people fear germs. No precaution was great enough. That was why they were meeting some thirty miles outside Minneapolis. That was why Stevens had left his car behind. Even if the FBI had not tailed him, they might have planted a microphone somewhere on the BMW.

Through the treetops Stevens caught a brief glimpse of the descending plane and its pontoons. The engine grew less noisy until it disappeared altogether. Fearing that it had crashed, Stevens ran forward. He emerged on the lake's sandy bank just in time to see the ultralight land like a loon

## THE RED ENCOUNTER

on the water's surface. Scanning the area, he confirmed that the lake was deserted.

As the craft glided to shore, Stevens thought how Viktor and the KGB believed that the plan to steal the GALA-1 specs was all their doing. At the same time, Hughes and the FBI were certain it was *their* idea to trick and then capture the KGB, with the hottest, most advanced computer in hand. Yet the only ones actually in control of every aspect were Stevens and the man who had just landed on the nameless lake. It was they who had designed it all, they who had lured both the FBI and the KGB into the operation.

As his employer stepped out of the aircraft and into the shallow water, he called, "Good afternoon, Mr. Lichton."

The risk of deceiving both the KGB and the FBI was worth it to Stevens. Tommy Lichton promised he would pay double whatever the KGB offered. All Stevens had to do was refine Lichton's plan, then simultaneously play along with Hughes and Viktor until the arrest.

The designer of the GALA-1 was so eager for an update that he shouted, "Has she arrived yet? She's here, isn't she?"

"Yes, sir," he said, referring to Vera Karansky. "She arrived yesterday."

Lichton laughed aloud and beached his aircraft with one strong tug. He knew that with or without encouragement, the Soviet Union would have gone after the GALA-1, just as they were going after every important piece of American technology. But Stevens and he were going to outsmart the Russians at their own game. There was no way, Lichton promised himself, they were going to steal his creation, the first all-gallium-arsenide computer successfully produced. He more than anyone had a duty to protect it.

"Well, how soon do you think she'll start work?"

"Probably toward the end of next week. The FBI already has her under surveillance."

"Excellent." A smile on his boyish face, Tommy Lichton added, "It's too bad we'll never be able to take credit for this because it's going to be fantastic. You and I, Richard, are going to accomplish what the White House and Congress have been trying to for years."

Stevens nodded. The impact would be nationwide. By using the computer behind the Star Wars defense system and a setting deep in Middle America, the severity of the problem would be widely publicized.

"American businesses are going to realize that they need to take immediate action to protect themselves. Just like you want, Mr. Lichton. Just like you want."

Lichton started toward the forest. "There's going to be so much publicity for this that when people think of spies they'll think of Britain's Kim Philby . . . and our Vera Karansky. Once they arrest her, she'll never be free again."

## Chapter 17

In his basement study, Anatoly lifted the RAM board to the bright light. The microchips, so perfectly made, so perfectly attached, glistened. He smiled. This was a work of beauty, something to be proud of. He would get top dollar for it, no doubt. This really was a great country!

There was a terse rap on the door and he threw a protective hand over the circuit board. He was sure he'd locked the door, yet . . .

*"Da?"* he said in a hushed voice.

"It's me," came Larissa's answer. She was to warn him if anyone unexpected stopped by. "It's okay."

He reached over, unfastened the lock, and his wife's head of bright blond hair poked in.

"Are you almost ready?" she said, her voice low.

*"Da, da, da."* As if it were a priceless work of art, he lowered the board into a foam-padded box. Two other pieces of microcircuitry already lay there. "Just finishing—"

From upstairs his mother called, "Anatoly?" Luba had been in the kitchen for the past hour, but now she was making her way downstairs. "What are you doing down there? Can you take me home now?"

"Right away, Mama."

His mother had no idea what was in this room—the advanced microcomputer, printer, modem, blueprints—nor why he spent all his free time behind the locked door. He wanted it to stay that way too. Larissa, understanding that she was to keep Luba away, backed out.

Anatoly worked quickly now. He finished packing up the items, making certain that they could not slide about. He shut off the light over the worktable, checked the computer, and placed the box under his arm. He made one final check of the lab, stepped out, locked the door and jiggled the handle. The room was secure.

Anatoly went to Larissa, who stood guard at the bottom of the steps. He leaned over, gave her a quick kiss, and called upstairs.

"All set, Mama. Let's go!" he said, barely able to hide his excitement.

Larissa latched on to one arm. "Just be careful, okay?" she whispered, referring to his imminent meeting.

Anatoly winked at her, planted a second kiss on her makeup-covered face, and headed out.

# Chapter 18

Nick just didn't like to be alone.

That's why he'd hardly spent any time in the efficiency apartment. Besides, it was a mess. He'd moved in three days earlier and was still living out of suitcases and boxes. The apartment was an okay place, on West Twenty-eighth Street, only a few blocks from Lake of the Isles, but he just couldn't stand to be there. So he stayed late at work. Or visited friends. Or cruised Lunds, the pickup grocery store, leaving with a free cup of coffee and a Scando cookie made with lots of butter and chunky sugar.

He saw movies, too, at the Uptown Theatre and the U Film Society. Tonight, though, he visited the evening English classes, something he was supposed to have done two weeks ago. On his way to St. Louis Park, he drove around the north shore of Lake Calhoun and admired the warm evening sun on the water. He wondered if Linda was out there sailing, roller-skating, or biking—in short, having more fun alone than they'd had together.

Even though he helped the teacher and became involved with a small group of immigrants practicing telephone conversation, Nick still felt unsettled when he left the class. Now, back in his car, he was alone again.

Immediately, his mind ran down his list of friends. Who could he visit? There was Laura, a waitress friend, but he didn't feel like crossing the Mississippi, going into St. Paul, then finding out she was at work. Didn't he know someone closer who'd like to see him?

Vera and Luba.

Nick checked his watch. Nine-thirty. He wouldn't even have to make up something. He could just tell them that he was visiting the English classes and was on his way home when he saw their light.

He'd seen Vera and Luba three times since their arrival a week earlier. First, he'd stopped by the following day with two more chairs someone had donated, and ended up staying for dinner. Then they came down to his office for the official first meeting, after which they had walked through downtown. He was supposed to tell them all the details; how long they'd be supported, that English classes were mandatory, that the job service would do its best. He tried to prepare them for the months ahead; Vera would be working soon while Luba needed more English before hunting for a job in chemical engineering.

Nick reached for the ignition. The last time he had seen Vera and Luba was the day before yesterday when he had taken them to the synagogue. It was there that he presented them to their host family—volunteers who were to introduce them to Judaism, show them the freeway system, and offer the definitive explanation of why American bread was so squishy.

The car, for once, started smoothly. He let it idle for a minute, then headed out of the parking lot. Virginia Avenue, where most of the Russians lived, was right around the corner. This was St. Louis Park, the Jewish *shtetl* of Middle America, complete with one bagel store, modern synagogues, a shopping mall, and homes that ranged from modest to glitzy. No wonder the Russians went into culture shock.

Nick stopped in front of the two-story walk-up and leaned over in his seat. Nothing, not a single light burned from behind the white lace curtains. Nick sighed, assuming that Vera and Luba weren't asleep but out, probably at Anatoly's.

He sat there, bent over, not knowing what to do or where to go, when a shadow darkened the windows from inside. The curtains parted slightly, closed, and the figure faded away.

Nick inched over for a better look at their apartment. Only the plain white curtains filled the windows. But he'd seen someone, hadn't he? Perhaps it was the wind. No, he'd seen a shadow. Perhaps it was a burglar.

Afraid for Vera and Luba, Nick climbed out of the car. Wouldn't that be a great welcome to the Land of the Free. You go out and someone robs you. That's what the Soviet press always picked up on. American papers highlighted Sakharov and other dissidents, while the Sovs reported all the gruesome stuff that happened to the average American. The message was simple: there might be a lot of *jeanzi* in America, but look at how Americans are afraid to go out at night. And if they do, they're mugged and often killed. Freedom is not worth your life.

Nick knew that fear was in the back of every immigrant's mind. The murderers, robbers, druggies. The horror stories they'd heard all their lives. Nick had seen too many Russians crack under the pressure of discarding the old life and then struggling to adapt to the new. There was the *babushka* who went wandering one night—right into a four-lane highway. The man, Sasha, who couldn't get a job, turned to drink, and drove a hundred miles an hour into a bridge. He lived, thanks to American medicine, as a quadriplegic.

Nick couldn't let that happen to any of his clients, not if he could help it. He pulled open the glass front door of the apartment building and started up the stairs. The walls, carpeting, and chandeliers were swimming-pool blue.

He passed through the heavy fire door and stood in the corridor, overcome by the odor of boiled chicken and Red Moscow perfume. Four apartments, four doors, and three Russian families were up here. A television blared through one of the doors, a scratchy record of Russian love songs came from another. The apartment with the handwritten words *Vera and Luba* beneath the doorbell was silent.

He stood silent, too, and listened. It was hard to hear over the TV next door, but he was sure he heard the whoosh of feet on the carpeting, then nothing.

Either Vera and Luba were home or they were out and someone had broken into their apartment. Unable to stop himself, he rapped gently, as if fearful of waking them. When no response came, he tapped again, longer, harder. With no answer, he reached for the doorknob. Without thinking, he twisted it and the door opened.

"Is anybody here?" he asked into the dark apartment. "Vera? Luba? It's me, Nick."

There was no response, and he briefly considered rousing someone from next door to help him check it out. Questions led to questions, however, and he didn't want the Russians to think he was a snooper. They'd think he worked for the FBI, Nick considered wryly.

Nick pushed the door open farther and stepped in. The hall light bounced off the walls and drifted across the gold shag. Someone was here. He could feel the stirred air, sense the coarse smell.

"Hello?"

He looked immediately to his right, through the galley kitchen and to the dining area. The black shapes of a teapot and a soup kettle rested on the stove. A basket of onions sat on the counter and one of fruit filled the center of the dinner table.

He swallowed and took a step toward the living room. This was as far as he dared go. He struggled to keep his sight on what was actually here and his imagination off some feared burglar with a gun.

Suddenly there was a dull noise. He froze, unable to pinpoint its source. Too late he realized that the sound came from directly behind him. He was trapped. Whoever was in the apartment was hiding in the hall closet. He spun around just as the closet door was thrown aside and a huge figure burst out. One hand grabbed Nick by his shirt, the other smashed into the side of his face.

Nick's head burst like an exploding star as the intruder hurled Nick back against the wall. Sprayed plaster scraped his scalp like gravel. Nick shook his throbbing head, managed to look up, and saw a deep scar on the man's right cheek. Above that cheek, Nick saw the man's fist poised again. Nick punched back, but could not stop the solid fist from smashing into his jaw. The power of the blow reverberated noisily in Nick's head, his body. And as the pain screamed through his senses, his eyes closed. . . .

## Chapter 19

Vera stood on the corner of Nicollet and Tenth wondering if she had confused the date Major Petrov had given her. If she were right, if contact were to be made that Wednesday night at 10:00 P.M., then he was late.

Nicollet Mall had emptied out and only the sounds of the fountains and the classical music from the bus stops filled the air. She felt ridiculously vulnerable here, standing in the open by a bridal shop.

Almost five minutes later she noticed the lights of a small foreign car move steadily down the street. She knew it was him. The silver vehicle slowed, pulled toward her. Still she did not move as the car's wheels rolled along the concrete curb and came to a stop. The curly-haired man behind the steering wheel pressed a button and the passenger window slipped down electrically.

"Vera?"

She checked the street as she reached for the door handle. No sooner had she settled in the leather seat than he pushed a button and the window slid upward, sealing her in. He plunged the gearshift forward and they pulled away.

A block later, he asked, "When did you arrive?"

"Eight days ago."

"How much did they tell you?"

"Enough."

He adjusted the air conditioning and reached up to the tape deck. As he turned left on Marquette toward the Mississippi, a Rachmaninoff concerto came over the four speakers.

"What's your name?" asked Vera.

The man checked both mirrors of the BMW. "So they told you enough . . . but not that much, eh?"

"I was simply told when and where you'd contact me. You were late."

"Sorry, got hung up."

"We have a schedule to go over," said Vera as they passed the base of the IDS Tower. "Where can we talk?"

"I'll pull off by the river." He glanced over at her with bright eyes. "Want to do your work and get back to the Soyuz as soon as possible, eh?"

Glaring at him, she said, "No."

"So you're not doing it for love of Mother Russia. Smart girl. I just hope they're paying you as much as they are me." Shrugging, he added, "I guess they didn't tell you anything because they didn't want to jeopardize me. How good of them."

Vera eyed the handsome man. He wore a pink knit shirt and light gray pants. Was this how he afforded the expensive clothes and car?

"I want to know your name."

"No need to be upset. It's Richard Stevens." He turned right on Washington and pulled to a red light. "You can start in a few days. It shouldn't take long if you're as good as they say."

The light popped green and Richard Stevens continued down to Portland. He turned left and the road deteriorated rapidly as he drove into this deserted corner of town. Empty, enormous flour mills loomed before them.

Stevens slowed as the car bumped over two pairs of railroad tracks.

"Listen," he said, "they asked me to do this—and they're paying me a lot of money. I requested someone who knew computers. So they sent you. I don't know why you're doing this, but we might as well cooperate. You just don't look very willing about the whole thing."

Vera braced herself. "I'll do my job."

"You're sure you can do it? They want the computer prints . . . and the manufacturing process of the gallium arsenide chip."

Vera knew she could handle the prints but the precise manufacturing details might require a chemist. Forcing herself to sound certain, she said, "The prints and the lab reports on the chip will all be in the computer itself. Get me to the computer and I will get you all the information."

This was not, she knew as she glanced at him, an ordinary man and he was not asking simple questions. He was judging her. She could tell by the tight muscles around his eyes. His mouth shut and his lips began to swell, too, as he clenched his teeth. The KGB had selected this man because of his connections, but already Vera wanted to have as little to do with him as possible.

He said nothing further as he steered the BMW behind a deserted flour mill and swung past a towering pile of gravel. He brought the car to a halt in front of the mill. Down an incline the dark Mississippi water foamed white as it tumbled over the concrete apron of St. Anthony Falls.

"That's the waterfall down there that started this city," said Stevens, switching off the car. "This was the flour-milling center of the world. Beneath us—beneath this entire area—is a maze of spillways that brought water power to all these mills. This was where the parent company of DataResearch got its start."

He tapped his window and Vera looked up. His sudden change of subject unnerved her. Immediately to their left, cement silos and an enormous flour mill of limestone blocks rose out of the ground. What few windows there were in the structures were smashed out.

"It was called General Milling and they made an enormous amount of money. The flour division is still one of their largest, but the company was always thinking ahead. So they used all that money to open an electrical division in the forties, which has become the largest part of the company. Then in the sixties they heard what Tommy Lichton was doing, so they took him out of his garage laboratory, built him his own building, and gave him free rein. The company's making hundreds of millions because of that decision." Stevens paused and turned to Vera. "They were always thinking ahead, planning for the future. That's what I like about this area. And that's what I'm doing. Taking the money from the Soviets and planning something good with my life. What about you?"

She stared out over the river, then turned back to him. "Comrade Stevens, I am obligated to the KGB to do a perfect job. I will do nothing less. My cover took years to develop and it is not the KGB's policy to divulge any more than is absolutely needed. I am not from California, you know. My personal feelings have no business here. Should you continue to press for unnecessary information, I will inform my superiors that you are a security risk and recommend a halt to this operation."

Stevens, seemingly unfazed, studied her in the dark. Vera shifted uncomfortably. Finally, his mind made up, he reached for the ignition.

"We'll start in a few days and continue as long as it takes. I'll pick you up on a different corner each night and then we'll proceed to DataResearch's downtown facility. Questions?"

"No."

The car engine came to life and Stevens switched on the headlights. Caught in the piercing beams were a dozen or so rats the size of kittens. Their eyes red dots in the black night, they screeched at the car. Then the rodents, fattened by years of grain that had fallen through the boards of the mills, scurried to a hole and disappeared into an abandoned spillway.

# Chapter 20

The smell of dirty socks—his socks—filled Nick's nose. The odor was so familiar that he couldn't fail to recognize it.

He opened his eyes and saw the worn black vinyl of a car seat. Above he could make out a familiar tear in the car's ceiling. Shit! He was in the back seat of his car. Someone had dumped him there and he was lying among his dirty clothes and books and pots. All the crud he had yet to move into his efficiency. He tried to roll over.

"Ah," he moaned.

Bullets of pain shot through his head. That big black shadow of a hulk hadn't spared any strength in smashing him. Who in the hell was he? A robber? A Russian? Nick ran through his clients. None of them were that big.

Nick twisted slightly and something fell onto the car floor. He started to push himself up but then froze. There were voices right outside. Voices speaking Russian.

*"Tri-sta, chtiri-sta, pyat-sot."* Three hundred, four hundred, five hundred. *"Xoroshow?"* Good?

*"Da."* Yes.

*"Poka."* See you.

Staring into his bag of laundry, Nick listened as two pairs of footsteps went in opposite directions. One pair stopped, disappeared, and was replaced with a car engine. The other came closer and closer. Nick clenched his eyes shut. Was it the goon who had bashed him, now coming to finish him off?

The leather soles trod nearer, slowing as they grew louder. The Russian was at the front of the car now, by the bumper. Then he proceeded to the door, right up to the open window. Nick's body went rigid, but the man didn't stop. He headed on, climbed into the next car. The motor started and the headlights flooded inside Nick's car. Seconds later, the lights swerved to the side as the Russian drove away.

Nick, clutching his head, sat up. A big American car he'd never seen before was speeding away. Rounding the corner up ahead, though, was a vehicle he recognized. It was a dark blue Saab, Anatoly's car.

Nick turned. Once again there was a figure in the apartment window, a figure holding aside the white lace curtains. But this time the lights were on and this time Nick recognized the person.

It was Luba. A blank expression on her face, she dropped the curtains and disappeared from sight.

# Chapter 21

Richard Stevens returned to the riverfront two evenings later. Stopping again in front of the deserted mills, he got out of his car and walked alone to a corner of the old General Milling office. He climbed one flight of wooden stairs and stopped on the platform outside the office door. He took out the key, unlocked the door, and pushed it open with his shoulder. He entered the unlit, musty room, stepped over a pile of boards, and crossed to the windows overlooking the Mississippi and St. Anthony Falls.

Something stirred in the corner and Stevens reached into his sports coat pocket. He lifted out the small, tape measurelike device, and slipped the ring of the coiled wire over his left forefinger. When he heard a slight shuffling on the wooden floor, he stuck his right forefinger into the second ring and pulled. Glinting light, the fine wire notched with

## THE RED ENCOUNTER

pointed teeth appeared between his hands. Efficient, noiseless, and, among other virtues, undetectable by airport X ray, the device ensured instant death. Such had been the case with Volodya in Moscow.

A rat screeched and disappeared into the wall, and Stevens let the wire recoil in its container. One day this office was slated to be an expensive restaurant and the silos condominiums, all overlooking the river, but for now it remained a megalopolis of rat dens.

He returned to the window and gazed down at the Mississippi. He was here tonight because of Vera, because he had too much money at stake on this operation. There was an aspect, a softness, of her personality that he didn't trust. She might grow to like it here, and he simply had to assure she wouldn't.

Below, a shadow moved, and Stevens sank to the side. It was him. Stevens watched as the slim figure took a step onto the brick road, checked both sides, then made for the wooden steps.

Before the young man was even a quarter of the way up, Richard Stevens had positioned himself. As the door slowly edged open, Stevens again had the wire stretched between his hands.

"Hey," whispered the young man, "are you—"

Stevens was upon him. He kicked the door shut, slammed his fist into the back of the man's head, and had the wire around his neck in seconds. The man tried to jump, pull away.

"I wouldn't do that, Joseph," said Stevens, pulling the saw-toothed wire tight against the man's neck.

"Hey, man! What are you doing? Ow!" screeched Joseph as the teeth took hold. "I come here to give you head and . . . and . . ."

Stevens caught Joseph's hand as it slipped into his jeans.

"That's what I want." Stevens reached into Joseph's pocket and pulled out the stiletto. "Sorry for the discomfort."

He lifted the loop over Joseph's head, then let the wire recoil. With his elbow he shoved the young man into the middle of the room. Joseph stumbled, regained his balance.

Rubbing his throat, he stared through the darkness at his customer.

"Not funny, man. Not at all. You want head, you get it. You want ass, it's yours, nice and tight. You want leather, it's yours, too, but no one takes my blood."

He'd never told Joseph his name and the young man had yet to see Stevens in full light. When he simply felt like paying for sex, Stevens called a number and told Joseph where to meet him.

Stevens asked, "Are you a fag when you're on your own?"

"What?" he said, rubbing his neck. "Me? Fuck no! I got a wife." Joseph's smile appeared in the dark. "I'm just a real freelancer, you know. Anything. And I sure as shit make good money doing this. I got a judge, some execs, a senator, a theater director, and some rich Wayzata boys. I take big cocks—a lot of old farts who can't get it any other way. People pay the best in these white-bread towns."

Stevens knew why Joseph sold his body. He had seen it in the young man's red nostrils, heard it in his sniffling.

"Cocaine?"

"You ain't as dumb as some of them." Joseph checked the room, noting that Stevens stood by the only door. "Hey, man, you gonna cut me more or you want to get down to fuckin'? Just call it like it is."

"Neither. I have a special job for you. And I pay by the gram."

"No shit? Clean stuff?"

"The best. All you have to do is rough up someone."

Joseph laughed. "This a fairy fight or somethin'? Someone give you the shaft in the wrong place or you got a boy friend sleepin' with someone else?"

Stevens reached into his coat pocket and took out an envelope. He tossed it across the room.

"A woman. Here's her picture and address."

"Listen, I don't do no rapes or murders."

"That's not what I want. I just want you to follow her for a few days and then rough her up."

"That all, man?" He laughed, picking up the photo.

Stevens nodded. "But you have to do a good job and you

can't get caught." Stevens lifted his hands and pulled the wire wide. "I mean it: don't get caught."

Joseph, rubbing his throat, stepped back. "This is serious shit, ain't it?"

"Yes, and I'll pay you well. I'll get you twenty-five thousand dollars' worth."

"Hot cocks," he said. "That much ain't easy to come by in this town. I'll do it, man. I'll mess up your lady friend just as good as I fuck."

"Fine." Tossing the knife at Joseph's feet, he knew he'd have to decide later if he'd let the young man live. "The woman's name is Luba Volshevetz. She has a daughter, Vera Karansky, but don't touch her by any means. Remember that. I don't want the younger woman hurt. You can do whatever you like to her mother, just don't do anything that will attract attention. And, by all means, don't kill her."

Joseph reached over and picked up his knife. "No way. Don't worry. I don't make stiffs. You got to draw the line somewhere, you know."

"A week?"

"Sure. This is a slow time—all the big meat's out at the lake." Confident, Joseph said, "A week and I'll meet you back here. But you better have the stuff, man."

"I already have it," lied Stevens. He'd get it when and if he needed it.

Joseph stretched out a hand and moved forward. "Hey, man, I'll give it to you real good right now if . . ."

Stevens hesitated, then backed away. "Next week. You'll get your payment next week after you take care of Luba Volshevetz."

## Chapter 22

"You say all this happened last night?" asked Hughes, his hands behind his back.

"Right."

Nick and the white-haired FBI man strolled through Loring Park on the edge of downtown. Clumps of people, feeding goldfish and ducks, were gathered around the small lake. Condominiums, hotels, and office buildings towered beyond the water and tall elms.

"I just stopped for no special reason." Nick was as confused about what happened at Vera's as he was about Hughes' response. "You're not very surprised."

Hughes raised an eyebrow. "Well, ah, you get used to this sort of thing."

"Sure. You try it sometime and see if you get used to it. My head's still attached, but just barely."

"Well, it wasn't a robbery. We know that much. We have to assume that if something were stolen, it would have been reported to the police."

Nick had hardly slept all night. It took hours for his head to stop pounding and longer for his thoughts to slow down. It wasn't Anatoly who slugged him, he knew that much; but it might have been a friend of his.

Walking on, Hughes said, "Did you get a look at him?"

"No, not really. Just a—"

Nick sensed something and spun around. A squirrel hopped up to him and then sat back, begging for food.

"Loring Park—home of the attack squirrels." Then he remembered part of that face. "Hey, wait. He had a big scar, a scar along the bottom of his right cheek. I forgot all about that."

"A scar?"

"Yeah, right here." Nick touched his cheek, and something else came to mind. "I've seen that guy before. At the airport when Vera arrived. He was there taking pictures. I think he photographed me, too, but I didn't see his face. Just that scar. I'm sure it's the same guy."

Hughes, for the first time, was disturbed. "Well, that's something. But not enough."

Nick glanced over at the other man, unable to believe his response. He'd called the FBI man first thing that morning and asked to meet. Hughes had told Nick to calm down, not to tell anyone, and to meet him late that afternoon. Nick had expected immediate action.

"So what do I do?" asked Nick. "Call Anatoly and ask him what in hell's going on? Tell Vera I was in their apartment when they were out—and some moron bopped me?"

"No. You do nothing."

"What!" he said in disbelief. He'd had a hard enough time keeping it to himself just for the day. "You mean, just forget it?"

"Exactly."

"But what if . . . what if . . ."

"Don't worry. He won't come looking for you." Cool, calculated, Hughes eyed a young couple who sat kissing on a bench. "If he'd wanted to do you any harm, he would have done it then. He wouldn't have put you back in your car."

Nick shrugged. That made as much sense as any of this. "What about Vera and Luba? Shouldn't I at least warn them, tell them someone broke into their apartment?"

"No."

Nick stopped still. "What are you—nuts? I could have been killed last night and now I'm supposed to pretend it never happened? Forget it. What if Vera and Luba are attacked? What then?" Glancing across the lake, he said, "How am I going to look them straight in the eye? And Anatoly and Larissa—I'm going to their house for Luba's birthday dinner next week."

Hughes pursed his lips. "All right, Nick. If you must do something, do this. When you have dinner at Anatoly's find out everything you can. Something's going on there we don't know about. Poke around. Look. Ask questions. Anatoly very well might be our man. But don't mention your suspicions to anyone—not to Vera, Luba, Anatoly, or to any friends. Absolutely no one. You're working for us and I'm telling you that directly."

Nick shook his head. "Like hell I'm working for you."

Theodore Hughes watched the rusty Chevrolet pull out of the parking place and head toward Lyndale Avenue. He wouldn't have involved Miller at all if he'd known how quickly Stevens might discover the identity of the Soviet agent. Now, however, with Miller involved—personally, perhaps, with the agent herself—he was forced to throw him a few curves, try and keep him from discovering who they were really after.

Hughes headed toward the other end of the park where his car and the two men sat waiting. If the operation went reasonably well, they'd arrest Vera Karansky within ten days. At this very moment the video cameras were being readied five stories beneath street level in DataResearch's software facilities.

Hughes passed a small picnic gazebo in the corner of the park and came to his car, a plain green sedan. He opened the car door and sat down. The man in the front seat hung up the phone.

"We have a bit of a problem," said Hughes. "We might have to remove our Mr. Miller. He could probably identify his assailant."

His assistant, a quiet, athletic man, turned and said, "Well, that might be the least of our troubles. That team you put on Stevens just called with some pretty interesting stuff. He's quite the swinging guy, just like you thought."

A dull throb crept up the back of Hughes' neck. "Get the aspirin out of the glove compartment, would you?"

# Chapter 23

Nick stood in the living room of Anatoly and Larissa's split-level home, his fists stuck in the pockets of his corduroy sports coat. Find out something. Find out whatever you can. That's what Hughes had advised. And that's what he thought he'd wanted to do too. But now that he was here for Luba's birthday dinner, he wasn't so sure.

He ran a hand through his light brown hair and walked across the room, which was filled with Scandinavian teak furniture. Anatoly was involved in something covert. But what did it have to do with the GALA-1 supercomputer? If only there were some direct, honest way Nick could find out, learn the source of the extra cash.

As if he weren't enough on edge, the atmosphere of the house was anything but tranquil. He was in the living room by himself, while Larissa, Luba, and Vera busied themselves in the kitchen. Anatoly, the source of the tension, wasn't home and no one knew where he was. Had he perhaps forgotten his mother's birthday, her first in America?

Nick stared at Vera as she came out of the kitchen, a plate of sliced cucumbers, green onions, and tomatoes in hand. Her expression was blank, withdrawn, as if she were here only physically. What was it, he wondered, that disturbed her so much, that made her so resistant to happiness?

"I can't believe all this food," he said. "No one can put on a spread like Russians."

He took an appraising look at the dinner table, every square inch of which was covered with dishes and platters of smoked fish, pâté, caviar, potato salad, pickles, sliced tomatoes, cucumbers, onions, black bread, and two bottles of chilled vodka.

Vera laughed, the morose look instantly disappearing from her face. That's what Nick liked about Russians. It was easy to get through. With Linda, as with all too many others, it was easier to get her into bed than to touch her emotions.

"This?" said Vera, with an exaggerated, very Russian wave of the arm. "This is just *zakuski*—hors d'oeuvres. There are three more courses. This is a special occasion—Mama's fifty-third birthday."

Nick grinned and shrugged. "Well, I still say Russians know better than anyone how to let loose and celebrate. You're a hundred times better at it than Americans."

"I'm glad we can do something right," said Vera as she took a glass of rolled-up napkins from a sideboard.

Nick turned and looked out at the dusky evening. The street, which offered no sidewalks, was deserted.

"This is really deep suburbia," he said over his shoulder to Vera. "It's awful. I can't figure out why people live out here. Minneapolis is wonderful—it has the lakes, parks, theaters, and downtown." Vera, pulling back her dark brown hair, came up the other side of the table and gazed out.

"I'm glad to hear you say that. This is the country, not the city. What are all the people doing?"

"Having fun without us."

She laughed. "Where?"

"Uptown, downtown. There're some good bars and clubs to dance." This was what he was hoping for tonight, a few minutes alone. The next opportunity wouldn't come for several days, if at all, when he was scheduled to take Luba to the doctor. "If you want, sometime I could show you a few places."

As they stood at the large window, Nick watched Vera's face drain of color. She seemed to withdraw.

Nick leaned toward her. "Vera, are you—"

She pointed out the window. "Look."

Headlights turned into the driveway, flashing their power against Vera's pale complexion. The car was dark blue.

"It's Anatoly," said Vera in a hushed voice.

Nick felt her fingers grasp his arm and gently yet powerfully sink into him. She held on, almost reluctant to let go. And Nick watched her eyes fall shut and heard her take a deep breath. He knew she wanted to tell him something.

He laid his fingers on top of her hand, and her eyes opened at once and stared directly at his. Luba rushed out of the kitchen, and Vera took a reflexive step away from Nick.

"Is he here?" asked Luba.

"Yes," answered her daughter.

Nick looked back out the window and saw the tall, slightly overweight Anatoly walking to the house. He wore a light gray suit and carried a box under one arm. Nick squinted but could not see if it was a box from Data-Research.

Anatoly came in and disappeared down the open half-flight of stairs into the basement. He rattled some keys and opened a door in the far corner, then locked that door and came up. In his hand was a bottle of cognac.

"I was worried," said Luba.

Vera tensed, and said, "You're late!"

Anatoly went directly to his mother and kissed her on the cheek. "Congratulations, Mama."

Larissa leaned her head out of the kitchen, and said, "He's late because of his work."

"Larissa, enough." Anatoly deposited the bottle of cognac on the table, took out a cigarette, and stuck it in the corner of his mouth.

Luba went over to Anatoly, studied his face, then took him by the hand, and said, "Shame on you, son. You have a beautiful house, an enormous stereo, a television that projects on a movie screen, and you've already had God knows how many cars. But look at how tense you are. Shame on you, Anatoly. You're growing old in America. Now come sit down at my birthday table and let's celebrate."

Anatoly turned on the stereo and pushed up the volume. They settled at the table, Luba at the head and Vera and Anatoly on either side. Stepping in before Larissa, Nick pulled up a seat next to Vera, leaving the other end chair for the blonde.

Vera glared at her brother. "Anatoly, the vodka."

He rubbed his long, tired face, and reached for the bottle. He poured vodka right to the brim of each juice glass.

"A toast," he said.

"To Luba!" Larissa, like a professional drinker, raised her glass without spilling.

"Happy birthday," added Nick, raising his glass.

Luba smiled and tossed back her entire glass of vodka. The others followed, draining their glasses. A platter of pickles was passed as a chaser. The dish of black caviar followed, in turn followed by black bread and a mound of unsalted butter. Each of them took a piece of bread, layered it thickly with butter, and crowned it with glossy caviar. Nick smashed the fish eggs into the butter with his fork, then poured a round of vodka.

"Another toast to Luba's birthday!"

The vodka fell on empty stomachs and rapidly lightened the mood of the party. Eating his caviar sandwich, Nick began to relax for the first time in weeks. Perhaps, he thought, it was good that he and Linda had separated. Maybe he'd learn something about himself.

The caviar quickly disappeared, as did the smoked fish. The cucumbers and tomatoes dwindled, only to be replenished. They drank a toast to family and friends, one to world peace, and Vera took a large pitcher of apple juice from the refrigerator and filled each of their water glasses.

"Imagine," said Luba, "I'm fifty-three and I feel like a little girl. I didn't know how much of the world I was missing when I was in the Soviet Union. And I've never met such nice people as Americans."

"You're going to do great here, Luba," said Nick, heaping potato salad onto his plate. "To a fault, Americans like people who smile."

Vera touched Nick's hand. "She smiles a lot, doesn't she?"

Leaning toward her, Nick nodded in agreement. He wondered, however, what made Vera different, what held her back.

Luba's face flushed red, and she pressed her hand to her chest. Her beaming face the only sign of the alcohol, she slowly and steadily pushed out the chair and stood.

"So a toast," said Luba, nodding to Anatoly, whose job it was to keep the vodka glasses full. "A toast to my new coun-

## THE RED ENCOUNTER

try, the United States of America, and to my children, Vera and Anatoly, and his wonderful wife, Larissa. I love you all so much." She paused, suddenly flooded with emotion. She had remembered something of the dearest importance. "You—you will all have won—wonderful lives here. I—I only wish little . . ." She rubbed her eyes slowly. "If only Vera's little boy could be here."

Nick almost dropped his glass. "Vera, you have a . . . a son?"

Vera stared at her plate. "Yes."

Shocked, Nick's eyes went from her to Larissa to Anatoly to Luba. They all sat stone-faced, no one offering any hint of explanation. He turned to Vera, wanting to pry the truth out of her. Had she left her son behind by choice or was this the source of her melancholy?

Vera, escaping from Nick, pushed back her chair and went to her mother's side. The older woman's joyous mood had vanished, and, her hands to her eyes, she was clearly holding back tears. Vera held her, then looked at her brother and nodded.

Anatoly understood the message. He reached into the pocket of his suit and pulled out a small package.

"Mama," he said, rising to his feet. "Mama, we have a birthday present for you."

Anatoly touched his mother's elbow and then carefully slipped the wrapped package into her hand. Luba studied her daughter on one side, her son on the other, and, gift in hand, settled again in her seat. One hand lightly to her lips, she held the gift in her lap, not quite sure what to do. Vera and Anatoly sat down and watched without speaking.

Finally, Larissa said, "Go on, open it!"

Luba's thick fingers tore through the silver gift wrap, dropping the paper to the floor. In her hands she held a small jeweler's box.

"Oh, such beautiful children I have." Enthralled by the box alone, she turned and kissed Vera and Anatoly.

Luba hesitated another moment before taking the box in both hands. Her fingers trembling, she lifted the lid. A barely audible gasp emerged from her motionless lips.

Nick sat forward, unable to see inside the box. "Well, what is it?"

Luba couldn't speak. She couldn't move. Tears came to her eyes and dropped unrestrained on the gift.

Vera laid her hand on her mother's wrist. "Are you all right?"

Luba nodded slightly and muttered, "The diamond." She held the sparkling gem to the light as if it had magical powers. "Dear Lord, I can't believe it. It's the diamond from my grandmother's, my mother's, and my own wedding ring! Oh, Anatoly and Vera, thank you!" She took her children under each arm and pulled them to her chest. "I can't believe it. I thought you'd sold it months ago!"

"I just couldn't," said Vera. "I'm sorry, Mama, but I was afraid to take the gold ring out too. The setting's new."

"Yes," said Anatoly, defensively, "but it's a very good ring. Pure gold. I had the best jeweler in town work on it."

Luba held the ring between her thumb and forefinger and thrust it out. "Look, Nick. Isn't it beautiful? It's been in my family since before the Revolution."

The many-faceted diamond caught the light from all directions, and Nick raised his brow in admiration.

"It's huge. How did you get it out, Vera?"

In the midst of sipping her juice, Vera choked, spraying the beverage back into the glass.

"Um, I just hid it."

Larissa poured herself some vodka, and said, "I don't know how you did it, Vera, but I thank God you didn't get caught. If they'd found that diamond on you, it would have been Siberia until the year 2000!"

"Enough!" The glow returned to Luba's face. "No more of such talk. We are here and we are safe. Let us be thankful for that." She paused. "My grandparents knew some Jewish prayers, and I think my father knew one too."

Nick, Vera, Anatoly, and Larissa bowed their heads.

"So I'll say what I know how to say, Christian or Jewish: *Slava Bogu.*" Thanks to God. "*Slava Bogu* for everything we have." Luba held up the ring. "This place will be good for my children, and that is why I came: for them and to be with them. Still, we have left so much behind. Friends, memories, and . . . our dear Vladik. I am fifty-three today. I left my entire fifty-two years of wonderful life and dear friends behind. But no more will I consider that lost."

She attempted to place the wedding ring where she had always worn it, on the fourth finger of her right hand. The new ring, however, was too small to go over her knuckle.

Nick spotted the problem. "Try the other hand. Americans wear their wedding rings on the left hand."

"Really?"

Luba's frown of disappointment turned to a smile as, with a nudge, she slid the ring on her left fourth finger.

"There, I'm an American now." She tugged on the ring. "American until I die."

Nick raised his glass. "A toast to the ring!"

Glasses were raised, clinked, and emptied.

Vera cleared her throat, and said, "We have to dance!" She took Nick by the hand and jumped up. "If this is a party, we have to dance between courses!"

*"Da, da, da!"* agreed Luba.

Larissa sprang to her feet. "Yes, before soup!"

They all followed Vera into the living room, where she put on a record of as-seen-on-TV original hits. At once Luba clicked her feet together and, her elbows stiff, she rotated her wrists. Vera, Anatoly, and Larissa moved in large, swooping, more modern movements, without the least bit of self-consciousness or inhibition. Watching them, Nick admired this very Russian characteristic—the ability to truly relax among friends. But he felt a little silly, a little too American, to let loose as they had. So he slipped over to one of the lamps, flicked it off, then turned up the volume on the stereo. With the environment a little more masked, he joined them.

And to the colorful sounds of "Disco Party," they all danced, loose and free.

Over three hours later, they finished the final course, *plov,* a Georgian rice dish with lamb, and sat full and relaxed. Luba, her eyes on the ring, rose and crossed through the living room and to the upstairs bathroom. Now, realized Nick, was his chance.

He stood and almost fell over.

"Are you going to be all right?" asked Vera.

Nick rubbed his forehead. "If we hadn't danced between courses I'd be dead. Aren't you even a little bit drunk?"

With a sly grin, she said, "A little."

"Anatoly, is there another . . ."

From across the table, he nodded. "Downstairs. Between the empty bedroom and the utility room."

Nick left the table and clung to the iron railing as he made his way to the bottom floor. One room, with Larissa's large television, occupied one half of this level, from front to back. On the right were two doors.

Purposefully, Nick walked past the empty bedroom door and went to the second. Closed tightly, this was where Anatoly had gone. This was where he had taken the box from the car. Nick reached for the knob and twisted, but the door wouldn't budge.

Quickly, Nick made his way across the brown-and-white shag carpeting and through the empty bedroom. Entering the bathroom, he found what he expected, another door adjoining the corner room.

First things first. He closed the door behind him, switched on the loud fan, and went to the bathroom. Standing still in front of the toilet, he put his free hand to his head. He'd stopped moving, but his head hadn't. Would he be able to drive home?

Having relieved himself, he went to the other door. He grasped the handle. It didn't move. The door was locked from the other side.

"Damn," he muttered.

He leaned his shoulder against the door and pushed, but without result. Shaking his head, he backed away. He had to open the door. Inside was the key to whatever Anatoly was involved in. Whether or not that was connected with DataResearch, Nick didn't know. It would more than likely tell him, though, why he'd been slugged and knocked out in Vera's apartment.

He reached into his coat pocket and extracted a credit card from his wallet. Then Nick dropped to his knees and inserted the piece of hard plastic between the door and the frame. Squinting, he shook his head to try and clear it. If only he could get the credit card in there and push back the spring-loaded bolt.

Coming up from the bottom, he caught it on the second try. Gently he lifted the card. The piece of brass hardware moved.

Suddenly there was a click. But the sound did not come from the locked door. It came from the door behind him, the one he had walked through.

Slowly, he turned his head and looked up. There, towering above him, was Anatoly.

"What are you doing?" demanded the scowling Russian.

Nick tried to pull himself to his feet.

"Was that door open all the time? Man, I must be drunker than I thought. I thought I was locked in here!"

# Chapter 24

Like a high-tech meteor, the DataResearch building seemed to have fallen out of the sky and lodged in the earth—five stories above ground, five below. While the GALA-1 was buried at the bottom, beneath tons of protective concrete, all that was visible on the street was a short mirrored structure.

With the bells of City Hall chiming 10:00 P.M., Vera met Richard Stevens at the entrance of Minneapolis General Hospital. They crossed Fifth Avenue and onto the triangular plaza in front of DataResearch, then passed a large red steel sculpture. Only as the glow of lights from the entry began to envelop them did Vera feel any hesitancy.

"Not a word as we pass the guard at the front desk," said Stevens as they neared the door. "He's been told you're being brought in to design a program to protect the GALA-1 from disloyal employees. He thinks you're starting tonight and will only be in during off hours. Don't worry, I'm his boss."

The uniformed guard stepped to the door and unfastened the lock. "Good evening, Mr. Stevens."

"Mark, how are you?"

There was no further exchange, and Vera, trying to hide her face, kept her eyes to the ground. As their steps bounced off the granite floor and hard walls, she was overwhelmed by a sense of sheer vulnerability. Here she was in the foyer of corporate America, seconds away from entering its body and spirit. What was done to those who betrayed capitalism?

They entered the elevator, Stevens punched a coded number into a keypad, and the doors eased shut.

As they rode to the bottom floor, Stevens said, "I was thinking about the lab reports last night. The manufacturing process of the gallium arsenide chip is very important, you know. And then I remembered your mother. She's a chemical engineer, isn't she?"

Vera froze and stared blankly ahead. "Yes, but not for this sort of thing. She was trained many years ago. Besides, a chemist won't be necessary. I'll be able to get everything we need from the computer itself."

"Let's hope so."

The elevator settled gently on the bottom floor, and Stevens stepped out. Vera followed.

"Well, what do you think?" he asked.

"What?"

She raised her head. They had stopped in front of a thick plate-glass window, through which she saw the largest collection of computer equipment she'd seen in months. Suddenly, she forgot about any treasonous activity and was instead filled with a warm glow, as if she'd just bumped into an old friend. This equipment—the rows of disk drives, the black-screened terminals, the mainframes—was her life, her work. She was not in the United States. She was back home.

Her eyes rested on the rectangular machine in the center, and she said, "That's it."

## THE RED ENCOUNTER

"Yes. The GALA-1."

Stevens cut to the left, opened a heavy metal door, and proceeded down a hall. Vera followed him to the second door on the right and into a small room. It was a plain space with concrete walls and fluorescent lighting. Vera's eyes immediately fell upon the table on which sat a terminal, keyboard, and printer.

"It's a direct hookup," said Stevens. "You'll be the machine's sole operator. Totally in control."

As if Stevens no longer existed, Vera crossed to the chair in front of the terminal, sat down, and took a spiral notebook from her purse. She ran her fingertips over the bottom of the plastic keyboard, then reached behind and pressed a switch. The video display clicked and a green cursor throbbed with life.

She had to search, hunt the digits, find the secret of the all-gallium-arsenide computer. The specifications and logic design were all stored somewhere in its electronic nerve system. Quickly, she ran down the list of what needed to be done. She just had to find out where the files were stored, break through the protectives. Then she'd have to write a program, open the locks, and take a look at each file. That would take two or three nights. There'd probably be a little more than a half-dozen files—the printed circuit layouts, logic, wire tabs, design equations, circuit buzzwords. . . .

Vera heard a voice behind her. "What?" she said, turning back to Stevens.

"Do you think you'll be able to do it?"

"Can I do it?" she said, her mind pulsing with energy. "Of course I can."

She had no choice if she ever wanted to see her son again.

# Chapter 25

It was lunch hour, and the streets of downtown Minneapolis were crowded with people sunning themselves on benches and gathered around food carts. Vera and Luba followed Nick as he led them down Nicollet Mall to the Doctors Building, where Luba had a one o'clock appointment.

They crossed Seventh Street and passed between the IDS Tower and Dayton's, the landmark department store that kept Minneapolis in fashion. As they neared Eighth, Nick glanced back and again spotted him, some guy with dark bushy hair and a faint mustache. The stranger looked at Nick, then cut into a store. Unless Nick was mistaken, that same man had been waiting on the street when the three of them had left Nick's office.

Vera's hand settled on his wrist.

"Nick, what is it?" she asked.

He tensed. "Just thought I saw someone I knew." That man couldn't be following them, he reasoned. This wasn't the U.S.S.R. "Come on, we better get your mother to the doctor's. It's almost one."

They hurried on, and halfway down the next block the sun broke over the buildings and spilled down on the street. Classical music, piped in at the bus stops, filled the air. Nick checked behind again, and instead of the man he saw clumps of blossoming flowers up and down the curving street.

Luba took a deep breath, and said, "I like it downtown. It's so pretty. And look at all the people, just like back home! Maybe this is a city after all."

They turned the corner and entered the Doctors Building on Ninth Street. As they passed through the second set of doors, they were struck with a gust of cold air and engulfed in subdued lighting.

"Brr," said Vera, rubbing her arms.

"Air conditioning." Nick, his eyes accustomed to the sunshine, struggled to see. "The elevators are over there."

Five of the six brass and chrome elevator doors, however, were locked open. A rope blocked them off and repairmen drifted from one lift to the next.

Nick scanned the green marble hall. "That one's working down at the end."

They boarded the elevator and rode it to the twentieth floor, the top. The doors opened into a penthouse suite of white offices that would have been stark were it not for the extensive artwork. Originals by Miró, Dali, and an array of other modern artists were on display every few feet.

Vera gasped. "Picasso. This is a signed print by Picasso!"

Admiring the next group of prints, Luba said, "No wonder medicine is so expensive here."

While waiting for the doctor, Nick helped Luba fill out a medical questionnaire. Speaking in Russian and English and simply pointing to different parts of the body, they completed the form. A minute later, a tall man with dark hair and a pale complexion appeared.

"Hello, I'm Dr. Feldman," he said, extending his hand. "You must be Luba."

Luba shook his hand. To Vera, she said in Russian, "What a nice man."

The doctor looked at her and said, *"Kenst ridden Yiddish?"*

Luba's eyes opened in amazement. That was the language of her grandparents. She hadn't heard it since they died, since before the war. She strained to remember and it popped into her mind.

"A *bissel!*" A little. "A *bissel,*" she repeated with amusement.

"Good." Dr. Feldman looked at Vera and Nick. "I'm sure we can manage between a little bit of Yiddish and English. I just want to give her a good physical, check that bronchitis she had—in Rome was it?—and make sure everything else is all right. Why don't you two wander off and come back in forty-five minutes or so."

Nick translated what Luba didn't understand, and asked if she'd mind if Vera and he went to get something to eat.

"Of course I don't mind. Now, go on," insisted Luba. "I'll be fine. You two go have fun."

"But—" began Vera.

Dr. Feldman, seeing the reluctance on Vera's face, added, "Don't worry, I'll take good care of her." He took Luba gently by the arm and, leading her away, said, "Besides, I know *ploxo*—bad—and *xoroshow*—good."

Luba laughed aloud. "B'ery, b'ery goodt!"

Vera watched the tall doctor and her mother disappear down the hall. Nick could clearly see the concern on her face.

"Hey, she'll be all right," said Nick, touching her elbow. "You don't mind going out, do you? I'm hungry, and I have to go right back to the office after this."

Blushing slightly, Vera said, "Let's go. There really isn't anything to worry about, is there?"

The man with the bushy hair and faint mustache paced back and forth in the lobby of the Doctors Building. Just rough up the Volshevetz woman, that's what Stevens had said. Just scare her a little. He had made it sound so easy, but how was he, Joseph, supposed to do that if he couldn't even get near her? For three days he had been following her and for three days she had yet to leave her daughter's side. Oh, he was sure he could do a fine job of roughing up Luba Volshevetz. He could handle her with no problem. It was her daughter he was concerned about. To make matters worse, the two women had picked up a third person today, some guy, and all of them had just disappeared into this building.

Joseph ducked down the hall and checked the time at the newspaper stand. After one. How long was he going to have to wait this time? He strolled back down the hall, trying to formulate a plan. As he neared the elevator lobby, he heard a ring, noticed the single working car open and saw Vera Karansky and her American friend step out. He panicked.

They were behind him, coming his way, while in front of him two women in wheelchairs blocked the front door.

Joseph spun to the side, saw the sign marking the stairwell, and lunged for that door. He pulled it open, slipped in, and plastered himself up against the wall. As the hydraulic hinge pulled the door shut behind him, Joseph got the break he'd been waiting days for. He heard the man and woman speaking in what he recognized as Russian although he didn't understand anything except the name "Feldman." As the door hissed shut Joseph could barely contain his excitement. He waited several minutes before checking the hall. Vera and her friend were gone, and Joseph cut directly across the lobby to the building's directory. He noted that Dr. Feldman's office was in the penthouse and started for the elevator.

He stopped. No. There probably was a reception desk right across from the elevators. They'd notice him at once and later be able to identify him. No, thought Joseph, he was smarter than that.

He turned around and made his way back to the stairwell. He had to do this one right, had to do it nice and smooth. . . .

# Chapter 26

Nick bought them each a sandwich and a bottle of juice, and they made their way up to the fountains at Orchestra Hall. Water bubbled from atop chrome pipes, slithered down to street level, and then fell from platform to platform to the reflecting pool below. Walkways and stepping stones jutted in and out of the water, and Nick and Vera made themselves comfortable between a waterfall and the pool.

Vera rolled her sandwich out of its plastic wrap and tried

to identify what she was about to eat. She lifted up a corner of the bread and stared at the concoction of cheese and strange vegetables.

To the roar of the falling water, she said, "I know Mozart, Tchaikovsky, Chopin, Rachmaninoff. I know Pushkin, Tolstoy, Shakespeare, and Molière. But I certainly don't know what these are."

"Well, first of all," began Nick, "this is what you call a veggie-sexual sandwich, an integral part of America's health kick." He leaned over, and said, "The big green thing is an avocado, the little green hairy things are alfalfa sprouts."

She closed her eyes and repeated the words to herself.

"I hope you don't think me stupid," she said in Russian.

"Hardly," he said, struggling to find the end of the plastic wrapping that held his own sandwich.

Vera smiled and brushed a wisp of hair out of her face. She took a bite of her sandwich, carefully tasting the new foods.

"Interesting," she said as she chewed. "Are they grown here in Minnesota?"

He laughed. "No. Maybe the alfalfa sprouts are—indoors that is—but not the avocados." He opened his juice. "They're from Mexico or California or Florida. From the south somewhere."

"The food distribution in America is incredible. I can't believe something so fresh came from so far away," she said in amazement. "What about you? Where are you from?"

A wind gust blew a spray of water on them, and Nick gazed out over the fountain. Beyond that and beyond the modern Orchestra Hall rose the irregular skyline. He wished he'd been born here. He wished he could simply say he'd been born and raised in one single place.

"No, I'm not from Minnesota, either. I've only lived here a year or so." He shrugged and his small mouth formed a boyish grin. "My father's a journalist and we weren't in any one city for more than a couple of years—Chicago, L.A., Dallas, Detroit. My mother died when I was a kid, and after that we moved even more often."

# THE RED ENCOUNTER

A warm breeze rushed over them, causing the young trees around the plaza to bend from side to side.

"Is that typical? Are you a typical American?" she asked.

"In a way, yes; in a way, no. I mean, Americans move around a lot, but not as much as we did. Dad's back in Detroit and I came here for the job. Unless you work for the CIA or the NSA, jobs that require Russian are hard to find." An expression of confusion and self-pity came to his face. "Who knows how long I'll stay."

Vera frowned and put down her sandwich. "How confusing. It must be upsetting not really knowing where you'll be."

Nick laughed. "Or where you're from. But that's me and that's America." He gazed off at the light red brick wall of Orchestra Hall. "I could as easily live in Minneapolis as in New York. Or Phoenix. Or Miami. There's nothing holding me here except my job, and that'll only last as long as the Soviet Union lets people emigrate. They could shut the doors tomorrow."

"Oh, yes," said Vera, quietly. "Jobs aren't guaranteed in America."

"No, they're not. But that's not what I'm talking about. I'm talking about mobility—trying to understand where I fit in in my own country."

The subject was one of the most disturbing to him. He needed a sense of place, and he wanted to belong, to understand his own country. Often, he just didn't feel a part of the United States, thought the government was far too shortsighted.

"Well, that gives us something in common besides Russian," said Vera. "We're both hoping to belong to America."

"What?" He raised his head. "Oh, yeah." He took a bite of his sandwich and, chewing, said, "This is a weird country. I love it, but it's weird. Sometimes I think we're suffering from one huge shopping-mall syndrome of complacency and banality, where if you withdraw and hide in a place where you can't see out, then everything's fine. You know, the U.S. was founded by people who wanted to escape and forget their past. They wanted to cut off their roots. And that's true today. People still think that their own actions don't have any consequences. It's changing, though."

Vera lowered her sandwich into her lap and stared off into the fountain. "The same with me, I suppose. There's so much in my past I want to forget but can't. I left so much behind."

"You mean your son?" he said, looking directly into her eyes.

Vera didn't move. Finally, she nodded.

Nick shook his head. "I'm sorry, it's . . . it's none of my business."

"I don't mind," she said calmly.

"It must be rough."

"Yes . . . very." She turned to him. "You see, my husband divorced me and, in the end, he was given custody of Vladik, our son." Forcing herself to smile, she added, "But I suppose that's the way it should be. A boy should be raised by his father, don't you think?"

"Well, not—"

"I think it's time," interrupted Vera, as she looked toward the Doctors Building, "that we get back to my mother."

## Chapter 27

Everyone smiled so much, thought Luba as she came out of the doctor's office. Everyone was so nice. And that doctor, what a gentle man. He had given her a checkup and he hadn't even hurt her! He had tested and probed, looked and felt, and she hadn't cried out once.

These American doctors—expensive but good. All that technology. All the lights bleeping on and off. Even an electronic thermometer. Incredible. And there must have been two nurses for every patient. If she were going to get sick in her life, America was the right place.

"Oi," she said to herself, pausing in front of a painting. "Such beautiful art. These American doctors have good taste too."

A young nurse came up to her, the girl's blond hair put up in a bun. She said something, her white teeth flashing as she spoke. There were, thought Luba, such beautiful white teeth all over America.

*"Shto?"* What, asked Luba.

The nurse spoke again, a little slower and a lot louder. Finally, Luba caught the gist of it.

"Sure, I'll wait in there, in the room," she repeated in Russian. "I'll wait and my daughter, Vera, will come for me."

"Yes," replied the nurse, "Vera."

"Thank you, thank you," said Luba, relieved to be away from the nurse's loud voice.

Luba headed into the waiting room, which looked like a small ballroom. The ceiling was high and decorated with carved plaster, and there was even an enormous fireplace at one end.

America was nice. The people were so friendly and so outgoing. Maybe it was trust. Maybe that was it. People were calmer, more trusting. And there was so much food. Food everywhere. All kinds. If people back in the Soviet Union were aware of how much food there was in America, they'd all want to come right away. With ease, Luba pushed away the memories of waiting in line for two hours just to get a kilo of beef, of eating nothing but potatoes and cabbage for dinner. Instead, she thought about the mountain of oranges she had seen in the grocery store just the other day. A whole mountain rising from the table and way above her head. Incredible. When and if they did have oranges in the Soviet Union—shipped from Africa—there were always such lines. Now, she couldn't wait to go back to the store to see if the mountain of fruit was still there. Perhaps it had just been a fluke, a display for some dignitary.

Luba glanced down at the diamond ring on her left hand and smiled. She was going to like it here. Now, if only her grandson could come, then her circle of life, like the ring, would be truly complete. In fact, thought Luba, she might have many more happy years left to live. She was still young in America—just look at how healthy and attractive the women her age were here! They looked at least ten years younger than her. Maybe, she hoped, she'd stop aging too.

Luba crossed through the waiting room and to the windows. Twenty stories below she saw little figures on the street. To her amazement, she thought she recognized two people. She squinted. Yes, even her vision was getting better in America, and down on the street she saw two people she knew. She was going to acquire many friends here—she'd had so many in Leningrad, always dropping in and staying for hours—but now she only knew a few, and there they were. There were Nick and Vera walking down Nicollet Mall.

Luba broke away from the window with excitement. She had to tell Vera all about the doctor and just how happy she was. She scurried back across the room and to the reception desk. An elevator was there, its doors were just closing. She rushed forward, but it was too late. She looked at the lights of the other elevators and remembered they were broken.

*"Yolki, polki,"* she said. Sticks and twigs.

All she wanted to do was rush down to Vera and Nick. Everything was so wonderful. She glanced to either side and spotted a solid door with a red sign above it. Yes, that's what she'd do, go out that way.

She burst into the stairwell, unable to recall the last time she had acted so childlike. Grabbing the metal railing, she practically skipped down the cement stairs two at a time. She had to stop on the next landing, though, and pat her chest.

"Well, maybe I'm not quite so young . . . yet."

The stairwell was empty and dimly lit, and the sounds of her breathing reverberated freely all around her. She rested just a moment before continuing her descent. Going on, her pace was slower but still filled with excitement. As she went down one flight, then another, all she could think of was reaching Vera and Nick.

But then she heard something. She stopped. There were

steps, either from above or below, and she looked up and down. Silence followed, filling the empty stairwell all around her. She dismissed the sounds as the last of her own faint echo, and headed on.

She didn't take more than another two or three steps when she thought she heard something again. Footsteps? She shouldn't be here all by herself. She touched her hands to her lips. Was someone following her? No, please, she thought. Don't let there be problems. Don't let it be the KGB or the FBI. She had only just arrived. She wanted to belong to America. She hadn't done anything wrong. Glancing up over her shoulder, she wished she'd waited for the elevator. . . .

Something grabbed her.

"Ah!"

She smashed right into someone. She had been looking behind her and as she came around a corner she ran into a man.

"Oh, excuse me," she said in Russian.

It was a boy, a young man, actually, with dark curly hair. But the young man with nervous eyes didn't move, didn't let Luba pass.

"Please, I'm going downstairs to my daughter, Vera."

The young man laughed and said something. Luba didn't understand, and instead focused on his delicate eyes and his sharp movements. This was a desperate person, she could tell, someone who needed friends and a good meal. He might even be ill and he needed to be—

Suddenly, he grabbed Luba by each arm and shoved her back against the wall.

*"Molodoi chelovek!"* cried Luba as she was hurled backward. She hit the concrete wall with a burst of pain. "What are you doing? What do you want from me?"

The young man laughed and spoke again in English. He was unlike anyone Luba had met in America. His eyes were sharp and mean and his whole body seemed to shake. And what pale skin!

He strode forward. Luba had no choice but to flatten herself against the wall. Now it was plain his intentions were anything but honest. He reached out and punched her shoulder, his fist shooting through fat and striking bone.

"Oi, that hurt!" cried Luba, trembling and unable to speak anything but Russian. "You, you . . . hooligan!"

The man flicked his hair out of his face and grinned. Power. He obviously loved it, craved it. He had something even more powerful, too, which he took from his back pocket. Holding the metal object up to the light, he turned it from side to side.

"What . . . what is this thing?" asked Luba in her native language.

As if he understood, he pushed a button. A silver flash of metal zipped out of the object.

"Oi!" gasped Luba.

It was a knife. A hideous knife. They had been warned against coming to America precisely because of such things, precisely because of the country's violent nature.

She knew what he wanted. But . . . but what little English she knew was gone. She couldn't remember a thing. She gasped and shut her eyes. Think. Think in English. But she couldn't!

Finally, she blurted, *"Dollari*—dollars—*nyet*—no. Please, dollars no!" Yes, that was it. "Dollars no!"

He laughed. He laughed at her garble and he laughed because he didn't believe her. He didn't care either. He raised the blade and slowly, like a snake charmer, waved the metal blade back and forth before Luba's eyes. Luba didn't notice his other hand until she felt his fingers walking up her hip.

"Oi, stop!" she cried.

She swatted him and lunged her heavy body sideward. She slammed into the other wall, her tired body crumpling against it. Famine. War. Stalin. Her parents. Her husband. Had she survived all these simply to perish in some stairwell in a strange country? Had she abandoned all her friends, her possessions, reduced her entire life to this moment?

She began to shake. This was America. And it was true. People hurt each other here. They killed right out in the open. She could scream, but no one would come. No one would help her. Just like that article in *Pravda* about the woman who was shot to death right out in the middle of a busy New York street. No one helped, despite her pleas. No one called the police. Kitty Genovese. That was it. Every Russian knew that name. She was murdered while people watched from their balconies. Dear God. This was America with all its freedom. Freedom to be hurt, freedom to be killed. At least in the Soviet Union you were safe. If you obeyed all the laws, did not upset the State, then you were safe. Why, oh, why had she ever left beautiful Leningrad?

"Please, *nyet!*" she said, tears spilling out of her eyes, her hands to her face.

The young man said something deep and coarse. He came straight toward her, his eyes narrowed, his mouth baring its cigarette-stained teeth. And then he spotted an object and, like a stalking lion, froze. He smiled greedily and pointed to the jewel on Luba's left hand.

Luba quickly clasped her other hand over her diamond ring, and shouted, "No, you can't have it! It was my grandmother's wedding ring and my mother's and mine too! *Nyet, nyet, nyet!*"

The young man jumped forward, whipped out his hand, and slapped her face. With the speed of youth, he threw her head against the wall. In the next instant the knife was at her throat, the blade slicing through the outermost layer of her skin.

"Please," sobbed Luba, "you can hurt me, but please don't take my ring. You don't know, you don't understand. I . . . I can't speak English. I came from Russia. Everything's gone. I came with nothing, nothing except this ring. If only I could tell you, then you wouldn't— It's all I have from my past. Please!"

He pushed the knife deeper. Luba felt the clean incision open deeper. Hot liquid rolled down her throat, intermingling with warm tears and cold sweat.

Pinning her head against the wall with the knife, the man reached down and grabbed the hand with the ring. He glanced at the diamond, felt it, and smiled. Then he tugged. But the ring didn't budge. He pulled harder. Still it did not move.

"Please, you see," gasped Luba. She was so weak and this

young American with the crazy eyes was so strong. "It doesn't come off except with soap. You see, my son, Anatoly, is going to get it made bigger. It's too tight now. It won't come off so you can't have it. Please, I'm just an old woman—"

He pulled the knife away from her throat, then jabbed his arm against her neck to keep her from sliding down the wall. He leaned his full body into her, plunging his shoulder into her stomach, and grabbed at the ring. He squeezed so hard that Luba thought her whole hand might pop off.

"Oi, that hurts! Oi!"

He grabbed her hair, yanked her forward, then hurled her head against the wall as if he were smashing a pumpkin. Luba's head roared with pain and she opened her eyes but couldn't see. Everything was black. She opened her mouth to scream but he leaned his shoulder into her more deeply, forcing all the air out of her. She gasped, strained for a breath. Her eyes fell shut. She couldn't breath! Her eyes burst open, and up above she could just make out the knife, light glinting from its blade. And she understood. She saw the young man's crazy eyes focused on her diamond and she understood.

As the knife went slicing downward, Luba opened her mouth and screamed. But there was no air in her lungs and her taut vocal cords could only gurgle helplessly.

# Chapter 28

*Moscow*

Viktor touched his crystal shot glass to his superior's, the gentle collision making a barely audible sound.

"To a great success, Major," said Colonel Orlov, "and your safe return to the Motherland."

Seated in the KGB office, Viktor Petrov nodded and drank the vodka in one refreshing swallow. He was leaving this afternoon for New York City. The day after tomorrow he would slip out of the Soviet Mission to the U.N. and Richard Stevens would take him to Minneapolis.

A frown clouding his face, the colonel returned to the subject of Vera Karansky and emigration. They had already been going back and forth on the subject for fifteen minutes that morning.

"Jews-schmews," said the other man. "I told them fifteen years ago we should never let them go. It set a dangerous precedent. And what a humiliation! Imagine, we housed them, educated them, gave them jobs, and then we let them leave. In the interest of détente, we let them flow out of here."

"The flow is down to a drip, Comrade Colonel." Viktor placed his empty glass on a silver tray.

"Only because our Olympics forced us to wrench the faucet shut—and they've been dripping out ever since!"

Yes, thought Viktor, staring at the floor, we can't let them leave because, unfortunately, we need them. Already some of the most learned and talented people were making computers and music in places from Tel Aviv to Minneapolis to Sydney. Not only was it a security problem because of all the information the Jews carried with them, but it was most importantly a critical drain of capable and educated people. Viktor hated to admit it, but his country needed the Jews. Perhaps they needed them as much as an all-gallium-arsenide computer.

"Some of the Jews have proven quite useful to us," said Viktor. "The Jewess from Leningrad in particular has been of great help."

"And well she should be! After all her country has done for her she should gladly serve the Motherland." Orlov shook his head in disgust. "Imagine, the President of the United States himself has proposed escalating the arms race into the last frontier—space! They want to ruin all our defenses, gain military superiority over us so they can conquer us at will! Can you believe the President's own words, what he said? He wants to outlaw Russia and start the bombing! I can't believe any responsible leader could say that."

"Fortunately," said Viktor in a placating tone, "we'll soon have acquired the brains, the very nervous system, to their space-weapons program: the GALA-1. Once we have that, we won't be far behind them."

Orlov propped his elbow on the side of his chair. "But we can't rest for a moment. And I have confidence in you. You'll do a fine job, Comrade Major, I'm sure. Oh, I almost forgot why I called you here."

With a spark of energy the colonel reached into his desk drawer and pulled out a pocket calculator and a Sony Walkman.

Handing the calculator to Viktor, he said, "Does this look right?"

Viktor accepted it, turned it over in his hand, tried to recall. "Yes, exactly."

"Good." Orlov shoved the tape player at him and settled back in his seat. "Now, don't forget to learn who this source is, this fountain of technical data behind your Mr. Stevens. We need that, you know, very badly. Almost as much as we need the prints to the gallium arsenide computer. Once we have the name, we can begin expanding our network in the American Midwest."

With a flash of excitement, Viktor said, "Don't worry, Comrade Colonel. I'll be in the United States in less than twenty-four hours, and I'll have that name for you by the end of next week."

Orlov reached for the bottle of vodka and poured them another glass. "If only half the workers in our country were as reliable as you, Major Petrov, then our Socialist Motherland would be the richest in the world." The frown returned to the colonel's face. "Now, you're sure we can count on this Karansky woman?"

"As sure as Lenin was a Communist."

# Chapter 29

*Minneapolis*

Heading down Nicollet Mall, Nick wanted to reach out, to touch Vera. He understood, even shared, her need to find a new home. He was American, but what difference did that make if he didn't even know which corner to call his own? Just taking her hand in his, he thought, or resting his arm on her shoulder would ground him here and now. There would be one more reason to call Minneapolis home.

Their shoulders bumped, repelled. His chance came and went in an instant, and after that Vera made certain to keep her lead. As he quickened his step after her, Nick wondered what he'd done, why she kept pushing him away. Perhaps he'd been all wrong. Maybe there could never be anything between them. He muttered under his breath, shook his head. Vera, alternately pulling him close and pushing him away, was as easy to love yet as difficult to understand as her native country.

They crossed the street like strangers, Nick outpaced the entire way, and entered the lobby of the Doctors Building. Five of the six ornate elevators were still not properly working.

"Oh, great," said Nick, sarcastically.

A crowd of over thirty people stood in front of the lone functioning elevator. On their way to the doctor, a handful of people coughed and gagged, while others sat impatiently in wheelchairs.

Nick peered through the crowd of people. "That thing has

got to go all the way up and back down again another five times before there'll be room for us."

"Let's take the stairs," Vera said.

"Yeah."

Nick pushed ahead of Vera, cut past a man with a bandaged eye, made his way around a woman in a wheelchair, and headed toward the staircase. He was just reaching for the door handle when, like a series of slot machines, three elevators lit up and rang in rapid succession.

"Look," she said.

"Yeah, bingo."

Automatically, they turned around and boarded the first car, which filled to capacity. One person got out on the second floor, two on the fourth, one on the sixth. No one got out on nine, but the elevator stopped there anyway.

"Talk about a slow boat," groaned Nick. "We should've taken the stairs."

Vera said nothing.

They were the only ones left on the elevator by the time they reached the twentieth floor. They stepped into the slick reception area, Nick breaking away from Vera. He crossed to the desk.

"Is Luba Volshevetz through with her physical yet?" he asked.

The young woman nodded and grinned. "Oh, yeah, she's a real sweetie, isn't she? She finished a while back. She's right in there, in the waiting room."

Nick proceeded down the bright hall and turned the corner. There were, however, only a few people in the room, two middle-aged women and an old man. Nick peered around a large lamp shade and found a fourth, a young girl.

Vera came in behind him.

"That's strange," he said, forgetting his disappointment with her. "Luba's not here."

She froze. "Oh, no."

"There has to be a simple explanation. Your mother's probably still talking with the doctor."

They crossed back through the waiting room, past the emergency exit, to the reception desk. Suddenly a voice cried out behind them.

## THE RED ENCOUNTER

"Hey!"

Nick and Vera spun around. An ancient-looking janitor, heaving air in and out of his body, emerged from the exit door.

"Dear Lord!" the janitor gasped. "Some medical building! Is there a doctor on this floor?"

"Yeah, sure," said the receptionist.

"Oh, shit," mumbled Nick, his hand to his forehead. It was Luba. She was hurt. He knew it.

"Well, get a doc quick. Some lady—she doesn't speak English—was mugged in the stairwell. And you better call an ambulance 'cause she's bleeding all over the place."

Vera was running. "Mama!"

Nick tore after her, charging past the janitor. "Get Dr. Feldman!" he called over his shoulder.

They flew through the door and down the cement steps, Vera more than a half-flight ahead. Nick leapt downward after her, two and three stairs at a time. He rushed down one flight, round the corner, and bounded down the next steps. He passed a heavy metal door with the number nineteen on it. Somewhere behind him he could hear the young woman and perhaps the janitor or doctor. Or all of them. Footsteps and moans and voices reverberated all around. Someone screamed from the stairs below.

Ahead of him, Vera shrieked, "Mama!"

Nick raced around the last corner and Luba's blood-soaked body burst into sight. She had to be dead.

"Oh, Jesus!"

She lay there, crumpled in a corner. A man and a woman in medical jackets were crouched on either side, a boy peered in from behind. Vera ran down this last flight so fast that she practically fell into her mother.

"Mama, Mama, what is it?" she cried, grabbing her. "What happened?"

Luba, her face ashen, didn't move. Finally, she came to life, inched sideways. She was huddled over, her left hand pulled tightly against her stomach. Her flowered dress was soaked with blood. She half opened her eyes, saw Vera, smiled.

"Oh, God," said Nick, rushing down the last stairs. "What happened?"

"We don't know," answered the woman in the medical jacket. "I just got here. I'm a dentist, but she won't show me where she's hurt. We called an ambulance."

"Mama, Mama, I'm here," sobbed Vera in Russian. She took her mother and rocked her. "You're okay. I'm here. We're here." Luba's warm blood seeped onto her daughter's clothing. "Mama, are you hurt in the stomach? Please . . . we need to help."

Luba gazed up at her daughter. "There was a—a man. And . . . he wanted . . . my diamond," she gasped. She paused, then shook her head. "I—I wouldn't let him have it. We've come so far, Verichka. And it . . . was my *babushka*'s wedding diamond. But—but he had a kn—knife."

As if to make it all clear, Luba slowly lifted her left hand away from her body.

"Ahh!" screamed Vera, falling backward.

Nick threw his head to the side and tried to stop the vomit.

On Luba's raised hand were not five but four fingers. Like a hellish fountain, blood bubbled up from the stump where her finger had once been.


# Chapter 30


Nick first saw the man in the plain blue suit ten minutes after the ambulance arrived at Minneapolis General Hospital. He didn't pay any particular attention to the stranger. There just wasn't time. Luba was unconscious, Vera couldn't be pried from her mother's side, and a team of doctors and nurses surrounded the two women and whisked them into a curtained emergency room. Pacing back and forth, pulling at the roots of his hair, Nick was simply too preoccupied to notice that the man with the round face and dark hair was attempting to learn exactly what had happened to Luba.

But then Nick, not knowing what else to do, ran to a phone and called the Jewish Family Service to report the mugging. When he returned he saw the man lingering outside the curtained area. Nick slipped behind a column and watched as the man listened to what the nurses and doctors were saying on the other side of the curtain. The stranger jotted something down in a small notebook, then cornered a nurse who was rushing back with a plastic bag of blood.

The man stuffed the notebook in his suit coat and quickly made his way out of the hospital. Nick followed, and peering through a corner of a large plate-glass window, saw the man walk directly up to a green car with solid black tires. He said something to another man in the car, then turned back toward the hospital.

Just as the stranger in the blue suit was entering, Nick tore across the lobby. He ran into the other half of the revolving door, shoved it a bit farther, and jammed his foot between the door and the ground. The anger tearing through him, Nick held the door tight, not letting it budge. The man in the plain blue suit jerked his head up, realizing that he was trapped in his quarter of the revolving door.

"What the hell do you want?" shouted Nick through the glass.

The man motioned toward the emergency room. "Is the lady all right? What happened?"

"I said, what do you want? You're not getting out of here until you tell me!"

The round-faced man glanced thoughtfully into the hospital. He reached slowly into his coat pocket.

Nick flinched, wondering if he had a gun. "Who the hell are you?"

The man smiled flatly and pulled out a black leather wallet. As if he had a great deal of experience in doing so, he flipped open the wallet with a flick of his wrist.

Nick leaned forward and read through the glass.

"No . . ." he muttered, backing away.

"Can I talk to you?" came the man's muffled voice.

Nick relaxed his brace on the door. He then pushed it backward, spinning himself into the hospital and forcing the man outside.

As he was pushed away, the stranger said, "Listen, for their own good I wouldn't tell them we were here."

Nick shook his head in disgust, unable to believe any of this. "Ah, crap."

Retreating into the hospital, he looked out the window again. The second man was now emerging from the green car, and Nick recognized him at once.

It was the man with the scar on the side of his face.

## Chapter 31

Vera couldn't believe it would be possible, but the doctor said they would try to sew Luba's finger back on. In the end, they were unable to. The knife slash had been too crude and, besides, the digit had been stepped on in the commotion. So the finger was discarded. Vera, seated at the side of Luba's bed, was numbed by all that had been lost that day.

Luba lay in the private room, still not awake, her left hand stitched and wrapped thick like a mummy's. She had been unconscious by the time the ambulance had arrived and since then had slipped into a coma. Dr. Sabelson, the attending physician, said there was no telling when she would rouse. She had lost a great deal of blood, he reported, and could be suffering from a skull fracture and perhaps a concussion. Not wasting any time, he had ordered a CAT scan and a series of other tests. Barring any major complications, the doctor felt that if she woke within the next thirty-six hours, she would be in the hospital for about a week.

IV bags of lactated ringers, packed red blood cells, and a saline solution hung on one side of Luba's bed. For over six hours Vera had watched the liquids drip at regular intervals into plastic tubes that looped gracefully in the air. Bit by bit, the fluids seeped through the needles piercing Luba's skin and into her body. Vera thought how the sun had burned its brightest, dipped and disappeared, and Luba had missed it all.

One night-light burned, and in the faint glow Vera studied the most recent drip of saline solution. Clear and shiny, it slowly bulged, expanded, burst, and fell like a tear into the tube. A chain reaction forced a drop at the other end into her mother. To Vera the small act seemed so violent, so intrusive, so grotesque, yet it failed even to stir Luba.

Anatoly, who had been there almost as long, broke the silence of the last hours. He slowly pulled back his sleeve and checked his watch. Almost in slow motion, his hand descended gently onto Vera's arm.

"We should go."

Vera, still staring at her mother, shook her head. "I don't want her to wake up and be alone."

Anatoly said, "But that might not be for several days. We need to get some rest so we can be here every moment after that."

"I don't want her to wake up and be alone," repeated Vera. "She'll wake up soon and I want to be here."

"She'll be fine, really." Anatoly's words were flat, reflecting his disbelief, and he did not move.

In the hours that the two of them had sat there—feeling closer than they had since Vera's arrival—doctors and nurses and visitors from the Jewish Family Service had come and gone. Larissa, as if she were crying for both of them, sobbed out in the corridor so as not to disturb Luba. And Nick paced the halls, pulling his hair, cursing, filling out medical forms, and talking with the police.

A shaft of light slowly made its way into the room and across the bed. Squinting, Vera glanced to the door. Larissa stood in the open doorway, her knotted blond hair and mascara-streaked face making her look as if she had just been in a fight.

"Nothing," whispered Vera to her sister-in-law. "She hasn't even moved."

Anatoly silently rose and left the room. He returned moments later. "Larissa is exhausted. I need to take her home. Nick said he'd stay as long as you wanted. Do you mind if we leave?"

"No."

Vera stood and embraced her brother. Wanting desperately to convey all that had been unsaid, she squeezed him as tightly as she could. He returned the signal, and for the first time in months, she almost cried.

"I love you," she said, kissing the side of her brother's whiskery face.

He kissed her forehead and left. The shaft of light appeared and disappeared as he went out, and Vera sank into her chair.

The room descended into darkness, and Vera was struck by an overwhelming sense of loneliness. Was she simply confused by the foreignness of her life here or was this the essence of America? It just seemed that there weren't any guidelines here, or if there were they were continually in flux.

The loneliness started in Vera's mind and then, like a fog, seeped throughout her body until she felt paralyzed. She had never felt so worn and exhausted, and she knew if she fell backward there would be no one to catch her. It was true, tonight she felt as if she had found Anatoly again. But would he be there tomorrow? Or would he be gone like her husband and then little Vladik and now Luba . . . ?

Her head fell back and she closed her eyes to try and press back the tears. And suddenly, as she slumped in the plastic chair in the dark room, the loneliness was gone.

Gennady, she called in her mind, I'm so sorry about the divorce. I wish . . . wish we were still married, still together. You're alone too. I know. I'm here and I love you. I'll always love you. And how is our child? He's beautiful, isn't he? I miss you both. I miss you both so much. . . .

"Vera."

She shook herself out of her trance and opened her eyes. Startled, she searched the room and saw her mother blink.

"Mama."

Luba's face was paler than the hospital sheets. There was a trace of a smile, though, and in an instant Vera flung herself forward and was at her side.

"Hello," her mother said uncertainly.

Vera, tears falling from her cheeks, bent over and kissed her mother. The atrocity had been done, but Luba had survived.

"I knew you'd wake up tonight."

"I . . . I . . ."

A puzzled expression overcame Luba. She searched the room, not sure where she was. Then she spotted the white lump that was her left hand and she remembered what had happened and realized where she must be. Her face constricted in pain.

"I'm in the hospital."

Vera nodded and forced herself to say, "Yes, and you're fine." She stopped crying and wiped the last of the tears from her face. "Anatoly and Larissa just left. They were here the whole time. They'll be back first thing tomorrow morning."

Luba stared at her hand. Gone was not only a piece of her body but the diamond, a piece of her soul.

"You're fine. The doctor assured us."

Luba rolled her head toward her daughter. For a long while neither of them said anything. It had been like this only once before—at the airport in Leningrad. That was the first time that their roles had changed, that Vera had assumed all responsibility and control. Now again, Vera had to be the strong one. Yet, as she stared into her mother's face, no matter how hard she tried, she could not find the strength.

Finally, Luba blinked once and understood who needed help.

Smiling, she asked, "Do they have nice art here too?"

"Oh, Mama," said Vera with a laugh. "I didn't notice. I never took my eyes off you."

"Well, you go out and look." Her eyes blinked heavily, slowly. "I want to sleep. And so must you. Do you have a way home?"

She nodded. "Nick is outside."

"A nice boy," said Luba, her eyes closing. "Now you go home and get some sleep."

"Are you sure you're all right?"

Luba nodded, her eyes shut, as she slipped away.

*"Spokoini nochi."* Good night, she said, and kissed her mother on the forehead.

When Vera reached the door, she turned. Luba was fast asleep or had retreated again into a coma. Praying that it was the former, Vera rested her hand on the door handle for several minutes before pulling it open.

Nick was slumped over in an orange plastic chair, his elbows on his knees and his hands in his hair. He felt guilty, sick at heart. Luba's injury extended far beyond the loss of her finger. How could she possibly ever like the United States after this? The hell of it for her—as with all Soviet immigrants—was that even if she wanted, she could never go back home, not even for a visit. In hope of a better life, Luba had hurled herself off a cliff, into a black void. And she had lost. The man with the scar on his chin—who still lingered outside with his partner—made that perfectly clear.

A nearby door eased open. The white light of the hallway cutting across her face, Vera stepped out of Luba's room.

"Is she all right?" he asked, rising immediately.

"She'll be fine, I think. She woke for just a few seconds and then fell back to sleep."

They stood only inches from one another, and Nick took her hands in both of his. If only they hadn't left Luba at the doctor's, if only he hadn't wanted to be alone with Vera, if only the United States weren't such a violent place.

"I'm sorry. God, I'm really sorry."

Her lips parched, Vera leaned forward and kissed him on the cheek, and he felt her warm, smooth skin linger next to his. He reached out, locked his arms around her, pulled her close. For the first time he sensed her relax, felt her tense body grow soft with relief. As his hands ran over her back he wondered if she could ever forgive him.

"Will you take me home?" she asked.

"Sure."

## THE RED ENCOUNTER

Nick waited while Vera reported to the nurse, and then they were off. It was after midnight and the empty streets glowed eerily with orange lights. His car was parked across the street from DataResearch's mirrored building, and as he started up the engine, a howling siren screamed in the night. Vera gasped.

"Just an ambulance on the way to the hospital," said Nick. The spinning red lights were now in view. "Don't worry."

Her eyes trained on the mirrored building, she muttered, "Of course."

Nick drove in silence across Nicollet, then turned onto First Avenue. He continued to Highway 12 and followed it out of the city. As the city lights fell behind them, the trees of the suburbs, black in the night, emerged all around.

Some fifteen minutes later, Nick stopped the Chevrolet in front of Vera's apartment. He shut off the engine and watched her. Not making the slightest movement to the door, she studied the apartment building.

"No one ever told me America was the loneliest place in the world," she said.

He rested his hand on her shoulder. "Would you like me to walk you in?"

She brushed back her brown hair and reached for the door handle. "Yes. But . . . I'm not afraid to go in by myself. It's just that I . . . I haven't even lived through one season here, let alone all four. At least back home . . ."

He kissed her lightly on the shoulder.

As they got out of the car, the humid summer air embraced them and absorbed the sounds of their steps. Vera silently led the way into the building, up the stairs, and to her apartment. Once they were inside, Nick fastened the lock.

He didn't bother with the lights and didn't take his eyes off Vera's dark outline as she rubbed her feet on the shag carpeting and made her way over to an open living-room window. She brushed aside the white lace curtain and stared out. A gust of wind blew through the window, lifting the curtains and her dark brown hair.

He started toward her at once, silently crossing through

the room. As he neared, she held out her hand without turning around. He quickened his pace, slipped his hand into hers.

"You should have been a doctor," she whispered, still staring outside. "You have soft hands. Softer than mine."

He pressed his chest against her back, wrapped his hands around her waist. She stiffened momentarily, then slumped back into his arms. He nuzzled his face against hers, kissed the strands of her hair.

"Vera. God, I'm sorry. I . . . I . . ."

She twisted her head and pressed her lips to his cheek. "Shh. You had nothing to do with it."

"But if only I hadn't asked you to go out, if only we hadn't left her. You know the truth?"

"No."

"I wasn't even hungry. I just wanted to be alone with you."

Vera was silent for what seemed like forever before saying, "And I was afraid. I was afraid of just the two of us together."

His arms constricted around her waist.

"I think I'd go crazy if you weren't here right this moment," she said. "I'm so tired of being strong."

"Yes . . ."

He buried his face deeper into the nape of her neck, kissed her skin. The pain was not his alone. They shared it, felt it together. It made him oddly happy and a surging arousal charged through him. He wanted her, couldn't let go of her. He kissed her neck, her cheek, her shoulder. He twisted her around and kissed her breasts through her clothing.

"Nick . . ."

A manic surge of energy overwhelmed them both. Their mouths met, searched, probed. Nick ran his hands up her back, over her shoulder. Slowly, he worked his hand beneath her blouse and across her skin. In a slow circle he rubbed his palm over her breast. She moaned deeply, sank her fingers into his shoulder. Then he gasped, almost cried out as he felt her hand descend and caress him. He furiously opened her blouse and found her soft breasts. He kissed her and, holding her close, pulled her down to the floor.

They scattered their clothes about, then stretched out alongside each other. Admiring her in the pale light, Nick pressed his body against her, feeling her warmth, her softness, her life. They held each other for a long time, still and quiet, as they grew accustomed to one another.

When he could no longer contain himself, he ran his hand through her hair, down her spine, then around to her firm belly and down again. She opened, drew him closer yet, and he slipped into her.

"I've wanted this to happen for a long time," he said.

"Yes. Me too."

But even though her words seemed honest and full of desire, Nick could hear the guilt hidden in her voice.

## Chapter 32

Twenty minutes before the scheduled meeting, Richard Stevens parked his car near Lake of the Isles, crossed the boulevard, and made his way toward the high knoll above the tennis courts. He headed directly toward an overgrown clump of lilacs and checked to make sure there was no one lingering about. To his satisfaction, there was not.

From his position, even in the dark, Stevens would be able to spot Joseph coming. It was exactly ten when he saw the shorter man trot across the grassy field and climb the knoll. The closer Joseph came, however, the slower was his pace.

"A little out of breath, eh?" said Stevens, smiling.

"I think I need to get some exercise," said Joseph, his hand to his thick chest. "Let me see it."

"Right here."

Stevens reached into the pocket of his jacket. Pushing aside the metal coil of wire, his fingers closed on the plastic pouch of white powder. He lifted the bag out, holding it up for Joseph to inspect.

"Hot damn." A grin shot across his face. His white teeth emerged in the dark. "What I won't do for toot."

"Well, you earned it."

Weighing his words, Joseph asked, "How much you know?"

Stevens frowned. Perhaps there was more to it than he had read in the paper. Had Joseph perhaps stolen money from the woman?

"Don't worry," lied Stevens. Only one thing mattered now. "You did a good job, took care of her nicely."

"Yeah, well, she got a little screamy, you know, so I had to shut her up. I didn't mean to cut her so badly, but it's done. Right?" Quickly, he added, "A deal's a deal, so give me the shit."

Joseph reached for the bag, but Stevens quickly stuffed it back in his pocket.

"First things first."

Joseph turned his head of thick, dark hair from side to side. He couldn't hide his disbelief.

"You want to do it up here, right out in the open?"

"No, this way."

Stevens led the way to the bush, which towered more than ten feet in the air. He held aside a branch, stepped over a short clump of leaves, and stepped into the hollow center of the bush. Joseph, obviously more at home on pavement than dirt, pushed and shoved his way in.

"Shit, man, this place has seen a few bare asses," said Joseph. "What you got to do, sign up just like down at those tennis courts?"

Stevens raised a single finger for Joseph to be silent. He knew what had to be done and he knew he couldn't be caught.

In a hushed voice he said, "Do it good and there's more where this came from. Do it great, and I'll keep you supplied for the rest of your life."

"Yeah, man. Don't you worry." Joseph took a step forward in the night. "I do it the best. Man, I'll blow you to the moon then suck you back down again. You just lie down and I'll take care of everything."

Stevens shook his head. "I'll stand. I wouldn't want to soil my clothes, would I?"

"That's the trouble with fags, always thinking about clothes. No offense meant, man." Within arm's length, Joseph began to sink to his knees. "Let me see the shit again, man. That'll get me going."

Stevens reached into his coat pocket. He fumbled with the bag, brushed it aside, clasped the wire, and quickly withdrew his hand.

"First things first," he said as he unfastened his belt. "You'll get your coke soon enough."

"You're the boss," said Joseph, dropping to the ground.

Richard's eyes drifted shut as the other man's hands landed on his thighs. He felt himself worked, stimulated under Joseph's professional kneading.

Forcing himself to concentrate, Stevens took a deep breath, raised his arms, and brought his hands together. Below, Stevens felt the thick fingers pulling at his zipper. He looked down and saw the head of bushy hair only inches from his waist.

"We'll get you standing hard real fast, man," whispered Joseph.

"Yes..."

He let Joseph prod for just a minute. Then he ripped his hands apart. The wire, tight and sharp, emerged into the air and clicked when it was fully uncoiled.

Stevens demanded, "What was that?"

"What, man, what?"

Joseph threw his head upward, exposing his neck long and clean. At the same moment, Stevens dropped his arms, the stretched wire pulled tight.

"That!"

With a long sliding motion, Stevens pulled the fine-toothed wire across Joseph's neck, slicing cleanly into the skin. Stevens pulled to the left, right, then jerked the wire out of the body. A dry gurgling sound emerged from Joseph's slit throat one instant, followed the next by a bubble of blood that popped with air.

The young man grabbed reflexively at his neck, stared in terror at Stevens. He tried to scream, but the last of the air rushed from his lungs and out of the gaping wound. His muscles tried to suck air back in, only to be flooded with blood.

Stevens stepped back out of the way as Joseph slumped to the side and fell dead on the hard ground. He recoiled the wire, wrapped it in a handkerchief, dropped it in his pocket alongside the bag of talcum powder.

"Sorry, Joseph," said Stevens as he fastened his pants. "But you shouldn't have done more than I said."

Stevens had no choice. He'd just wanted Joseph to rough up Luba, to frighten the old woman and her daughter, to ensure that Vera would remain loyal to the Soviet Union. But Joseph had gotten carried away. Luba's mugging had attracted far too much attention, stirred too much concern. The police were releasing little information and had their best detectives on the case. And the press was asking questions. Stevens couldn't allow someone like Joseph to jeopardize everything.

Pushing aside several branches as he made his way out, Stevens knew he could now comfortably leave town in the morning. He had a nine o'clock flight to New York City, where he was to meet Viktor. Then the two of them would return to Minneapolis, and the transfer of the GALA-1 specs would be accomplished by the end of the week.

# Chapter 33

In the two days since Luba had been mugged, Nick's anger had been growing steadily. Walking with Hughes through Loring Park, the only thing he wanted to do was punch the

FBI man in the face. Hughes was such a bastard. Nick should never have had anything to do with him.

"Why are you following them?" demanded Nick.

He had called Hughes first thing Friday morning, less than twenty-four hours after Luba was mugged. Nick had to know what was going on, why the FBI was following Luba and Vera, why Hughes had not revealed the identity of the man with the scar. To aggravate Nick's anger, though, Hughes had put him off, making him wait until this morning, Saturday, to meet.

"We're watching plenty of immigrants," said Hughes. "I can't tell you anything more than that."

Nick stopped. The still air carried his voice above the calm lake and trees.

"Who in hell do you think you are? What do you think you're doing?"

The older man tugged on his mustache and glanced from side to side. He was not so much concerned with Nick's words as with the chance that they be overheard.

"Now, just calm down," said Hughes smoothly. He took Nick gently by the arm. "There's no need to get excited."

"What do you mean?" Nick broke away and started off at a fast pace. "Luba Volshevetz was almost killed—and your goon could've killed me too."

Nick's mind went back to the night he had entered Vera's supposedly empty apartment. The huge figure had flown out of the closet and attacked Nick.

"I couldn't figure out why you were so calm about the whole thing." But it made complete sense now. "You weren't upset about it because you already knew. That guy with the scar on his chin is FBI. One of your people. And he'd already told you about it. Shit, he probably even contacted you after he knocked me out and asked where he should dump me. No wonder the only thing that disturbed you was that I recognized him as the guy taking pictures at the airport."

"I'm sorry, truly I am. But there was simply no way any of us could have known you'd be stopping by."

"Just casing Vera's apartment, huh? You knew they were out so you thought you'd have a little look-see. That's disgusting. What did that guy do, plant some microphones in the apartment?"

As Nick stared out over the lake, his stomach constricted in pain. He had to assume Vera's apartment was bugged. That meant the FBI had been listening in—possibly even watching—when he'd spent the night with Vera.

A more hideous thought occurred to him.

"You guys didn't have anything to do with Luba's mugging, did you?"

"What?" Hughes shook his head. "You must be kidding! My people were downstairs waiting the whole time. The first we learned about it was when the ambulance arrived."

A grassy hill rose on their right, topped by a senior citizen high rise. Groups of elderly women, out enjoying the morning air, sat on benches on either side of the walk. Nick was silent until Hughes and he passed.

Nick tried the direct approach. He had nothing to lose. "I want to know why you're following them and what's going on. You've got me involved in something and I have a right to know. So do Vera and Luba."

Hughes said, "As I said, we're watching a number of immigrants." He took a handkerchief out of his pocket and blotted his forehead. "I can't tell you anything more. But I can assure you that you've nothing to worry about."

"What about Vera and Luba? They're my clients. I have to be honest with them."

"No."

Nick stopped again and turned to Hughes. "What?"

"No. You will not tell them anything. I can't allow you to jeopardize our work."

Nick couldn't believe it. "You're crazy. I suppose you're going to tell me not to talk to the press or the police, either."

Hughes' bushy eyebrows rose in alarm. "What are you talking about?"

"The *Tribune* picked up on what happened to Luba. They're going to do a big human-interest story. The police are doing all they can, too, and they want to hear everything I have to—"

"Absolutely not. You are to tell them as little as possible and to have as little as possible to do with them. In no way

## THE RED ENCOUNTER

are you to mention anything about your involvement with the FBI, our dealings, or what you have discerned about our operation. Mr. Miller, this is a most delicate situation and I—"

Nick interrupted him this time. "You can't give me any orders because I don't work for you. And if I agreed to do something . . . then, well, I quit. Got it? I quit. I work for those immigrants, Vera Karanksy and Luba Volshevetz included, and I'll do whatever is in their best interest."

"You will not."

"I will." Nick spun around. "Screw this, screw the FBI. I don't want to have anything to do with you!" he said, stomping off.

"I warn you, don't say anything to the press or the police!" called Hughes, raising his voice for the first time.

Heading toward the edge of the park, Nick shouted over his shoulder. "I'll say whatever I want to whomever I want, and you can't do anything to stop me!"

Or at least that's what Nick hoped as he stormed back to his car.

"Idiot," muttered Hughes as he watched Nick charge off. There were more important things than Russian immigrants and people starting new lives and, yes, even a mugging. National security overshadowed everything. And if they could arrest Vera Karansky with the GALA-1 prints in hand, publicize the arrest as much as possible, then they might be able to prove to Congress, the White House, and the American public that immediate steps needed to be taken. Soviet theft of American technology, after all, was the ticket to Russian military domination.

Something had to be done about Miller. The FBI couldn't let him go around spouting off, potentially ruining everything. And something needed to be done soon.

Hughes cursed out loud. As if he didn't have enough to worry about with Richard Stevens, now there was Nick Miller.

## Chapter 34

Vera knew she should have gone ahead without her brother and Larissa. She should have left early and taken the bus down to the hospital instead of waiting for them to finish their business. But she hadn't, and here she was in the back seat of Anatoly's dark blue Saab.

Pulling into a development of aluminum-clad row houses in St. Louis Park, Anatoly said, "This is the last stop."

"I hope so," said Vera, catching her brother's eye in the rearview mirror. "Mama's probably been up for hours."

Vera wanted to be there first thing that Saturday morning. She would stay all day talking and tending to her mother, just as she had done yesterday when Luba had come fully out of the coma.

Anatoly brought the car to a stop at a corner house. He shut off the engine, opened the door, and hurried off. A waiting *babushka* greeted him and Anatoly disappeared inside. Meanwhile, Larissa once again counted the wad of money—the take from this morning's run.

A few short minutes later Anatoly emerged from the house. The tall Russian glanced in either direction, then quickly made his way to the Saab. Seated again behind the wheel, he handed a fresh roll of money to Larissa.

"How much?" asked the blonde.

"Six hundred." He reached down between the seats and started the foreign car. "What's that leave us with?"

"We took in exactly $3,100 and paid out $1,450." She smiled and crammed the money into her purse. "That leaves us with $1,650. Not bad for a few hours' work."

"Not bad at all," agreed Anatoly. "Vera, we're going to

be rich here. You too. We'll be rich in America, just like we dreamed."

Vera shook her head as her brother reversed the car and drove away. That's not why her once idealistic and impulsive brother had come to the United States. It was not why she had come either.

"No, Anatoly, you've forgotten. You didn't dream of being rich. You dreamed of being free."

"Of course," he said and laughed. "But in America you measure the size of the dream by the number of dollars in your hand. Money is freedom."

For the first time that morning, Larissa turned around and spoke directly to Vera. Flapping in her hand was the roll of fifty-dollar bills.

"Don't be silly, Vera, and don't listen to him. We're doing good with this—good for someone back there in the Soyuz and good for us. In case you didn't realize, Luba doesn't have health insurance. We'll get all we can from the Jewish Family Service and the U.S. government, but this will pay for the rest. Luba is going to have thousands of dollars in medical bills. You won't believe how much her week in the hospital is going to cost."

Larissa turned around, having said all she wanted. But then she remembered something.

"I almost forgot," she said, reaching into her purse. "I have a present for you."

Lipstick, thought Vera. Her sister-in-law had probably seen just the right shade for her and thought her life would be incomplete without it. Or maybe it was eyeshadow. Or another pair of earrings.

"Here. But be careful."

Larissa turned around and handed Vera a small, cylindrical plastic case. Vera took it, turned it over in her hand, unfastened a snap on one side. Inside the vinyl case was a metal tube. Vera had never seen makeup like this before.

"What is it?"

"Mace."

She jerked back. "What?"

Her brother glanced at her in the mirror. "Don't play naïve, Vera. It's like tear gas. Use it to protect yourself."

As if she were holding a live gun, she tensed, almost dropped the container, then shoved it back to Larissa.

"No."

"Vera, what's the matter with you?" asked Larissa. "You saw what can happen here. Keep it. Carry it in your purse. Use it to protect yourself. You might need it when you're waiting for the bus or if a burglar breaks into your apartment. If someone attacks you, just spray some in his face."

Vera looked down at the container in her hand. Everything she understood had been thrown out. She was like a child, starting all over again. So was this Mace one of the things she needed for her new life? Did all Americans carry this?

She sighed, snapped shut the case. Reluctantly, she reached for her purse and dropped in the container of Mace.

*"Spacibo."* Thank you, she said.

If the streets of America were so unsafe, she probably needed a poison like this. Especially, she thought, since she'd be working late every night next week at Data-Research.

# Chapter 35

## New Jersey

Richard Stevens made his way through the dim hotel room and toward the bathroom light. He checked and smoothed his hair in the mirror, then took two glasses from the sink and returned to the low dresser.

Stevens lifted a bottle of Scotch from his leather carry-on and poured a generous amount into each glass. He reached into the ice container, which he'd filled when Viktor and he arrived some five hours ago. He scooped the last of the ice into the glasses.

The ice cubes clinked together, and behind him the sheets moved and twisted. Stevens looked over his shoulder with one eye and saw the naked Russian stretching. A glass in each hand, Stevens made his way to the other double bed and sat down across from Viktor.

"To your health," he said, handing Viktor a Scotch.

The Russian sat up, nudged a pillow behind his back, and pulled the sheet up to his navel. He took the glass, rubbed his hairy chest, and sipped the whiskey.

"I forget where we are," said the Russian, his eyes swollen with sleep.

"Still outside of Newark. We leave for Minneapolis first thing tomorrow."

"And I'll be back at my consulate by Saturday night?"

"No problem. The exchange is all set up for Friday night."

An awkward silence fell between them. They sat there sipping their drinks, each waiting for the other to broach the subject.

"Richard, who are we kidding?" said Viktor, a sad smile on his face. "How long are we supposed to go on like this? Let's just leave now. Forget everything. I won't go back to Moscow and we can just take off. Right now, tonight."

"You can't be serious," said Stevens, laughing.

"But I am. Absolutely. If we don't go now, then when? What happens if I go home and they never let me out again?"

"Don't panic. Everything's going to work out. But we can't go tonight. We'll go soon . . . in a year. Half of the money I'm making is yours—I promise. And right now we stand to gain a quarter of a million dollars. Think of it. That's what we're going to get for the GALA-1. Think of what we'll be able to do with all that money."

"Don't you have enough already? How much more do we need, Richard?" Viktor shook his head and downed the rest of the Scotch. "Don't be a greedy capitalist. Enough is enough."

"But we can't stop halfway." This couldn't happen now,

thought Stevens. Everything would be ruined if he didn't get Viktor to Minneapolis. "If this were the beginning of the operation, then maybe. If this were the end, then we certainly could. But too much is in motion."

Stevens stared down at the red carpeting, then pushed off from the bed and came to his feet. He headed directly for the bottle of Johnny Walker Red Label.

"Besides, Viktor, if we can just hold out for another year or so then we'll have it made. It's not just the quarter of a million dollars for the GALA-1. There's more. A lot more. Soon too. For a small cut, I've been promised a number of wonderful things we could sell to your government. Then we'll be able to retire to a place where neither the CIA nor KGB can find us."

"The infamous supplier of Richard Stevens." Viktor drained the last of the whiskey and forced himself to laugh. "You are incredible, Richard. Really, you are. What is it next? More computers? Lasers? Perhaps something to do with bioengineering?" He shook the ice in his empty glass. "You Americans really use too much ice. It's not good to drink everything so cold." Looking directly at Stevens, he said, "So, where are you obtaining all these technical things? My government wants me to scout Minneapolis and St. Paul, you know. They want me to find out what may be buried in the Middle West. And we're a team, aren't we? Tell me, who is this supplier of yours?"

Stevens made his way back over, the bottle of Scotch in hand. He sat down on the edge of the bed next to Viktor and filled the Russian's glass.

"That, my dear friend, I shall never tell," said Stevens. "After all, we all have our little secrets, don't we?"

"Fair enough." Viktor grinned and raised his glass. "I'll toast to that."

# Chapter 36

## Minneapolis

Vera spent all Tuesday at Minneapolis General with her mother, as she had done every day since the mugging. She fed Luba, tried to ease her pain, watched her sleep. The farthest she would go was the hospital cafeteria, which she visited several times a day for a cup of tea. There, on the first floor, Vera always sat at the same table with the same view: the DataResearch building and its plaza across the street.

As she had done the nights before, too, at 10:00 P.M. she left her mother and crossed the street. This was her third night at DataResearch. And again she'd be here until one or even later coding, decoding, searching, programming. Little by little she was succeeding, too, in learning how to instruct the GALA-1 to release its secrets. The green cursor, begging for more information, now throbbed on the screen before her.

Of course she'd be able to do it. She had no choice. Or rather, now more than ever the choice was all hers and she chose to do everything in her power to milk the specs and lab reports from the hard disks in the computer room.

Vera had never felt so vulnerable before. She had never imagined it possible that she would lose both her husband and son. But she had. And she had come so inconceivably close to losing her mother; Luba would have bled to death if they had not found her so quickly.

America was so frightening. Anything could happen. At least back in the Soyuz she knew whom to fear and how to avoid them. Here, however, the insanity could pop up anywhere and its randomness made it that much more terrifying. There was no protection. She didn't understand how Americans tolerated it.

That's why she couldn't survive alone and that was why she had to succeed in this work on the computer.

Vera yawned and rubbed her eyes, the glare from the screen having made them ache. It was after 1:00 A.M. and she'd spent hours in this room five floors below ground level. The keyboard—black plastic keys with white English letters—and a black screen sat before her. Plug into it, she told herself. Plug yourself into this keyboard and probe the GALA-1.

It had taken the first two nights to write a program that would open the locks of each file; after hours of jotting notes, trying one command, then another, she succeeded. The following night she typed in the program again, then went through each file hunting for relevant information. First had been the printed circuit layouts, next the logic design, then a half-dozen others. It had gone much faster than she had expected. It was, she knew, because she had direct access to the machine. Anything she entered on the keyboard went directly to the heart of the GALA-1.

Only a few more hours of work and then she'd have everything. Only two more files—the equations design and circuit buzzwords, both of which she'd already found—needed to be coded. Then she'd check everything and scan through the files one more time.

After that it would be over. Her head fell forward. It was only a matter of days maybe even hours.

*"Raddi Boga."* Thank God.

She hit the intercom button. Stevens appeared in the doorway moments later.

"I'm finished for the night." She massaged her forehead and spun the chair away from the terminal. "There's not much left to do. First I have to finish with the files, after which I'll transfer everything to magnetic tape. I'll need a blank reel."

"That's no problem," said Stevens. "You've done well, Vera. My compliments. All of this is way beyond me. I don't understand how you've done what you've done, but then again, that's why you were needed."

"I'll be back tomorrow night—Wednesday—and Thursday night too." Her mother was due home from the hospital on Friday. Somehow, though, Vera would have to slip away from the apartment that evening and finish up her work. "You'll have everything transferred onto tape by midnight Friday."

In silence, Richard Stevens escorted Vera up and out of the building. They crossed the plaza, Park Avenue, and made their way to the taxi stand at Minneapolis General's main entrance. He handed her a twenty for cab fare, waited until the yellow vehicle disappeared down the street, then turned back to DataResearch. As he neared the entrance the bells of City Hall chimed 2:00 A.M.

Downstairs on the fourth level—one floor above where Vera had been—Richard Stevens tapped twice on a door. His knock was answered with commotion and voices before Theodore Hughes pulled open the door.

"Richard," said the smiling FBI man. "A good night. We got it all. Come on in."

Stevens gazed around the room, which was outfitted with an array of recording instruments.

"Now what about Major Petrov? Everything all right?" asked Hughes.

"Not to worry. Friday night Vera, Viktor Petrov, and the GALA-1 specs will all be yours."

Stevens stepped over to a low table where two technicians, Denise Lawson and Mark Howard, were rewinding a VCR. To their side were several television monitors, another VCR, blank tapes, extra microphones, and coiled wires.

"I should have found you a larger room," said Stevens. "I didn't expect you'd have so much equipment."

"Well, we brought in a backup for every piece," said Hughes. "I just want to make sure we don't miss anything."

"Is that it for tonight?"

Hughes turned around. "Everything copied?"

"Just rewinding one of the videotapes now, sir," said Denise Lawson, the senior technician.

Five minutes later, Hughes and his crew were all packed up for the evening. Stevens led them down the hall to the elevator.

As soon as the doors closed, Richard Stevens boarded the second elevator and rode it to the top floor of the DataResearch building. This was quite slick, he thought. Vera was doing the work under the belief that Stevens had no other way of obtaining the GALA-1 prints. But of course other copies existed. There were extras in his office safe. And as a security director, all he had to do was ask if he needed any more. Even Hughes was aware of this. But that didn't matter. All that did matter was that Vera didn't know of the other copies nor, of course, of the FBI's ploy to trap her as she attempted to steal the specs.

He passed down a hall, took out a set of keys, unlocked his office, and entered a plain but functional room. He crossed to a second door in the far corner, turned a lock with another key. A small keypad emerged, and he punched in a code. The door opened into a brightly lit space, the main security office for this building and also for the lab, located some fifteen miles away. It was from this control room, filled with video monitors, speakers, keyboards, and computer terminals, that DataResearch security oversaw what went on in its own buildings.

"You should start an escort service," said Tommy Lichton, in front of a video monitor.

"Are they out yet?"

"Almost."

Lichton touched a different corner of the video screen. At once the picture changed to a different angle of Hughes and the technicians passing through a side entrance. As soon as they were out of the building, Lichton flicked off the screen.

"So much for them," said Stevens. "How did she do tonight?"

"Pretty good. She's smart. Wish I could've had her working for me." He indicated the keyboard in front of him, which he used to ensure Vera would find everything she needed. In the instances when she was stuck, he overrode her commands and instructed the computer to give her more information. "I had to give her a little help here and there."

"But she'll be on schedule?"

"Absolutely. She'll have the specs Friday night without fail, and then . . . then it's up to the FBI."

"Don't you worry, Mr. Lichton. They're going to blow the whistle good and loud. Hughes has already planned a news conference for Saturday morning. Hell, he's already got the brief written up. The story will be on the front page of every Sunday paper across America. And by next week Vera Karansky's picture will be on the cover of *Time* and *Newsweek*. If this doesn't get some action against the Russkies stealing our stuff, nothing will."

But Stevens didn't really care. All that mattered to him was that Saturday morning Lichton was going to pay him double what the Russians would have. That meant that by the end of the week he'd be five hundred thousand dollars richer. Tax free.

## Chapter 37

Nick slept poorly. As if his mattress were full of pebbles. He tossed, kicked aside the sheets, stretched in discomfort all through the night. His sleep was confused, full of thoughts that would not melt into dreams and dreams that would not take concrete shape. What prevented him from slipping into a restful sleep, however, wasn't his bed. It was Vera. He'd been looking for her for two days.

Yesterday, he missed her at the hospital by a matter of moments. Last night as well as tonight he had circled past her dark apartment a half-dozen times. He called Anatoly too. The first three times the Russian said his sister was staying with friends; after that Nick's calls were greeted by

Anatoly's latest purchase, an answering machine. Tonight it was almost midnight before he retreated to his apartment.

Somewhere back in his mind he heard a tapping noise. He rolled over in the old Murphy bed and was confronted with an exact statement of time. He hated that digital clock, wished he had his old one with the wobbly hands that would not have read 3:09 A.M., but simply very late.

The noise repeated itself. He glanced toward the open french doors. A shadow moved on the tiny balcony. He stiffened and sat up. It was a tree, swaying as the summer air stirred into a storm.

When he heard the noise a third time he knew what it was. He rose naked out of the bed, crossed through the main room, passed the kitchen, and stopped at the arched front door.

"Who is it?"

*"Eto ya."* It's me.

Without bothering to clothe himself, he dropped the chain, fumbled with the lock. The hall lights burned like lasers into his eyes and he could only make out a solid figure. He quickly shut the door and at once felt her jeans and her cotton blouse press into skin. She held one arm back, and he spotted a small black container held deep in her fist.

"What's that?"

"Mace."

He loosened it from her grasp, reached around the corner, and set the container on the kitchen counter. He supposed she was right to carry it at this time of night.

"How many lakes did you walk around?" he asked.

She laughed. "Three."

"Harriet, Calhoun, Isles?"

Vera nodded.

"I've been that upset before. Tired?"

She shook her head.

"Come on, I'll get you a glass of—" As he reached for the kitchen switch, she intercepted his hand, pulled it down.

"No."

"Good. You won't be able to see what a mess it is." He still hadn't unpacked everything.

## THE RED ENCOUNTER

He bent down and kissed her on the back of her neck. Vera touched her hand to his face, then broke away.

"I don't want the lights on because I don't want to see anything more," she said. "Everything's different here—from the light switches to the people. I'm . . . I'm so confused."

Nick crossed to the metal-framed Murphy bed, his eyes all the time following Vera. He lay down as she pulled back the french doors, looked out into the pale night light.

"Every moment there's something new."

"Vera . . ."

She turned around, her blouse already open. He held out his hand, and by the time she reached the bed she had undressed completely.

"Love me." Her plea was sad, scared.

But before he could take her in his arms, she sat at the end of the bed. She arched over, and he shuddered as her warm, moist mouth closed over one toe, another. His eyes drifted shut, and he felt her breasts press into his feet, drag slowly along his legs as she worked her way upward. When she was only inches away from his groin she lifted away, seemed to disappear. He opened his eyes, saw her working her way on top, straddling him, then taking him deep within her.

He groaned as she worked herself up and down faster and faster; she did not respond. Feeling the delight spread further and deeper with each moment, he looked up at her. She was staring at him, concentrating on his pleasure. Not seeking any physical stimulation herself, she only wanted to watch him want her, have him fill her with life, to discover if she could be loved.

The pleasure screamed deeper in Nick's body, radiating outward to his stomach, his legs, his chest, filling every sense. Then she seemed to be pumping not just one part of his body, but all of it and every corner of his mind too.

"Vera . . ." he forced himself to call.

She did not respond. Focused totally on him, she worked quick and frantic.

"Vera . . ." He was so close. "Not yet."

He reached up, tried to slow her. She resisted, wouldn't

stop. He grabbed at an arm, she leaned back. Finally, he pulled her down, brought her against him, pinned her to his side.

"Just lie still."

Her skin was cold and dry. She shook, but not with excitement, not with pleasure. He brought the sheet over them both and forced her to lie still. She was tense, ready to burst away, but he wouldn't release his hold.

Gradually he felt the warmth of his body seep into hers. Bit by bit, too, he felt her muscles soften, relax. She sighed, deep and long, as if she were breathing evil out of her soul.

"Nick . . ."

He kissed her cheek. She wasn't shaking anymore.

"Yes," he said.

"Nick, *ya tebya lubloo.*" I love you.

He brushed back her hair with one hand, the strands soft and light between his fingers, and studied the relaxed lines of her face.

*"Ya tozhe tebya lubloo."* I love you, too.

The truth made him grin, but he could never have said it in English. Uttering the words in Russian simply identified the emotion most accurately for him: mysterious and foreign and magnetic. Like Vera.

"You all right?" he asked.

"Much better. Normal again."

As she lay in his arms, he felt something begin to ebb from him. It was an outlook or a feeling he'd never realized was part of him, that he could only now sense as it began to detach itself.

"I've . . . I've never thought of myself as angry."

"What?"

"I don't know. But I think I've been angry for a long time. Years. I don't know what about. I only know that it's beginning—now, tonight—to go away."

"Good."

"Yeah, I think I'm about to lose some excess baggage." Laughing he said, "Maybe I should do all my serious thinking in the middle of the night. Of course, that's in addition to . . ."

He rolled her onto her back, skimmed his hand over her stomach. She sighed long and low.

"Can we start over?" he asked.

She rose, pushed him back, and shook her head.

"No," she said, smiling as she worked her way on top, "let's just continue."

# Chapter 38

"It's disgusting," said Nick, into the phone in his downtown office.

"So you'll meet with me?" asked Susan Clifford of the Minneapolis *Star and Tribune*.

Inspired by Luba's mugging, the paper was going to do a series of four articles about Russians in the Twin Cities. The first would be an expanded story of Luba's family life—what things had been like in Leningrad; why she, Anatoly, Larissa, and Vera had left; what they were hoping to find. The other articles were to cover the one thousand or so immigrants in Minneapolis and the seven hundred across the Mississippi in St. Paul.

Nick leaned back in his chair. The story was one that needed to be told. Forget about Hughes. Forget about secret this and that. Luba's great American dream had turned into a nightmare. Perhaps this would somehow help make things right again.

"Sure." He'd do it for Luba and Vera because they deserved any chance they could get. "I'll tell you everything I know."

"Wonderful," said the reporter. "Do you have any time today?"

He leaned forward and checked his calendar. Every hour into the evening was filled with client meetings.

"How about tonight around nine?"

Susan Clifford agreed and suggested they meet at the Monte Carlo for a drink.

"And if you know of anyone we can talk to about Russian immigrants and their new lives, please bring their phone numbers," she said.

Nick said he would, and as he hung up the first name that came to mind was Theodore Hughes. That's who the media really needed to talk to, and that's what he'd do. Tell the *Tribune* reporter everything he knew about the FBI surveillance of the Soviet immigrant community.

In a building only three blocks away, a man rewound the tape of the telephone conversation he had just recorded. He took the tape, swiveled his chair around, and inserted it in another machine. He added a blank cassette in the second compartment and pressed a button. Fifteen seconds later, the copy was complete.

The man took a manila envelope from a drawer and quickly wrote a name on it. He then dropped the second cassette in the envelope and pressed a button on his phone. Seconds later a younger man appeared in the doorway.

"Deliver this at once. It's urgent," said the man as he handed the envelope to his assistant.

# Chapter 39

Major Viktor Petrov's first three days of covert activity in the United States were spent at the Minneapolis Public Library. His labor was well rewarded. Not suspected, not questioned, he gathered data on almost every technology-oriented company in the Twin Cities' area. At a dime a page, he spent almost forty dollars at the photocopy machine.

## THE RED ENCOUNTER

Adding to his stack of information were copies of the Minneapolis and St. Paul phone books and over five hundred pages of information from the chamber of commerce. Back home he'd turn all of this over to analysts, who would decide what products would be of use to the Soviet Union. Then it would be up to the KGB to obtain them.

Now, seated in his comfortable room at the Marquette Inn, his eyes strayed over the white walls and rich red carpeting. It wasn't bad. Quite pleasant, actually. He hadn't expected something so luxurious in the American provinces. Back home, the comforts shriveled dramatically with each kilometer you took from Moscow. The service here was excellent too. Not only at the hotel but also at the library. He'd had a cadre of librarians helping him almost nonstop.

As soon as he heard Richard turn on the shower he pushed himself out of the deep chair, crossed the room, and opened his black leather briefcase. Lifting out a stack of papers, he reached into one corner and pulled on a scrap of material. The bottom came free, and from the exposed compartment the Russian took the Sony Walkman and the calculator. He replaced the false bottom, always listening for the sound of running water, and filled the case again with his papers.

He cut a direct path across the expansive room. Swinging open the bathroom door, he was hit with a cloud of steam.

"What are you doing in there, *tovarisch?*" joked Viktor, his eyes on the figure of the large man behind the glass shower door.

Stevens responded with a laugh and ducked his head under the hot stream of water.

Wasting no time, Viktor pulled the door shut, grabbed the calculator from the chair, and reached for the American's attaché case. He lifted it onto the bed, popped open the latches, raised the lid. There, right in the pocket where it always sat, was Richard's calculator. Viktor studied it, then checked the identical one in his hand. His people in Moscow were to be commended. Now if the contraption only worked.

The Russian upended the calculator and turned a small screw one quarter of a rotation with the nail of his index finger. With one hand Viktor pulled Richard's calculator from its pocket and with the other he slipped the second electronic device in its place. He then carefully closed the American's briefcase and returned it to its exact former position. By the time Viktor stashed Richard's calculator back in his own briefcase—he'd have time later to place it beneath the false bottom—Stevens was just turning off the shower. By the time the American had dried himself and, towel wrapped around his waist, opened the bathroom door, Viktor was seated in the chair. In his hands was the Walkman, on his head was a set of earphones. Rock music blared in his ears.

"I didn't show you my latest purchase," shouted Viktor, holding up the small stereo. "Bought it last time I was in Zurich. It's amazing."

"Aren't you the little closet consumer. Somehow I don't think Lenin would approve." Stevens reached for his white shirt and blue suit. "Viktor, can you hear me?"

"What? Did you say something?"

"Never mind."

Viktor's eyes followed his friend as he disappeared into the bathroom. He didn't want to go through with this. He just wanted to go away, live his own life for once. But Richard wouldn't even consider his proposal.

Stevens came out. He tucked in his shirt, fastened his pants, then reached for his watch that lay on the bedside table.

"Damn, I'm late," said Richard.

Not paying Stevens any attention, Viktor fiddled with the radio dial. To his surprise he came upon classical music he recognized, a piece by Rimsky-Korsakov. As the symphony filled his ears, he turned and stared at the massive stone and glass buildings of the financial district. A moment later Stevens, straightening his tie, came over and gave him a friendly pat on the shoulder.

"I'll be back in an hour and a half."

Viktor slipped off the earphones. "So you think this supplier of yours will meet with me?"

"We'll see. That's what I'm going to try to set up. In any case, Viktor, you'll be going back to Moscow with a stack of information."

## THE RED ENCOUNTER

He nodded, a sly grin on his face. He hadn't even visited the University of Minnesota's science libraries yet; he was scheduled to go there and to several state agencies tomorrow. Everyone was more than eager to help him once he told them that he was scouting the area for a branch of his San Francisco firm. He was shocked how trusting Americans were. No one even questioned his accent.

"See you," said Viktor, watching the American put on his coat and grab his briefcase.

Richard waved and headed out of the room. As soon as the door clicked shut, Viktor slipped the Walkman out of its case. He inserted a fresh tape on which to record, then flipped a small switch on the bottom. Transmission from the calculator in Stevens' briefcase began with a single click.

Over the earphones Viktor listened to the mechanical sounds of the descending elevator, to Richard's bright greeting to the doorman, then finally to the sounds of his BMW roaring to a start.

Viktor wasn't happy about doing this. He'd tried so often to persuade Richard that they should abandon the GALA-1 operation. But the American wouldn't listen and soon Viktor was wasting valuable time arguing. He decided that business would have to be business. And Viktor's assignment was to make certain he found out with whom Stevens was dealing.

Richard Stevens parked his car across Hennepin from Loring Park and, briefcase in hand, proceeded on foot toward the Walker Art Center. Squinting in the bright sunshine, he studied the modern, dark-brick stucture. Somewhere inside was Tommy Lichton.

He entered the bright white lobby the museum shared with the Guthrie Theatre, turned left, and immediately spotted Lichton lingering in the gift shop. The tan-faced man, bent over a glass case, appeared deep in thought.

Without breaking pace, Stevens continued toward the broad steps that led to the second gallery. He was to meet Lichton there in several minutes.

Suddenly, Stevens heard running steps and voices calling out.

"Sir, sir!"

Christ, he thought, did they want him? He kept walking, trying to appear fascinated by the Picassos and dead to the summons. Then he felt a hand on his arm and had to keep himself from bolting. Forcing himself slowly around, he was confronted by a female guard in a blue uniform.

"What?" He was certain that everyone in the lobby was looking at him. "Did I forget to pay admission?"

"No, there's no charge, but I'm sorry, sir, you'll have to check the briefcase. It's not allowed in the museum. You can leave it in a locker."

Five minutes later, Richard Stevens found Tommy Lichton in an empty gallery. His chin in one hand, the computer designer studied a large oil painting, done in blue, of three horses.

"Can you feel the creativity in the building?" Lichton said when Richard was only a few feet away. "It throbs, pulses. I come here to get recharged."

"You knew about that, didn't you?"

Stevens smiled. Lichton, he knew, always went to great lengths to calm his security fears.

"What?"

"The briefcase."

His employer was always in control—of the people around him, of the computers he designed. Included in his stylized security measures was the demand that nothing be exchanged on DataResearch grounds.

Avoiding his question, Lichton asked, "How's your friend?"

"Fine. He's found quite a bit of information at the library. He keeps asking about my source, my contact, though. He thinks I'm out trying to set up a meeting for you two."

"Never." Lichton laughed. "Oops, you dropped something."

Grasping something in his hand, the computer designer bent over and pretended to pick something up off the floor. He stood, then handed the item to Stevens.

"Looks like a key to a locker." Lichton lowered his voice and said, "Remember, Mr. Stevens, I'll be watching from the security control room Friday night. Do a good job and you can claim your money anytime Saturday."

Accepting the key, Stevens palmed it and watched as his employer, grinning, wandered away. Stevens pretended to admire the blue horses for a few more minutes, then headed downstairs. There, in a second locker, he knew precisely what he would find: the bank account number holding his half-million dollars.

## Chapter 40

Thunderheads darkened the summer sky earlier than usual that night. After nine o'clock—Susan Clifford was probably already waiting for him—the late northern sun was blotted out and it was darker than midnight.

As Nick turned onto Washington and drove farther into the warehouse district, he spotted white lightning crackling on the horizon. Within his first month of living in Minnesota he had learned firsthand of the storms—snow and rain whipped horizontally by arctic blasts—that rolled over the area like a bowling ball scoring a strike.

At Third he turned right and slowly passed the Monte Carlo, in front of which sat an idling sedan. Toward the end of the street he took the last parking space in front of the Colonial Warehouse loading dock. His rusty door screeched as he opened and shut it.

A few lofts lit up the surrounding turn-of-century buildings, but the main activity came from the Monte Carlo Bar and Grill. As he crossed the street a misty rain began to fall, and the bar's neon sign glowed a steamy red.

Over the course of the day Nick had thought about, considered, and then again rejected Hughes' warning. Although he'd softened a bit and might only allude to FBI surveillance of the immigrants, he'd tell Susan Clifford everything else he knew.

A shadow darker than the night moved in the alley. At first Nick thought nothing of it, but then his heart flinched. A thick man, his dark-dotted eyes staring at Nick, emerged into the red glow of the neon. Nick knew that man, recognized the square chin with that familiar scar on the side.

"Damn!" muttered Nick.

He knew that man's punch, too, and at once Nick began to trot toward the entrance of the bar. He couldn't fight the guy but perhaps he could outrun him. Just then, though, a door on the idling car was thrown open. Another man of equal size heaved himself out, blocking Nick's passage. Nick froze. His eyes went from the man with the scar to the other man. They started to close in on him.

Nick spun around. Screw the drink, he thought. He'd call the reporter in the morning and this time he'd tell her everything—Hughes, GALA-1, and all. He scanned the lifeless buildings around him, reached into his pocket for his keys, and bolted for his Chevy.

Suddenly a motor roared and the lights of the large sedan were upon him. Nick tore as fast as he could, but the powerful car closed in on him. His Chevy was just across the street, only a few feet away. If he could only reach it, lock the doors. But the sedan kept racing forward, threatening to block the way. Nick could feel its lights burning in on him when finally the car skidded silently on the wet pavement. Nick, unable to stop himself, smashed into the fender, his hands slipping across the wet hood. He pushed himself up and around.

The bathwater-temperature rain turned to a steady drizzle, sliding with the sweat down Nick's face. The two FBI men continued to close in on him, their pace slower, more assured. The man with the scar went directly to the rear door of the sedan. He popped up the handle and held open the door like a Mafia chauffeur.

"Get in."

"Stick it in your ear. You can't do this!"

"Get in."

"No."

## THE RED ENCOUNTER

The front door of the bar opened. A woman and her date stepped out. Nick started toward them but the second FBI man was on him before he could open his mouth to yell. A solid fist of bone and muscle plunged into his stomach, and every bit of air shot out of him like the burst of a cork on a champagne bottle. He doubled over, his empty lungs shriveling with pain. Two hands hoisted him into the sedan.

The car sped off, and a half-block later Nick still had his head between his legs. He braced one hand on the seat and pushed himself up. The first thing he was aware of was the batting of windshield wipers. The second was the four other people. In the front sat the driver and one of the men. On Nick's left in the back was the other, the one with the scar. On his right sat Theodore Hughes.

Nick stared at the man with the white hair and gasped, "Bastard."

Hughes looked over at Nick, shook his head in admonishment, then gazed out the window. The driver drove swiftly up Washington.

"I warned you," said the other man, the smile noticeably absent from his face. As if it were all Nick's fault, he added, "I told you to stay away from the media."

"You can't do this."

"Of course I can." Hughes groomed his mustache with one finger and then stared over at Nick. "Do you have any idea what Vera is involved in?"

One hand still to his stomach, he sat back in alarm. "What are you talking about?"

"Well, do you know where she is tonight?"

He had no idea. His mind churned for an answer but he didn't have one. Suddenly afraid, he couldn't even speak.

Smugly, Hughes asked, "Do you know what she's been doing at night? Aside from screwing you?"

Nick lunged at him, ready to kill. The man with the scar hurled one arm out and pinned Nick back.

Nick wanted to scream out, to fight back, but, his mind racing backward and forward, he knew what this was all about. This was where the search had led. He knew but he didn't want to know, he thought, eyeing the door handle.

Hughes volunteered, "She goes directly to Data-

Research. One of our agents has provided her—with my consent, of course—with access to the main memory of the GALA-1. She's been extracting the specs for it. And doing a very good job, I'm told. You see, she's the Soviet agent we've been looking for."

Over an hour later, Nick, Hughes, and the other three men sat in the parked sedan halfway between Minneapolis General and DataResearch. A large thunderstorm had charged through town, washing the buildings, the cars, the streets, and filling the lakes. Nick stared into his lap, unable to look at the plaza in front of the mirrored building.

"There," said Hughes, lightly tapping the very bottom of the window.

Automatically, Nick pulled himself forward, his fingers sinking into the vinyl seat. He jerked his head around. There she was. Vera.

"No," he mumbled.

Her head low, she walked directly to the corner, checked the street, jumped over a puddle, and crossed. On the other side she checked again, perhaps, thought Nick, to see if anyone was watching her. Then she made her way directly to the front entry of DataResearch. The guard greeted her at the glass door, let her in, and she disappeared from sight.

"Now do you believe me?" asked Hughes.

Could it be true that the woman he had made love to less than twenty-four hours ago worked for the KGB? Were sex and espionage once again entwined? It couldn't be so, yet with his own eyes he had just seen her....

"I . . . I . . ."

"I thought you'd be convinced," said Hughes as he signaled to the driver to start the car. "I'm sorry to do this, but we're going to have to take you out of town for a few days until this is all over."

"What?" demanded Nick.

The car started up and began to pull away from the curb. He knew they'd do it. This would be his only chance.

"Hey!" he said, and pointed outside, past the man with the scar. When the guard turned, Nick grabbed the thick head and smashed it against the glass. Caught by surprise,

## THE RED ENCOUNTER

the man didn't react. Nick brought his elbow back and hurled it into the guard's face. He cried out and grabbed at the flow of blood from his nose.

"What in the hell are you doing?" shouted Hughes.

Nick twisted around, lunged over the white-haired man, and grasped the door handle. Hughes wrapped his arms around Nick, tried to contain him. The two of them pressed up against the door and Nick jabbed Hughes in the stomach. At the same time, he shook his feet, kicked, tried to free himself of the other hands now grabbing for him. Nick clawed at the handle, heard it pop open, and saw a crack of pavement beyond Hughes' shoulder. Just then the driver braked to a sharp halt and the momentum swung the door fully open.

"Ah!" cried Hughes, his hands still grasping Nick, as he tumbled onto the street.

Nick rolled on top of Hughes, landing on the other man's stomach, then tumbling onto the pavement.

"Sorry," mumbled Nick as he scrambled to his feet.

He jumped over Hughes and started running as fast as he could. Behind him he heard the FBI man gasping for air, then doors slamming. He looked back. The driver was by Hughes' side, the two guards were running around the end of the car and chasing after him.

Nick ran up Seventh Avenue not knowing where to go, how further to elude the two men. When he came to Portland, a number 16 city bus crossed the street. Immediately, he cut through traffic and after it. The vehicle stopped at the next corner and he was almost there when the doors hissed shut. He just reached the back of it when it spewed diesel exhaust in his face and started off. The two FBI men were closing in behind.

"Like, are they cops or something?" a voice shouted.

Nick looked up. Two punkers with Mohawks were leaning out of the side rear window.

Nick shook his head, and yelled, "FBI."

"No shit?" said one.

The other shouted, "Well, grab on."

Laughing, the two kids stretched out their arms. Nick

ran forward, jumped up. His fingers sunk into studded leather and he felt himself rise in the air and carried along.

Engulfed in a cloud of fumes and exhaust, he looked back and saw the FBI men slow to a walk.

# Chapter 41

The list of files Vera had succeeded in locating and opening suddenly vanished Thursday night. Erased in a computerized flash, the secrets of the GALA-1 disappeared, never to return. The screen glowed for a few short seconds where the lettering had been, then the black void of the GALA-1 computer loomed before her. All that was left was the green cursor.

Vera's hands fell from the keyboard. Lost was just not a week's worth of work, but everything. All these months of anticipation and hope were gone. It was over.

She took a deep breath, sighed, sat back in the chair. She reached for the phone, pressed the intercom button. Moments later, Richard Stevens rushed in.

"What is it?" he demanded.

"There's been a problem." She rubbed her eyes, tried to relax. She thought of her mother, who lay in the hospital across the street, and wondered what this would mean for her.

"What?"

She tapped the black screen and he rushed up behind her.

"What?" he repeated.

"Everything's . . . gone."

"What do you mean? What in the hell happened?"

"Everything's lost. Gone. I had all but one of the files located and identified. I was almost ready to copy them over to magnetic tape. But there must have been some security lock. A warning flashed on the screen and then it just went blank." She shook her head. "I'm sorry. Everything disappeared. I can't retrieve anything."

"But the specs are supposed to be delivered tomorrow night. You—you mean all the work you've done is ruined?"

She nodded, feeling his anger in the air behind her.

"Oh, my God. It was supposed to be delivered tomorrow night and—and . . ."

"Perhaps it was a disk drive. Or some mechanical problem. I don't know. I don't know. It could have been some master security lock too." She put her head in her hands. Everything was ruined. "I'm—I'm sorry."

"Don't leave this room," ordered Stevens. As he hurried out, he mumbled, "I'll be right back. Maybe one of the mainframes went down."

"She's lying," said Tommy Lichton.

Stevens, who had rushed upstairs to the security control room, said, "She told me there was some sort of lock that was activated."

"Goddamn it all, she's lying!" He lifted his hand to the display terminal. "She had it all. Everything. And then she just eliminated it. Deleted everything. There wasn't any goddamn security lock. She had everything up there, everything ready to go. Just a few more steps and she could have copied it all on tape. But she didn't. She sabotaged it all!"

Stevens' mind reeled. "Wait . . . I think . . ."

"Get her out of here! Get the FBI out of here. It's all ruined. We can't go through with it now. I mean, there aren't going to be any damn GALA-1 specs and no Russian to arrest."

"Yes there is. Perhaps not Vera, but . . ."

Richard Stevens spun around and hurried out. The extra copies. There was still a way to deliver to the FBI a Russian immigrant—computer specs in hand—and a KGB major.

Without responding, Stevens listened as Vera told him she couldn't do any more tonight. Or this week. She was exhausted, she said, and she needed a few days off; she'd return Monday night for certain. Barely acknowledging her, he escorted her out of the building and dismissed her with a few terse words.

As soon as she was gone, Stevens proceeded to the room where Hughes and his crew sat with the video cameras. Quickly he explained that there had in fact been a mechanical failure. An emergency crew was coming in, and Stevens said there was no further need for the FBI this evening. In fact, he said, it would be best if they left before the crew arrived. And, yes, he promised, everything would proceed tomorrow as scheduled. Whether or not Vera completed her work didn't matter at this point. There was another way to complete the operation, a way that promised even more success.

Once Stevens was certain Hughes and his people had left, he returned briefly to his office. There, he took a Swiss Army knife from his desk drawer, then headed out of the building. He bade good night to the guard and headed directly across the street to Minneapolis General Hospital. The FBI report he had read stated that Luba Volshevetz was not due to be released until the following morning. Her room number had also been conveniently listed.

He thought himself fortunate when he arrived at the emergency entrance at the same time as two ambulances bearing victims of an auto accident. In the chaos of running nurses and doctors, neither the desk clerk nor guard noticed Stevens grab a physician's robe and slip into the main wing of the hospital.

By the time Stevens reached the main elevators, he had the white jacket buttoned snugly over his suit. He checked the name tag and assumed that Dr. Lars Peterssen, as the tag read, was on break. Stevens was confident, however, that the jacket wouldn't be missed for the next fifteen minutes.

On the sixth floor, he smiled at the woman at the nurse's station.

"I left my stethoscope up here. I hope," said Stevens, moving down the hall as if he had been here hundreds of times before. "I lose more of those damn things than I do gloves in winter."

## THE RED ENCOUNTER

The nurse stifled a yawn, and said, "Don't go waking anyone up. We just got the last of 'em calmed down."

Already past her, Stevens raised his arm and waved back at her as he rounded the corner. The lights were dimmed for the night in this corridor, and his eyes went from door to door. When he reached room 633, he checked behind him. A patient was hacking away in another room, but there was nothing else.

He eased open the door and there she slept in the bluish glow of the night light. He recognized her at once from the photograph in her file. She lay flat on her back, the bed slightly elevated beneath her head. On her stomach lay the gauzed clump of her left hand.

The door hissed shut. He took the knife from his pocket, opened it, and step by step made his way to her side. When he was within a few feet of her he cleared his throat. He wanted her awake.

Luba's head moved slowly from side to side on the starched sheet. Her eyes quivered, then opened, fixing immediately on the tall figure of Richard Stevens now towering over her. She seemed not to know if she were dreaming or awake.

"*Vui vrach, shto-li?*" Are you a doctor?

"*Nyet.*" No.

Slowly, he raised his hand that held the knife. She noticed the motion and glanced to the side. Her eyes opened in terror as the silver blade came into view. It had the effect he wanted.

Stevens threw his free hand down, clamping it tight over her mouth. She squirmed and tried to scream under his force, but he leaned his full weight over her, pinning her to the bed. Slowly, very slowly, he brought the knife down to the corner of her eye.

"Don't move," he said in Russian, "or you'll lose your eye just like your finger."

Her body froze. Nothing moved except her terrified heart.

"Luba, are you listening?"

Her eyes flicked to him. He sensed a slight nod of her head.

"Good," said Stevens. "Now, do as I say and you'll live."

## Chapter 42

Nick didn't return home that night. He followed the punkers into First Avenue, a nightclub, hung out there until it closed, then carefully made his way toward the Monte Carlo Bar. He slipped behind a neighboring warehouse, studied his car for ten minutes, and moved around to an alley. He emerged from the shadows only when he was certain Hughes and his men were not around. He started the Chevy as fast as he could and headed out of town on Highway 12. Twenty minutes later he found a quiet lane on Lake Minnetonka, stopped his car, and sprawled out in the back seat.

Images of Vera haunted his sleep. He wanted to escape, to try and gain some perspective. He couldn't. Though never clear, her presence was with him like his own shadow—always there yet always elusive. He knew what he had seen, he knew what Hughes had told him, yet he didn't believe it. Perhaps because he didn't want to.

He woke early Friday morning and drove to a public beach. He stayed there until almost one, sleeping in the sand, wading in the water, hoping to come to some conclusion. When the only thing he was certain of was the emptiness of his stomach, he headed off to an old café in a log cabin.

It was almost four o'clock when he realized that the week hadn't ended yesterday, that it was still Friday, and that he had missed work. Finishing his coffee, he found a pay phone in the corner of the dirt parking lot. Billowy puffs of clouds sped through the blue sky as he found a quarter in his pocket and dropped it in the phone.

"My God, Nick, are you all right?" asked Nancy Adelman, his coworker, on the other end of the line. "All of us

## THE RED ENCOUNTER 163

have been worried sick about you. Where are you? What happened?"

"What do you mean, am I all right?" Her alarm spread to him. Had Hughes stopped by? "I'm okay. I just had a rough night and I—I—"

"Nick," interrupted Nancy, "your landlord called this morning to say your apartment was broken into last night."

"Oh, shit."

"Your place was trashed. We all thought something happened to you."

"Nancy, I'm—"

"And Detective Montrose of the Minneapolis Police Department called four times."

"What—"

"I don't know what he wanted, but he sounded pretty damn excited. And worried. Oh, and Luba Volshevetz went home from the hospital today and Vera's been trying to reach you."

He didn't want to talk to Vera.

"Give me the detective's number."

Nick caught Montrose just as he was leaving for a reception with the city council and mayor. He told Nick it was urgent, however, and wanted Nick to meet him back at the station at seven o'clock. Assured that he was free to come and go—and as certain as he could be that Montrose knew nothing of the FBI's dealings—Nick agreed. As he passed through the arched granite entry of City Hall, he hoped that the detective was right, that he had found something major in regard to Luba's mugging.

Now seated in the detective's office, Nick's question was answered immediately.

"Holy shit, that's it," he said, staring at the tiny object in the direct light of the desk lamp. "I'm positive."

Pinched between the detective's thick fingers was Luba's diamond ring. The jewel drew light toward it like a magnet, then broke the beams apart and cast them back out like glitter in the wind. A small paper tag with a penciled number hung from the bottom of the gold setting.

"That's what I thought," said Montrose proudly. "I told

you I wouldn't stick around here on a Friday night if I didn't think it was important."

"Where in hell did you get it?"

Nick reached out to try and touch it, but Montrose was too quick for him. He picked up a plastic bag, dropped it in, then ran his finger along the zipperlike seal as if the bag held nothing more than a sandwich.

"Mrs. Volshevetz was just discharged from the hospital today at noon," began the lieutenant, "and I didn't want to disturb her unless I was sure I had something. Didn't want to get her hopes up, you know, so I called you since the Jewish Family Service is still looking after her."

Nick couldn't believe it, and again demanded, "Where in hell did you get it?"

"We got a call from a jeweler who'd been approached by a woman trying to sell this. That's why we didn't tell the media about the ring. We didn't want whoever had stolen it to know that we were on the lookout." He tapped his head with his finger, quite pleased with himself. "I arrested her on suspicion alone, and you know what?"

Nick shook his head, just wanting to hear the rest.

"Seems the lady is a recent widow. Her husband was found murdered by Lake of the Isles just last week. Throat slit. He was a cocaine freak who supported his habit by selling himself. A male prostitute. According to his wife, the guy received this ring as payment."

"You mean payment for—for . . . ?"

Montrose shrugged. "For some sexual act? Maybe. Maybe not. She swears that all he told her was that he did something for someone and this was how he was paid. That was last Saturday afternoon. He was murdered that night."

Nick blurted: "Luba was mugged last Friday. Christ, you don't think this guy was hired to mug Luba, do you?"

"I was thinking the exact same thing. Our mugger very well might already be dead." Detective Montrose picked up a pencil and rolled it between his fingers. "He might have been hired to attack Mrs. Volshevetz, and then whoever hired him killed him. Somehow, though, the diamond ring was overlooked."

"When I took Luba to the doctor I thought I saw someone

following us. I spotted him near my office and then saw him again on the street. Do you have a picture of him? Maybe it's the same guy."

Detective Montrose tilted his chair forward and reached into a stack of files on the corner of his desk. He flipped through one, then another.

"I have a number of pictures of his body, but only a few of him alive." He lifted up a stack of papers and came to several black-and-white shots. "Here. His name was Joseph Scarpelli. His wife gave me these."

Nick grabbed the glossies and stared down at them. Looking blankly up from the paper was a fine-boned man with thick curly hair. Like a flash, Nick saw that face on the Mall.

"That's him. I'm positive. We were going down Nicollet and I thought he was following us. I looked right at him and he looked right at me. Then he ducked into the IDS Center and that was the last I saw of him. I forgot all about it."

Nick studied the face a moment longer, then handed it back to the detective. Things were beginning to fit. Occurrences that seemed illogical and random, that Nick had thought would never have any rational explanation, were suddenly making sense. It wasn't just the events of the last week that were coming together, either.

"So we have a loose link," said the detective, breaking Nick's thoughts, "between one dead man and Luba Volshevetz, which seems to indicate that it was not a random mugging. But why?"

Nick raised his head. "What?"

"Why? I mean, this Joseph Scarpelli had no previous record of violence. Assuming he's the one that attacked her, why did he choose Mrs. Volshevetz of all the people in the world?" He pointed to the ring. "It's a nice diamond but certainly there are plenty bigger. Was someone after the ring or was this Joseph guy hired to go after the lady for some other reason?"

Nick's thoughts were tripping over each other.

"Because—"

Nick cut himself off. He knew why. Or at least he hoped he did. Didn't it all have something to do with Vera? Didn't it have something to do with computers and the KGB and the FBI and Vera's family?

The detective leaned forward. "Because what?"

Because Vera isn't willfully cooperating with the KGB, thought Nick. She's an honest person, a good person. He knew that, sensed that absolutely. She wouldn't be involved in the world of espionage unless she were forced to.

"Oh, shit," he said aloud.

"Oh, shit, what?" demanded Detective Montrose. "What's going on?"

Forced. That's what was going on. Vera was being forced to cooperate with the KGB. But how? And what could he tell the police?

"There's a lot of . . . of weird stuff going on in the Russian community," mumbled Nick.

"Such as?"

"Well, there's been something going on with money. And odd meetings."

"Great. It might be the Russian Mafia moving in from Brooklyn. That's all we need. Pay up or else. I heard they're running money out East."

Suddenly Nick remembered Misha Rozen. "Something happened a few months ago. A Russian died because he wasn't taken to the hospital. They were broke—they said they'd sent all their money to the Soviet Union—and didn't know how they'd pay for the doctor. But I could never figure out how they sent money home. I knew it couldn't be a legal way. Maybe it was some sort of Russian Mafia link or connection."

"Yeah, yeah, yeah," said Montrose, taking notes.

There was something else. Nick searched his mind, pulled at the fragments of the memory. Roza had said something else that hadn't made sense back then. Was it . . . was it . . . ?

"Yeah . . ." he mumbled.

"Yeah what?"

Nick looked up. Montrose was staring at him. Nick shoved back his chair and started for the door.

"I got to check on something right away."

"Wait!" said the detective, starting after him.

"I can't. I'll call you as soon as I find out something," lied Nick.

This was business not for the police but for Hughes. First, however, he had to find Vera.

He charged out of police headquarters, hoping that he wasn't too late.

## Chapter 43

Riding in the front seat of the sedan, Theodore Hughes was driven to DataResearch shortly before seven o'clock. One hand pressed to his right side, Hughes slowly and painfully climbed out. Then he carefully bent over and reached back for his briefcase. He shook his head in disgust. Even shutting the car door was difficult. It wasn't simply the ribs he'd broken tumbling on the pavement last night; it was the tight, rigid corset he'd been fitted with.

Briefcase in hand, he made his way directly across the plaza and to the front entrance, where he was greeted at once by the guard.

"Good evening," said the young man who held open the door.

"Evening," muttered Hughes.

As if there hadn't been enough problems last night—less than twenty-four hours before the arrest was scheduled to take place—Vera Karansky had encountered difficulties with the GALA-1. All her work had been lost, or so she claimed. Fortunately, however, Stevens had had his wits about him and was able to salvage the operation. They wouldn't be able to arrest the Karansky woman with the GALA-1 specs in hand, but they'd bring her in later. And her substitute would serve equally well. Perhaps even better. Now there would be two Russian immigrants and one Soviet agent to bring to trial.

The only possible complication, he thought as he boarded

the elevator, would be Miller. He had simply disappeared, and Hughes hoped he'd stay that way. At least for the next few hours, at least until the arrests were made. Hughes shook his head. His only mistake in all of this was involving Miller in the first place.

Theodore Hughes rode the elevator down, then made his way through an empty corridor. He stopped at the fifth door on his right and tapped with his knuckles.

"Hughes here."

The door eased open, and Hughes was greeted by the senior technician.

"Good evening, sir," said Denise Lawson.

Hughes stepped in, closing the door tightly. He surveyed the row of monitors, recording equipment, and the long panel of switches.

"Is everything all set?"

"You bet. Everything's all checked out." She turned to her assistant, Mark Howard. "Bring up a shot, would you?"

The man flipped three switches. At once the monitors burst with light. In clear focus were the terminal and desk where Vera had worked.

"Good," said Hughes, his hand on his side as if to hold in the pain. "Let's hope we won't have any more trouble tonight."

Over the past week Vera had spent countless hours in the hospital cafeteria. Once again she sat at the same table, same chair. Luba was no longer here, however. A cold cup of tea in hand, Vera stared out the window at the broad plaza and reflective glass building of DataResearch.

This was Vera's second time at the hospital today. At noon Anatoly and she had come to take their mother home. Vera had then helped her settle in at the apartment and had only hesitantly left, ostensibly for the library. Luba appeared glad to have Vera go, though. She wanted to sleep, she said, before Anatoly and Larissa came over that evening.

After that Vera took the bus directly to the hospital. She hadn't come to see a doctor, though. She hadn't come for any medical purpose. She'd come to Minneapolis General for the chair, the tea, the view. She had watched the DataResearch building empty for the weekend, seen a few people go in, such as the older man with the rim of white hair who'd just entered. Soon, too, she hoped to decide on the right course of action.

Gazing out at the mirrored structure, she was lost in thought. She wasn't going to have anything more to do with Stevens. She wasn't going to have anything more to do with the GALA-1. She had no intention, either, of returning Monday night. Everything was gone. With a few simple commands last night she had destroyed all of her work. Destroyed, too, were all of her hopes. There was no going back now, no returning.

That accomplished, she simply needed to determine how she could prevent Stevens from passing any information at all to the Soviets. . . .

## Chapter 44

Nick whipped his car in a U-turn, hit the curb, and shut off the engine. He jumped out of the Chevy and stood on the sidewalk looking up at the apartment. There was no sign of life. He checked his watch. It was going on eight. Praying he wasn't too late, he charged into the building, up the steps, and into the pool-blue corridor. He pounded on the apartment door, heard shuffling inside, movement, a voice. The peephole darkened with a magnified eye. The bolt flipped open.

"Nick." Luba, clutching her bandaged hand, brought a quivering smile to her face. *"Kak pri'yatno."* How nice, she said, her voice quivering. "I just came home after lunch. We—we tried to call you, but . . ."

"Where's Vera? I have to talk to her!"

Nick pushed past her and entered the apartment. He checked the kitchen, the dining area. In the living room, he turned around, scanned every corner.

"Vera!" he called back to the bedroom. "Vera, it's me, Nick!"

A deep voice behind him said, "She's not here."

Nick turned, expecting some stranger. Instead, he saw Luba, standing motionless at the edge of the front hall. Her eyes were piercing, angry. Finally, a tight smile slowly reappeared on her face. This time her lips were steady.

"She's not here, Nick."

"What?"

"She's out."

"Well, where is she?"

"I don't know."

"When will she back?"

"Not for a long time."

Nick caught himself, stopped himself. She knew. She knew exactly where Vera was. But she wasn't going to tell him. She was a *babushka*. She had survived Stalin, World War II, and few things were tougher.

"Listen, Luba, it's very important. I have to talk to her."

She shook her head and looked directly at him. "I don't know where she is, Nick."

He felt the anger swelling in her heart. He clenched his fists, started toward the older woman.

"Goddamn it, tell me!"

Luba's eyes narrowed into tight bands. She stood firm without saying anything further. Nick could tell she would offer no more no matter how long he pleaded. The only way would be to break her some other way, then get the information out of her.

"I just came from the police, Luba," said Nick in a calm tone. "They found your diamond ring."

Her eyes opened wide. "What?" She gasped, clasping her good hand over her mouth. "My wedding ring?"

"Yes. The gold ring with the beautiful diamond. And they think they know who attacked you. But that man's dead now. He was murdered the day after he cut your finger off and stole your ring."

Luba shook her head. "No . . ."

Nick watched the fine wrinkles around her eyes deepen, then fill with tears. He hated doing this, but he had to find Vera. He had to find her before it was too late.

"And the police think he was hired to attack you. Luba, someone paid him to mug you. It's true, isn't it? We both know it."

"No," she sobbed, taking a step back into the hall. "No, it's not!"

"It is true." He stepped forward and lowered his voice. "Vera was forced to leave her son, wasn't she?"

"No."

"Yes she was. She was forced to. And there's more, isn't there? I know it now, Luba. I know the truth, I know what happened. And I know all about the computer."

Luba shook her head violently. "No!" She took another step back, reaching the door to the galley kitchen.

"Don't pretend, don't lie, Luba. You know exactly what's going on. You know what Vera's doing and you know about Anatoly too. I'm not sure how he's involved, Luba, but I do know Vera is in a great deal of trouble. You must—"

"Get out!" She stepped into the kitchen, clearing the hall to the door. "Get out of here right now!"

"No. Not until you tell me. Luba, you have to, you must help me so I can help Vera. She's in danger and I have to find her!"

He reached out to grab her. But before he could touch her, Luba's hand reached to the kitchen counter. She grabbed a long steel knife by its wooden handle.

"Get out of here right this minute! Out!" she screamed, holding the knife above her shoulder. "It's none of your business! Get out and leave us alone!"

Luba jabbed the knife in the air, and Nick fell back, bumping against the folding closet doors. She plunged it farther. Nick ducked. She'd stab him. To protect her family she'd even kill him.

"Out!" she screamed, starting toward him.

Nick scrambled to the side, lunged for the door. He grabbed the knob, twisted it, pulled. The door flew into him. Sensing Luba and the knife nearly upon him, he dove for the opening and out. The door slammed behind him with Luba's full body weight behind it. The next instant the bolt was slammed shut, the safety chain noisily thrown across the door.

Nick slumped against the corridor wall. What now? he thought. What the hell was he supposed to do next?

And then it came to him. He'd go right to the source to stop this madness. With a new burst of energy, he ran down the steps and out of the apartment building. He headed straight for his Nova, climbed in, inserted his key into the ignition.

"Come on, you sucker. Don't stall on me."

The engine came to a racing-start roar. Nick popped it into gear and tore away. Coaxing the engine with the gas pedal, Nick had to stop at Minnetonka for traffic. When the road cleared, he pressed the pedal again, and the car shot forward. But the engine died. The momentum, however, was enough to carry the car up and over the road and into the parking lot on the other side. Nick coasted to the side and braked to a halt. In a flash he got out and ran to the phone booth on the side of the grocery store.

He dropped a quarter into the phone, checked the number on the business card one more time, and dialed.

"Hello," said the nondescript voice, again without any identification.

"Give me Theodore Hughes. It's an emergency!"

"Who's calling, please?"

"It's Nick Miller. Hurry!"

Deep hold. Permanent hold. That's what he was on, he thought, as he paced back and forth on the concrete sidewalk. Hughes was never going to answer. It was probably too late, anyway. They probably already had her.

The line clicked.

"Where are you?" said the familiar voice.

"Is this you, Hughes?"

"Yes, what is it? What's happened?"

"She's innocent. Vera's not doing it because she wants to. Don't arrest her," he half yelled into the receiver. "They're blackmailing her."

"What?"

"They're blackmailing her. Forcing her to get the computer prints. The KGB's doing it. And the guy who mugged Luba was paid to do it. He was murdered over the weekend."

"What do you mean? What are you talking about?"

"I was just at the police station. They found Luba's diamond ring. And the guy who did it had his throat slit the next day. The detective in charge of the case is almost positive that the guy was paid to go after Luba and . . . and . . ."

"Wait a minute, go back." Hughes' voice was calm, as if none of this surprised him.

"No, you wait," said Nick. "Just stop the whole thing. Just for one night, all right? We can get this whole thing straightened out."

"I'm afraid it's too late."

"No. Stop it now. If you don't, I'm going to call every TV station in town and send them right over to DataResearch. I'll blow the whole thing up. If you don't meet with me right now, that's exactly what I'll do."

Silence. "Yes. All right. We should talk."

"But no funny stuff. None of your goons dragging me away." After the other evening he knew he had to protect himself. But how? "We're going to meet out in the open and . . . and a friend of mine is going to be watching from the side. If he sees anything . . ." That's how he'd do it. "If he sees anything happen to me, he's going to call every media person he can and get them right over to DataResearch."

"Yes. I understand. But that won't be necessary. Nothing will happen," said Hughes. "So where do we meet? And when?"

## Chapter 45

Luba didn't step away from the door until she heard him leave. Only then did she really see the kitchen knife clutched so tightly in her right fist.

*"Bozhe moi."*

She would have stabbed him. Dear Nick. Thank God he had left. She pressed her bandaged hand against her forehead as if to force that bit of insanity back into its hole, back into its dark place. Was she crazy? No. No, she wasn't. She just wanted her family together again.

Her eyes fell upon the silvery blade again. She had to get rid of it, separate herself from the evil instrument.

She ducked into the kitchen and opened the cabinet beneath the sink. She tossed the knife back beneath the pipes, then covered it with the plastic garbage bin.

There, she thought, that instrument is out of sight, buried as deeply as anything could be in an apartment. She didn't want to hurt anyone. Not unless she had to. And certainly not Nick.

Luba reached up to the counter with her good hand and pulled herself up. Breathing heavily, she straightened her plain blue dress.

Nick's mere mention of the diamond caused the bandaged stump of her finger to throb. Unconsciously, she stroked the gap in her left hand and for an instant thought that the digit had floated back on. She looked down and was surprised to see nothing. A hole. Like a stomach growling at the thought of food, so did her hand painfully yearn for the finger. She longed, too, for the weight of the ring, the alternating coolness and warmth of the gold against her

## THE RED ENCOUNTER

skin. Had they really found the diamond? Might it actually be returned to her?

She shook her head. She couldn't allow herself to think of the diamond. It was just a material thing and mattered so much less than everything else. As long as there was even the faintest of hopes that they might all be together again, she should think of nothing else. She could not think of what Nick had told her, could not consider the meaning of his words. It would jeopardize too much. No matter the risk, she had to do as the man told her. Besides, Nick might have been wrong. Or he might have been trying to trick her. No, she couldn't pay any attention to anything he had said.

Luba clutched her left hand to her body and started for the window. Let this be over with, she prayed. Only a few more hours and everything would be all right. Or as all right as things could be.

She peered through the light curtain and did not see Nick's car. Good. She'd be able to make the meeting without any problem. To be certain, she pushed aside the curtain and looked up and down Virginia Avenue. The summer evening light was subdued by a front of billowy clouds, and Nick was nowhere to be seen. He had left. The street, as usual, was empty.

Luba checked the kitchen clock and was surprised how little time she had left. She ran through the things she would need: pencil, paper, her glasses, pain medication. The first two items she took from a kitchen drawer—three pencils just to be safe and a spiral-bound notebook—and set them next to her purse on the living-room couch. Then she checked her purse just to be certain her glasses and pills were there.

Everything was set. She had telephoned Anatoly and Larissa and told them that she was fine but that she didn't want visitors tonight. The pain pills were making her sleepy, she said, and she just wanted to go to bed.

Luba had told her daughter the opposite. She told Vera she had spoken with Anatoly and Larissa and they were going to come and watch over her. Vera could go out and not worry about a thing. The sooner, Luba had told her daughter, things returned to normal, the better. She would be just fine here with her son and daughter-in-law.

But what if Anatoly called and found no one at home? What if Vera did the same thing?

That's it, thought Luba. She went directly to the black telephone and took it off the hook. If Anatoly called, he would think either she or Vera was on the phone. If Vera called, she would assume Anatoly or Larissa was talking.

Luba dropped the pencils into the purse and stuffed the notebook into a side pocket. It was almost eight. She had to hurry. She couldn't be late. Rushing to the window, she checked one more time to make sure Nick hadn't returned. Satisfied, she dropped the curtain, grabbed her purse from the couch, and headed for the door. If only no one saw her leave. If only Nick was really not in the area. If only she could do the work. . . .

She rushed out the door, closing it behind her. The keys. Her keys to the apartment. She looped her purse over her left forearm, jabbed her good hand into her bag. What had she done with the keys?

"Oi, *ni vazhno.*" It's not important.

Forget about the door. Forget about every silly possession. So what if a burglar came and stole everything, she thought as she hurried down the steps and out the rear of the building. The man was waiting and she had to go, had to get there, so she could start work. There were more important things than locking her apartment door. More important things, such as her family.

Luba hurried out the back door, past a row of parked cars, past the dumpster. She proceeded along the parking lot, leaving her building and the next two walk-ups behind her. At Thirty-second Street she turned left.

There, parked by the alley, was the silver BMW and Mr. Stevens.

"Please . . . please," she prayed as she neared the car. "Let me remember it all."

For tonight she was going to need everything she'd ever learned about chemical engineering.

\* \* \*

## THE RED ENCOUNTER 177

Vera sat in the hospital cafeteria for over an hour before she came to a decision. Her mind made up, she rose, and stretched. First she'd call her mother. Then she'd phone the police.

She went directly to the pay phone, deposited a quarter, and dialed the apartment. A clear, steady busy signal answered her call. She hung up, then dialed her home number a second time, and a second time found the line busy. She tried again and again as if she were a mindless robot.

Some five minutes later, she returned to her table in the cafeteria. It was obvious that Anatoly and Larissa were at the apartment. Larissa loved the phone and she could chat for hours. Well, thought Vera, she was going to have to wait out her sister-in-law because she wanted to talk with her mother one last time. Once she contacted the police—who would surely connect with the FBI—Vera had no idea what would happen to her or when she would see Luba again. . . .

After he parked in DataResearch's underground garage, Luba followed Richard Stevens to the room, five stories beneath street level, where Vera had worked. Luba listened as he said but a few words before stepping out.

Left alone, Luba stared at the flat, round case on the table. Inside was the long magnetic tape on which, Stevens had told her, Vera had had copied the prints and specifications of the GALA-1 computer. She didn't know why the Soviets wanted it so badly. All she knew was that they were missing one part of the computer specs and they needed Luba to find it.

Turning to the pile of manuals and reports before her, Luba tried not to panic. How was she going to do it? She was just a chemical engineer. She'd been trained decades before computers came into use. She didn't even know where to begin. She didn't even stand a chance of accomplishing this. It was true, she'd be able to read most of the formulas because of their similarities to Russian. It would take her hours, however, to make it through anything written in English.

But you have to try, she told herself. You have no choice.

Luba took a deep breath, held it, exhaled. She glanced at

the computer terminal on her right where her daughter had worked. Then, images of her grandson in her mind, she quickly opened her purse and took out her pencils and notebook. She placed her things on the table and reached for the first lab report.

Stevens said Vera had located most of the specifications for the computer and put them on the magnetic tape. For some reason, though, Vera hadn't been able to identify all of the manufacturing information. So that's what Luba had to do now. Go through these lab reports and figure out the manufacturing process of the gallium arsenide chip.

That would be it. That would be the last thing. Once he had that, Stevens promised Luba's family would all be together again.

Tommy Lichton held no doubt that he himself was a computer genius. And he now held no doubt that Richard Stevens was a genius in his profession.

There, filling the video monitor before Tommy, was Luba Volshevetz. For three hours he had sat—not daring to leave the security control room for fear of running into Hughes—checking every camera, watching every monitor, and waiting. Not for a moment did he stop wondering if Stevens would actually succeed. But Stevens had. Luba Volshevetz was there, working on the lab reports.

Tommy Lichton flicked off all the monitors except the one trained on the Russian woman. He leaned back in his chair, felt the tension ebb. Stevens had done a remarkable job. He had succeeded in bringing Petrov to Minneapolis and he had gotten Vera Karansky to do a large amount of work—all of it videotaped. And when she had sabotaged her work and refused to return to DataResearch, Stevens had not panicked. Instead, he had salvaged everything. Indeed, he improved it. Now there would be a family of spies to arrest.

Yes, thought Tommy Lichton as he watched Luba and waited for her arrest. Richard Stevens had earned every cent of his half million dollars.

## Chapter 46

One floor above Luba, Stevens was greeted by Hughes with the words "We have a problem. Miller just called."

Stevens listened in shock as Hughes recounted Miller's suspicions and demands.

"That's absurd," Stevens responded.

Almost as if he were testing him, Hughes said, "But I think he may be on to something . . . don't you? Perhaps Vera Karansky is being blackmailed."

"Perhaps." Stevens was quick to add, "But we can't let Miller ruin this whole thing."

"Absolutely. I suppose he does have to be dealt with." Referring to Luba, he said, "Do you think she'll be able to do the work?"

"Of course not, but she'll serve the purpose. After we see to Mr. Miller, then I'll pick up Major Petrov. You can make the arrests anytime after that."

Stevens ran to the room where Luba was working and explained that he'd be back in an hour. As he shut the door, he saw the confusion, the fear on her face. She stroked her bandaged hand, seemed ready to protest, but she was silent as he locked the door.

By 9:15 Stevens and Hughes were moving quickly through Loring Park and toward the pedestrian bridge that spanned the narrows of the lake. Miller had said he'd be on the east side of the bridge, only a few feet from a small stucco building housing restrooms.

Stevens, waving bugs from his face, inhaled and was assaulted by the smell of fishy water and urine.

"Great place," he muttered.

In nervous anticipation, Stevens slipped his right hand

into the pocket of his coat. His fingers closed on the metal container of coiled wire.

"Don't worry. I understand your concern."

Hughes said, "I have no doubt."

The FBI man stepped onto the bridge and scanned the area for activity. The leaves rustled overhead and a light rain began to fall.

Holding out his hand to verify the precipitation, Hughes said, "Good. This should keep people out of the park, send everyone scurrying home."

The droplets fell harder with each moment, and the two men moved toward the small building. As if they had rehearsed this a hundred times, Stevens disappeared into the men's room and Hughes took position in the doorway.

Stevens moved across the gray floor without a sound. He scanned one wall, noting the two urinals and one doorless toilet stall. On the opposite wall, above the sink, burned a naked bulb. He went directly to it, stepping through a puddle, then licked his fingertips, grabbed the bulb, and twisted it. The room fell black, and the smell of urine was more pungent and acidic than ever. He stood in the dark, blinked once, twice, and moved back toward the faint flow of light from the doorway. Miller would be here within minutes.

From his coat pocket, Richard Stevens withdrew the coil of wire. He slipped his middle finger of his right hand into the ring attached to the container, inserted his left middle finger into the ring at the end of the wire, and pulled. The saw-toothed strand of metal, taut and sharp, emerged between his hands.

Stevens peered down the short hallway at the squat shadow that stood in front of the door.

"Ready?"

Hughes nodded.

"Any sight of him?"

The figure looked in both directions. "Not yet, but soon. He sounded awfully nervous."

"Move in a little more."

Hughes nodded. "Yes, I want you to hear everything he says."

The FBI man was now no more than five feet away. It was

the opportunity that Stevens was waiting for and he did not waste a second.

"Is it going to rain any more?"

Hughes raised his head up, exposing his smooth neck. "No, I—"

The wire tight between his hands, Stevens rushed forward, not allowing Hughes to finish his sentence. He raised his hands with a single movement, looping the metal wire over Hughes' head. Then he came to an abrupt stop and jerked back. The only protest that came from Hughes was a hissing noise from his slit throat that sounded like water spilled on an electric stove.

Stevens used all of his strength to pull the FBI man back and into the building. When the last of life had rushed from Hughes, Stevens used the wire to pull the collapsed body down the hall. When just the bottoms of the dead man's shoes were showing in the doorway, Stevens freed the wire and rinsed it off in the sink. After he had shaken off the excess water, he walked over to the body.

Smiling, he said, "You sly bastard. You knew something was going on. Just trying to smoke me out, weren't you?"

There was, he knew, no longer a chance for the FBI to make a simple arrest. That meant, of course, that he wouldn't receive his payment from Tommy Lichton. Depending on how much Hughes had told his subordinates, however, Stevens thought there might be another alternative. He still might be able to return to DataResearch and arrange for a handful of FBI agents to take Luba into custody. During the commotion he'd simply pick up the GALA-1 specs and walk out. Later, once he was out of the country, he'd sell them to the Soviets.

When Richard Stevens heard steps outside, he stretched the wire again between his hands.

## Chapter 47

Hughes put him off until nine-thirty, so Nick stopped at a doughnut shop in St. Louis Park, got a cup of coffee, and tried to sort things out. He started into town just after nine and did over seventy coming in on Highway 12. The road was slick with fine rain but he didn't slow. He had to get there. He had to stop Hughes. Vera wasn't an agent of the Soviet Union. At least not of her own accord. Before they arrested her, before she was thrown in prison, every angle had to be checked out. He had to help her. If only he weren't too late.

The Cooper Theatre. Lincoln Del. Highway 100. Wirth Park. As the landmarks clicked by, so did the things Vera had said to him in the past weeks. Her husband left behind. Her son. In spite of what she had told him, he knew she wouldn't voluntarily leave them, forget about them. Nick knew Vera. He had walked with her, talked with her, slept with her. Their souls had touched. Something much more profound than immigration had been disturbing her. It all made so much sense now. It explained so much. Fit so neatly. Now Nick understood her reticent laughter. He understood that look of hopelessness in a new place that for her should have been filled with hope. The KGB had some sort of hold over her. She was being forced to steal the GALA-1 specs.

The windshield wipers beat back and forth with annoying regularity. Nick pulled off at the Hennepin exit, passed two cars, swerved in front of a bus, and turned right. At the Walker, he slid on the pavement as he went left through a red light. He pulled over, shut off the engine, and ran through the rain and into Loring Park.

Hughes had better be there, thought Nick as he ran down a grassy bank. He had better be there and he had better not try to haul him away again. No. Hughes wouldn't do that. He was a reasonable person. He'd listen, then agree when he heard all Nick had to say.

Two figures moved off to his left. Hughes' men? Nick froze. No, it was two wet kids taking advantage of the empty park to skateboard down the paths.

He hurried on. The darkness seemed to fall with each drop of rain. Nick cupped his eyes, struggling to see past the clump of trees, past the bridge. Was Hughes there? He had to convince him and then he had to find Vera. He shook his head, hoping that she wasn't this very minute being arrested at DataResearch.

Nick ducked around a flower bed. He reached the paved path, came around a clump of bushes, ran faster. Just past a grove of doomed elms he came to the bridge and raced up and over it.

No one.

He sucked the humid air in and out of his lungs. He clasped his chest and leaned against the end of the bridge. It was so hard to breath. He was so hot—was that rain or sweat rolling down his cheeks? And Hughes wasn't here yet. Screw the bastard!

Every minute mattered. The park lights were just coming on. He saw the kids on their skateboards, ready to shoot down toward the lake. But no one else.

He paced away from the bridge, toward downtown. Maybe Hughes was coming from that direction. Maybe he wasn't going to come at all. Perhaps he was right now arresting Vera.

Nick heard rustling bushes to his left. Nothing caught his eye at first.

And then he saw the small stucco building with the red and yellow and blue trim. He stopped. The doorway was open, black, inviting. Drawn to it, he moved closer and closer. He heard no other noise as he drew nearer. Squinting, he could make out something shiny on the floor. Shoes? No, they were too scuffed. The bottoms of shoes perhaps.

Maybe this was a drunk, a homeless bum sleeping in the men's room to get out of the rain.

Nick stopped at a fork in the path. He turned from the building, scanned the park. No sign of Hughes. He didn't like this at all. He was being set up. Hughes hadn't come through on his word. Any minute, Nick knew, one of the FBI goons was going to emerge out of the dark and try to drag him away.

There wasn't much time. He knew it now. He had to get out of there, call the press as he threatened, before the FBI locked him up and Vera was arrested. He turned to bolt out of the park, but looked back at the bum sleeping on his back. Suddenly he realized that that couldn't be a tramp. The pants weren't torn and tattered. Nick took a hesitant step forward. By the cuffs alone he could tell that they were fine gray slacks.

"Hey," called Nick, now within six feet of the man.

The figure did not move. Nick stepped off the path, proceeded carefully along the edge of the grass. He reached the building, touched the cool bumpy stucco with one hand, tried to peer into the dark hallway. It was too dark. He couldn't see anything except a pair of shoes and the gray slacks that disappeared in the blackness. Behind him, a park lamp flickered with light, burst to life.

"Oh, shit . . ."

There lay Theodore Hughes, his face as white as his mustache. A puddle of red-black blood oozed onto the floor.

Leaves rustled. Something bit sharply, deeply at his neck. Nick slapped at a mosquito. Then suddenly, from out of nowhere, someone rushed up behind him. But Nick didn't have a chance to move. A razor-sharp wire was thrown over Nick's head and it cut into his skin like a knife through cheese. The pain was hot, white. Nick grabbed at the metal, but the pointed teeth bit to the bones of his fingertips. He twisted, tried to pull it away, and gasped but could not scream.

And as he fell to the ground, all he was aware of was the roaring sound of the two kids bombing down the path on their skateboards. . . .

# Chapter 48

Vera couldn't stop thinking of her mother. She took a last sip of her cold tea and started out of the cafeteria. Again she went directly to the pay phone, only to find someone using it. Determined to reach Luba, determined to lay her worries to rest, she cut down a side hall in search of another phone. She found none, so she turned down another hall, passed through a set of doors, and found herself in the emergency room. And there in front of her, covered by a sheet, was a lifeless body slabbed out on the table.

She recognized it.

No. It couldn't be, she thought. Please, no. But the shape beneath the sheet was so familiar. The hairs poking out so known. And that bit of exposed clothing—hadn't her mother bought a skirt just like that in Rome?

"Excuse me, ma'am."

Slowly she raised her head. It was an ambulance attendant. He tried to roll the table past her, but Vera caught hold of the metal top and stopped him.

Seeing her shocked face, he said, "Oh, I'm sorry, is this your . . . ?"

She couldn't answer, and her eyes sank down to the table. Beneath the haphazardly tossed sheet was the body of a middle-aged woman. Just the shape of it looked so much like her mother's—not tall, full at the chest, round at the waist. And the hair. It was exactly her mother's color.

God, no. Please, she prayed. Please don't let that be her.

Unable to stop herself, she took hold of a corner of the sheet. She lifted it without blinking and there, before her, was the dead, twisted face of a woman in her fifties. But the face was too narrow, the nose too long, the eyes too deep.

"Thank God."

"Not yours, huh?" said the attendant, gently pulling the sheet from Vera's hand. "You're lucky. You would have just missed her. This lady poisoned herself and died not more than an hour ago."

Vera glanced one more time at the yellowish, latex-looking skin. No. It wasn't Luba. She was at home, wasn't she?

Vera backed away. Death was so close in America. It was right here, right now. It was everywhere—on the streets, in the homes, in this hospital. Was there no escaping?

She turned and ran down the hall. All she wanted was to talk to her mother, make certain that she was all right. Forget about Stevens and the computer and the KGB. She had to find out if any harm had come to her mother.

Near the entrance she found another phone, deposited a quarter, and dialed. The line was still busy.

Vera slammed down the receiver, then picked it right up, and dialed again.

Why, she wondered, had they ever come to America? They had hoped for so much, yet gained so little. She wished she were depositing two kopecks—not even three cents—in a Russian phone instead of a quarter here. Everything was so expensive and so dangerous here. If only things were familiar again, if only they were all together. . . .

The busy signal throbbed over the line. What did that mean? Was it just her sister-in-law talking and talking? Was Anatoly on the phone with a doctor? Was something wrong?

She replaced the receiver and made for the door. A bus would take forever. Transportation here was so terrible. She had to get home sooner. A taxi. That's what she'd do. There was a cab stand right out front. She just had to get away, away from death, and find her mother. . . .

## Chapter 49

Stevens huddled behind a large oak tree and searched for his escape route. The two kids on skateboards had shot right over to a police alarm box, and now Loring Park was lighting up like a carnival. Cherry-red flashing lights glistened on the rain-wet grass and search lights cut powerful white beams across the placid lake. Sirens blared, screeching through the night. Police cars were arriving each second from every direction. Curtains in the surrounding apartments parted. Peering faces appeared. Another murder.

Stevens knew only a precious few seconds remained before it would be impossible to get away undetected. His eyes followed the most recent police sedan as it raced around the east side of the park, sped around a corner, and accelerated toward the other squad cars.

In the faint light of a park lamp, he took note of himself and thought he looked as if he had just cleaned a fish. His hands were smeared with blood and his suit was sprinkled with red spots. There was no hope if he were caught.

Coming from the direction that Miller had appeared, the police ran their powerful flashlights back and forth. Then a handful of officers began to swarm around the building, studying the ground, the gore. If only, thought Stevens, he'd had a chance to take care of those damn kids too.

Richard Stevens ducked away from the tree. As he ran down a small knoll, his feet slipped on the grass. His legs shot out from under him and he tumbled to the wet ground. Almost in the same movement, he scrambled up and was off again. He moved rapidly toward a gathering of small pine trees and stopped. He studied the open area, saw no one, and dashed toward a shuffleboard court. Bent over, he moved quickly along the fence enclosing the court, then headed up toward the fountain. He froze behind a bush as a car passed. The quickest way for him to reach his car was to cut down Grant Street. But there was a car stopped there and a handful of people.

He slipped off his coat and felt the coiled wire in the pocket to make sure it would not fall out. Dangling his jacket over his arm so that the blood spots on his pants were obscured, he strolled around the edge of the fountain. He stopped on the other side, looked past the spraying water, and shrugged.

As if he were out for an evening stroll, he proceeded up the Greenway, a pedestrian walkway that led from the park to Nicollet Mall. He passed between a row of houses on his left and a brick condominium building on his right. At the corner of that building he stopped and listened to another approaching siren, perhaps that of an ambulance. He glanced up and down the Greenway, then ducked down a muddy embankment. He headed across an open parking lot, across a street. Just one more block and he'd be safe.

His throbbing heart shot blood through his body. He closed his eyes, breathed heavily, and wasted not a moment. Finally he reached his BMW. He threw his jacket in the back seat and slipped behind the steering wheel. Coolly, he started the engine and checked the mirrors.

There was no time to think, only act.

# Chapter 50

Vera froze in disbelief. From the back seat of the taxi she could see that there weren't any lights on in the apartment. No one was there. What had happened? Where were Anatoly, Larissa, and Luba?

"Thirteen dollars, lady," said the cab driver over his shoulder.

She jammed her hand into her purse, grabbed a ten and a five, threw it at him, and was out. As she ran up the cement walk, her mind was like a slide projector flipping rapidly through the images, searching, hoping to find the right scene. Could they all have gone back to Anatoly's? Was Luba asleep? Had they taken her back to the hospital?

But the answer was not that simple or safe. Nothing was anymore. Something had happened. The terror of the last months was too familiar to her, and suddenly she saw herself cuddled against her mother in the stairwell of the Medical Building. She smelled the blood, felt its penetrating warmth seep from Luba and through her own clothing. Her ears ached as she heard again her screams there, in the stairwell, and in the Leningrad Airport. The KGB. The CIA. Stevens. Who was it now tearing apart her life?

She ran up the stairs. A note, a message, some indication of where they were, what had happened. That's all she wanted. Please, she prayed, let them all be safe.

Her last hope for their well-being vanished, however, when she reached her floor, rushed to the apartment door, and turned the knob. The door was unlocked, and when she eased it open and saw the darkened, lifeless rooms before her, she knew something was wrong. Without stepping into the apartment, she called out in a hesitant voice.

"Mama? Mama, *tee zdess, tee doma?*" Are you here, are you home?

Her neck tightened, her body tensed as she struggled to hear something, anything. There was no answer, only silence.

The stairwell light cut around her figure, throwing her stark shadow ahead and into the apartment. Following her own outline, she stepped once, twice into the short hallway of her apartment, reached the edge of the kitchen doorway, and stopped, touched the molding. Still she could detect no one. Was her mother at Anatoly's?

Suddenly she heard a deep, hissing noise. It was the sound of strained breathing. Someone was here, waiting for her. She lunged for the light switch. But a man's hand shot out of the darkness, caught her. The fingers wrapped around her mouth, clamped deep into her skin. Blood streaked across her face, filled her with its rich, deathly smell. She tried to break away, but the man kept pulling her back, kept smothering her face in his viselike grip.

# Chapter 51

Luba felt the fear spread through her body like a paralyzing disease. She couldn't do this. All these manuals, all these reports. They were nothing but gibberish to her. There were a few things she recognized, but only a symbol or a code here and there.

No, she'd never be able to do it. There was no chance she'd be able to discover the manufacturing process of the gallium arsenide chip.

She felt as if the bandages around her hand were not soft cotton, but leather. Wet leather that was drying and shrinking and squeezing her hand and the wound, trying to make it all just rot off.

She bent over, clasping her hand to her stomach. She wanted to tear that hand right from her body and hurl it into a pit. She cried out. The stump was raw and hot, the nerves burning where the ring finger had been severed. She could feel the warm blood beneath the bandage. It wouldn't heal. The skin was refusing to grow back as if her body refused to admit defeat.

Oh, dear God, she prayed. Let me have my finger back. Please. And my family. Dear God, do you exist at all? Do you hear me?

Tears in her eyes, Luba spun around. She hurled herself out of the chair and ran across the room. She couldn't even take the doorknob in both hands. This is terrible, she thought. I don't want to live anymore. She grasped the handle with one hand, twisted it. But, as she knew and feared, it was locked. That man had locked her in here beneath all these thousands of tons of concrete.

Fresh air. That's what she needed. What she had to have. If she could only get outside. That would make her feel better. Calm her. Like a caged animal, she pawed at the door. Out. Please let me out. Just for a few minutes. She turned and twisted the handle until her sweaty palm slipped right off and she fell up against the door.

She was trapped. Just like she had been trapped in Leningrad by the Nazis. For nine hundred days the Fascists had held the city under siege, shelling it, cutting it off from all supplies. The food stock had rapidly dwindled until there was nothing but rationed bread—a few slices per day per person—made of sawdust and rotten wheat. Neighbors and friends collapsed in the kitchen, the hallways, the streets, and died on the spot. She remembered trying to drag them away. But it took too much energy. One million people died all around her, shriveling into piles of bone and flesh. Dogs and cats were consumed. People whispered the neighbors made soup out of a little boy. And still the bombs came, destroying palaces, Socialist monuments, and the linden trees.

But she had survived. She and her mother fought every day for life and had won.

The realization shocked her. She turned her back against the door, put her good hand to her chest and tried to catch her breath. The air flowed in and out of her as if she had just run ten kilometers. She closed her eyes, sucked in, exhaled, the oxygen rushing to her head, her heart. Nourished, her body loosened with relaxation. She opened her eyes.

*"Bozhe."* God.

Although the war seemed like another lifetime ago, she had lived through it. She had lived through Stalin too. Both had ripped through her soul, ruined every physical thing around her, then reduced what was left to one of two things. Black or white. Good or bad. Life or death.

But she had survived before and she could again. The choice was hers.

She rushed across the room and took her seat. Grabbing a manual, she bent back its cover. She had work to do. There was no time to panic. If she couldn't make any sense of it, well, then, she'd just have to make up something. She'd pretend as if she knew and she'd conjure up some great formulas and numbers and symbols and say, here, this is how you make the stupid chip. Quite easy, actually. Just like this. Just like I have it written here. She'd be strong. Confident. She'd be so sure of herself that she wouldn't even allow Stevens to question her. She would give him some formula for manufacturing the gallium arsenide chip and the Soviets wouldn't be on to her for weeks, months.

And by the time the scientists back home realized her scientific scribblings were nothing but gobbledygook she, Anatoly, Larissa, Vera, and Vera's son and husband would be together again. The KGB had done their dirty work, kept them apart long enough. Luba would bring them back together again.

Tommy Lichton tapped his watch to make sure it was still running. Hughes and his men had better be here soon, had better make the arrest within the hour. Luba Volshevetz wouldn't last that much longer.

His eyes fixed on the monitor, Tommy had just witnessed her panic attack. He had watched her rush to the door. He had heard her heavy, desperate breathing. He thought she might faint or scream out or do harm to herself. Finally, just at her very worst, the Russian woman had calmed herself. She was back at work now. But Tommy had no idea how much longer she would last.

He tapped his watch again. Stuck up in the security control room, there was nothing he could do but watch. And he wasn't going to take his eyes off Luba Volshevetz until the FBI had her under arrest.

## Chapter 52

"Vera, it's . . . me. Nick. Quiet."

Pressed against his rain-soaked clothes, her pulsing body froze in his hands.

"I'm going to—to let you go." Numb with pain, he found it hard to stand, difficult to speak. "But don't turn on any lights and don't make any noise."

"Nick, are you . . . ?"

"Shh. We—we have to be careful. Your apartment is bugged. There might be someone outside watching too. Understand? Okay?"

She nodded.

"Now," he whispered.

He gently opened his hands, then fell back against the counter. Vera took a step forward, bracing herself on the stove. She took a deep breath before turning around.

"Nick!" she cried out when she saw the blood. She reached for him.

"Don't!"

He jumped back, drawing in his injured arm and hand, but Vera didn't stop. Nick hesitated before extending his arm and the blood-soaked dish towel that covered it.

"Nick, what happened?"

He pulled away from her, crossed through the kitchen and living room, and turned on the television. With the volume turned high to blur what the microphones might pick up, he returned to the galley kitchen. Leading Vera toward the front door, he rubbed his forehead, tried to recall what had just taken place.

"Someone . . . tried to kill me." In his mind he saw the

193

bottoms of Theodore Hughes' shoes. "Whoever it was murdered another man just before he attacked me."

As he spoke, she reached out for his arm. He lifted it, making it easier for her. For the first time he realized that he was covered with mud and blood and that every bit of his clothes was soaked through to his skin. Closing his eyes, he didn't know how he'd made it here. All he remembered was a mosquito, a fight, and then running to his car.

He flinched as she unwound the last of the towel.

"Dear Lord!" she said in horror.

The gash—cutting across the back of his hand from his forefinger to his mangled watch—throbbed with reddish life and burning pain. Nick stared down at the wound, a clean, swollen cut that looked like a split-open slash on a loaf of French bread.

"Thank God for Minnesota mosquitoes." The scene was coming back and he spoke as if he were recounting a movie he had just seen. "I—I was supposed to meet someone. Someone from the FBI. I saw him there, dead, his throat slit. And . . . and then this mosquito bit me on my neck and then some guy rushed behind me and threw a wire over my head and . . . tried to kill me."

*"Bozhe moi!"*

"But—but my hand was on my neck." He couldn't stop himself. "The wire got caught on my watch. Then there were these two kids on skateboards that almost ran us down. . . ."

"Who? Nick, who?" she asked, afraid.

"I don't know. I didn't see his face. But he was tall . . . and with curly hair. That's all I know. All I could see."

Vera recoiled. "Richard Stevens."

"What? You know him?"

"Nick, I . . . I . . . think so. Maybe. Oh, God. Richard Stevens works at DataResearch and . . . and I was helping him get these prints to—"

"I know."

"What?" She didn't turn, didn't move.

"You're not a KGB agent, are you?"

In the dark, he watched her head drop and furiously shake. "No. I'm not."

"I didn't think so. You see, the FBI came and asked me questions. Questions about immigrants. I told them a few things. Cooperated a bit. I wanted to look out for my clients. They knew one of the immigrants was a Soviet agent." Ashamed of himself, he shook his head. "I didn't want to talk to them, tell them anything. If I had it to do over again . . ."

"You wouldn't be here with me right now."

"I guess so." He shrugged. "I'm worried about Luba. Something's wrong. Really wrong. She was here only a few hours ago. She wasn't when I returned. The door was open."

Vera put her hand to her mouth and shook her head. "Mama was supposed to stay home all night. Anatoly and Larissa were going to come over. I called but the line was busy."

"The phone's off the hook."

"Oh, no. I knew something was wrong. I called and called. I was down at the hospital cafeteria trying to figure out what to do. And—and then I saw a body that looked like my mother and . . . I came here as fast as I could."

"But it's not safe here. Come on. We have to go. If someone's looking for us, this will be the first place they come."

They left the television blaring and slipped out the back of the apartment building. Without the headlights, Nick drove out of the parking lot, down the wet street, around the corner to Texas Avenue. Using only one arm, Nick turned left, accelerated, and checked the mirrors. He saw nothing behind except a broad, empty concrete street.

Vera asked, "You didn't see Anatoly and Larissa at all?"

"Nope. Luba was alone. And upset. Very upset." Nick glanced at her, knew he couldn't tell her about her mother charging him with the knife. "I asked her if you were being blackmailed somehow. She went nuts and forced me out."

"She knows." Vera rubbed her eyes, shook her head. "I didn't want her to find out. I didn't want to hurt her. But she knows." Vera grabbed Nick by the shoulder. "She might be at Anatoly's. Can we go right there?"

"Sure."

As Nick turned on Minnetonka, he looked over and saw Vera slump back against the door. A dazed expression on her face, her lips trembled, parted. Her voice—flat, monotone—emerged from deep within her throat.

"Nick, I'm still married."

His hopes sank. "Wh-what?"

"Gennady and I . . . we, I mean, we were divorced. Legally. But not really. We pledged to each other that we'd always be married. No matter what. That's why I tried to keep away from you."

Nick tried to drive, tried to make sense of her words. "Vera, I . . ."

Tears in her eyes, she turned to him. "We didn't choose to divorce, Nick. We didn't want to, but we had no choice. We were forced."

It struck Nick how little he actually knew about her.

Her words quick, she was desperate to make Nick understand. "Gennady and I tried for years to leave Russia. Almost four years. But we were refused every time. We were losing hope. You see, when they found out at work that we were trying to go, Gennady and I both lost our jobs."

"Vera—"

"No, listen, Nick. I want you to understand. You have to understand that we were running out of money. We were eating nothing but potatoes and cabbage. Oh, we were given little jobs—I was given one sweeping halls in a school. But we couldn't live on that. Then Mama lost her job and things became worse than ever. We had a great deal of money saved for our exit visas. They're so expensive. The whole process of emigration costs thousands and thousands of rubles. Three or four years' salary. We applied three times to leave. Anatoly and Larissa got permission, but we didn't. Then we bribed an official with a whole month's salary just to find out why. He told us it was because of Gennady. He said we'd never get permission because Gennady worked on too advanced a computer. He knew too much. So you know what?"

Nick shook his head. He didn't want to hear this. He didn't want to know that the world could be so wrong.

"We realized our future there was ruined. We'd never be given good jobs or apartments or anything again. We'd always be suspect. But we still had a wonderful son and we didn't want his life to be ruined too. So for our son's sake, we decided that Mama, Vladik, and I would try to go. It was either then or never. We would have had to use our savings if we stayed, and then our visa money would be gone. We knew we'd never earn enough money to buy another one. So . . ."

"You were divorced." As Nick turned onto Highway 100, he thought of Roza Rozen's brother Misha, who had died of a heart attack. Though he had divorced his wife, Misha never gave up hope that his family would come. "They made you?"

Vera nodded. "If only one spouse is leaving, there's no other choice. You have to divorce. It's a Russian law. That's how the Soviet government protects itself. That way nobody can accuse them of splitting up families." Vera wiped her eyes. "We were divorced and Gennady moved out. We prayed that somehow we'd be able to get him out later. But then . . . then . . ."

Nick forgot about driving, about where they were going, when he realized what was still missing.

"Your son."

"Vladik." She nodded, choked back the tears. "Emigrants keep a notebook, a diary. After one person leaves, he passes it on to the next. Each person writes down their whole process of emigration and you use it for advice—from what kind of pots and pans to take to which officials you should bribe. And how much. It's an underground guide. Apply here at the beginning of the month. Ten days later see Ivan Ivanovich. Stay away from Pavel Iosivich—and pay him one hundred rubles. From Mila you can get good cameras to sell in Vienna. From Grisha you can get caviar to sell in Rome." She sobbed. "I did just as it said. Everything. Everything! We were almost out, almost there . . . and then they took my son, Nick, they took him!"

Vera sat forward, twisted around, grabbed him by the arm.

"Nick, the KGB set the whole thing up—from our being refused the very first time to losing our jobs. They just steered us here and there, put us in position. Nick, the KGB is holding my husband and son! They told me . . . told me in Rome that they'd free them if I cooperated. And if I didn't..."

Nick pulled off at the next exit. He steered onto the side of the road, parked, and took Vera in his arms. He rocked her and she cried, glad for the relief. She wouldn't be calm, though, until she drained herself of the last of the truth, the reason they had sought to leave.

"You know, many people are content there, but we weren't. And it wasn't just that we ran into problems as Jews. Gennady and I and our friends—we were real *intelligentsia,* you know, and we didn't believe what they wrote in *Pravda* or said over the radio. Instead, we saw that communism was a beautiful dream. That was all. A beautiful dream that could never be. And once you see that in the Soviet Union, you can never be happy. It sits heavy on your heart." She wiped her eyes. "A few immigrants leave because they're practicing Jews. Most leave for a better life— and being Jewish is the only way out. And a few leave because they have a conscience. That was us, Nick, and that's why we wanted to leave."

He kissed her on the forehead and asked, "Are you all right?"

"Yes."

Thinking of Luba and how little time they had, he started the car. They were only a few minutes from Anatoly and Larissa's.

"One last thing, Nick. I just want you to know that you helped me realize that if I did as the KGB asked, I'd soil this place too. It all became clear Wednesday night... when we were together. After that I knew that even if they did release my husband and son, America would be ruined for us. I went in last night and destroyed all the work I'd done."

As he steered around a corner and then headed into Anatoly's subdivision, he remembered the ring. He explained to Vera when and how the police had found it, how he had spoken with the detective earlier in the evening.

"And the guy who they think stole the diamond was killed the day after he mugged your mother." Nick looked down at his hand. "His neck was slit. Just like Hughes. Just like that guy tried to do to me."

They pulled into the driveway of Anatoly's house.

Nick said, "That means Richard Stevens probably hired that guy to mug your mother, then killed him so he couldn't tell anyone. Stevens must not have known about the diamond ring. I found out about that, told Hughes what I thought, and that's why Stevens killed Hughes and wanted to kill me too."

Vera sat in the car staring up at her brother's split-level house.

"My mother's not here. I know she's not."

Nick didn't move, couldn't move. "If you're here, then who's the FBI going to arrest tonight?"

He shook his head. The answer was all too obvious.

# Chapter 53

Richard Stevens drove through downtown, crossed the Mississippi, and went directly to his apartment. There he stripped, washed, and put on a fresh white shirt and clean gray suit. As soon as he had knotted the red and blue silk tie, he bundled up his soiled shirt and suit and carried them into the kitchen. From beneath the sink he took an empty grocery bag. He stuffed the wad of clothes into the bottom, then took out the half-filled garbage container and poured the trash over his soiled clothes.

After he had rinsed his hands off in the kitchen sink, he dialed a number on the wall phone. He spoke one brief sentence.

"I'm leaving now."

He quickly returned to the bathroom and, checking himself in the mirror one more time, smoothed his curly hair.

As he headed out the door, he grabbed his briefcase in one hand and the brown paper bag in the other. In the hallway, he tossed the trash and clothes down the garbage chute, then rode the elevator to the basement garage.

It was going on ten-thirty, and he was late. But there was nothing he could have done. Miller's phone call and threat to contact the media were as unexpected as his resistance. Of course everything had changed now. The police would connect the body of Theodore Hughes to the FBI. The FBI would connect Stevens with Hughes. They would know he had killed Hughes and soon they would also realize he had killed the cocaine addict with the same wire. It was only a matter of time, too, before they would be able to piece it together as Miller had done—the blackmailing of Vera and all the rest. They might even dig up his dealings with Lichton.

That wouldn't be until tomorrow, however, at the earliest. He'd have left by then. He'd be gone by late tonight, GALA-1 specs in hand. The opportunity no longer existed for a simple operation followed by his payment from Lichton. Had it all gone smoothly, Vera, Luba, and Viktor would already have been arrested. Now the best he could make of it was to divert the FBI and Tommy Lichton—who would be watching it all from the security control room—with Luba and Viktor. He would obtain the copy of the specs that sat on the table next to the Russian woman, and then leave the country. He'd miss out on the money from Lichton, but he'd approach the Soviets within the month. It would be a direct sale and he might even be able to get more than the original price of $250,000.

He climbed in his car, sped across the Hennepin Avenue bridge and looped around to Marquette. He pulled up opposite the hotel. Taking a deep breath, he tried to clear his mind. All he'd told Viktor was that Vera had completed her work and now her mother, a chemist, was helping with the lab reports. He hoped the Russian believed it.

He looked over and saw Viktor dogtrot out of the lobby. Viktor came around the side of his car and climbed in.

"You're over an hour late," said Viktor, shutting the door. "What happened?"

## THE RED ENCOUNTER

"Don't worry. Nothing's wrong. It just took me a while to collect the lab reports. As I said, Vera thinks she might have missed something. She had trouble with one of the files, so her mother came down to go over the lab reports. I don't know if it'll help, but it's worth the try." He checked both mirrors and was relieved to see no one following them. "After all, the process of making the gallium arsenide chip is part of the deal. Actually, it's even more important than the logic design."

Viktor shrugged. "It's true, Richard. The KGB likes you for your thoroughness."

Less than ten minutes later Stevens parked in the DataResearch garage. He led Viktor to an empty office and instructed him not to leave. Then he took the elevator down two floors to check on Luba. He had to make sure everyone was in place. And he had to make certain Tommy Lichton, who was undoubtedly watching his every move, suspected nothing.

"I wonder where in hell Hughes is," said Denise Lawson. She pushed back her chair, stepped over some camera wires, and began pacing about the small room.

"He should've been back by now," said Mark Howard.

The woman pushed back her shirt sleeve to check her watch. They had been filming Luba Volshevetz for well over an hour.

"I'm going to call the office. Hughes was supposed to call in his crew half an hour ago for the arrest," said Mark Howard, rolling his chair over to the phone. "Perhaps something came up and everything was canceled for tonight."

"Could be."

The woman shrugged and went over to the control panel. She heard a noise from the speaker, looked up at the video monitor, and saw someone coming into the room where Luba was working.

"Hey, here's Stevens."

He stopped dialing and put down the phone. "Anyone else?"

"No, just him."

Mark Howard pulled his chair back over and hit a series of buttons on the recording units.

"So where is Hughes?"

"I don't know, but they must be just about to arrest her."

The man continued to adjust the volume levels. The speaker next to the monitor cracked and hissed. Suddenly a voice came over it. Speaking in a slow, calm voice was Richard Stevens.

"I apologize for being gone so long," said Stevens. "Is everything going smoothly?"

Denise Lawson checked the monitor. She watched the older woman nod and point to a pile of manuals.

Lawson said, "Think we should call the office and try to find Hughes?"

The other technician's eyes darted from the video monitor to the volume levels. He shook his head.

"No. If Stevens is here, Hughes must be around somewhere. He must've just gotten a little hung up."

"Right."

## Chapter 54

Glad that Anatoly was driving, Nick braced himself in the back seat, his wounded hand cradled in his lap. There was no way he could squeal around corners, race in and out of cars like this. It took Anatoly's Saab, his concern for his mother, and his only recently developed skills behind the wheel to risk what he did. The Russian came to a line of cars waiting to turn onto Highway 12 and swerved around them. He charged into the opposite lane of traffic, back around, and, punching the accelerator, through the red light and onto the highway.

## THE RED ENCOUNTER

"There's only one thing I don't get," said Nick. "And that's you, Anatoly."

His eyebrows shot up. "Me? I'm just a regular employee of DataResearch. It's a huge company."

"Yeah, but what have you got going on the side?"

Anatoly, keeping his speed constant at seventy-seven, said nothing. Nor did Larissa. No one spoke as they shot through Golden Valley and past Wirth Park. The highway turned and the towers of downtown, looking like Oz, sprang into view.

Finally, Larissa eyed her husband. "We have friends in New York."

When she offered nothing further, Vera volunteered, "Powerful friends. The Russian Mafia."

"No kidding." Nick sat back. So it really existed. "Is that where all your money comes from?"

"There's no legal way to send or receive money from the Soyuz," said Anatoly, his eyes bouncing off the rearview mirror. "So we provide that service to the immigrant community. For a fee we move money between the two countries."

"But what are you doing down in your basement?"

Anatoly glanced at his wife and nodded his approval.

"We're using that money," explained Larissa, "to start our own companies. That's how I started my beauty salon and how Anatoly's going to produce the computer he's designing."

Nick shook his head. So Anatoly and Larissa, flung from the socialist homeland, were John and Jane Doe, chasing a golden dream.

Anatoly swerved past the green copper-topped basilica. Then the highway dumped abruptly onto a downtown street. The light ahead turned yellow and Anatoly, along with just about every other car, sped up and raced through the red light.

"Watch out for the *militsiya*, Anatoly," said Vera.

Nick moved closer, held her hand between his wounded, towel-covered hand and his good one. The warmth of her, the softness, made him forget just for a second.

"Nick," she whispered, "I don't know what's going to

happen. Maybe they'll arrest me tonight, maybe . . . who knows. But my mother should be spared and I have to do everything I can to help her. And I just want you to know—"

Nick shook his head and cut her off. He was going to say it first.

*"Ya tebya lubloo."*

Her body pressed against him and he took her in his arms. Perhaps it would be the FBI that would pull them apart, separate them. Or perhaps Vera's husband and child would cause the end of their relationship. He didn't know. But as they raced down street after street, Nick didn't want to stop holding her. He'd already lost too many people and places.

When they reached the other side of downtown, every ramp and parking place was filled.

"What's going on?" asked Larissa. "Where did all these cars come from?"

Anatoly said, "There's a Twins game tonight."

Nick sat up. "Circle around the DataResearch building. The car they pulled me into was a big brown Pontiac. Look for anything with people just sitting there."

Anatoly slowed on Sixth and proceeded past the rear of the low reflective-glass building. Trying not to be conspicuous, Anatoly and Vera studied the cars on one side of the street and Nick and Larissa examined the other side. They came to the large, brooding Minneapolis General Hospital, turned right on Portland, right on Seventh. They approached the front of the building, but the triangular plaza with its modern steel sculpture was as empty as the parked cars.

"Nothing," said Nick, when they had circled the building.

"I didn't see anything either," said Vera. She pointed toward the bright lights of the lobby. "That's where I went in. That's where the guard is."

"Just one more time around," said Anatoly. "We might have missed them."

They drove clockwise around the block again, and when

they still saw no one, Anatoly pulled in front of a fire hydrant.

"Well, now what?" asked the Russian man.

"From what Hughes told me, I'm sure they're videotaping her."

*"If* Luba's in there," said Larissa.

Nick studied the front entrance, a glowing mass of dark glass. He had to assume that the guard sitting at the reception desk had orders from Stevens or Hughes.

Nick rubbed his forehead and was seized with an idea. "Vera, do you still have the Mace?"

"Sure," she said, opening her purse. "It's right here."

"Would the guard recognize you . . . enough to let you in?"

Understanding, she grabbed the mace. "Let's go."

To Anatoly and Larissa, Nick said, "Wait here."

Crossing the street, Nick took Vera's hand in a tight clasp. He scanned the parked cars, but there was no movement. If they were being watched, he wondered, what was the FBI waiting for?

They made their way up the side of the building, out of sight from the guard inside. Up on the top floor, Nick saw a band of light. Just the janitor, he hoped, sweeping up a day's debris.

Their footsteps bounced off the granite plaza and their reflections bounced off the mirrored building. Slowing as the wall gave way to the lobby's smoke-colored glass, they checked the street yet another time. No movement came from any of the cars; no men appeared. There should be FBI agents stationed out here, thought Nick. Vera and he couldn't be more visible. Why was no one stopping or even questioning them?

"I don't see anyone," said Vera.

"Maybe they don't know Hughes is dead. Or maybe they're waiting for us inside," said Nick in a hushed voice. "You all right?"

The Mace held tightly in her hand, she nodded and took a deep breath. "You couldn't stop me even if you wanted to."

Nick sunk back against the wall as Vera started off. Her

steps firm, she went directly to the regular door alongside the revolving one. She quickened her steps at the last moment, then started to run.

"Hello? Please?" she called, pounding on the door.

Nick pressed himself flat against the wall and watched. She was certain to get the guard's attention before he alerted anyone to her presence.

"Please, please let me in!"

Her pounding ceased, her voice relaxed. Apparently the guard was not phoning anyone. A moment later he appeared and cracked open the door.

"How are you tonight, ma'am?" said the young man.

"I'm fine but—but I," she paused and pointed toward the far corner of the plaza. "I thought someone was following me. I was frightened. Is Mr. Stevens here tonight?"

"Yes, but I'll have to call him before I can let you in. Those are his orders."

"Well, could you just give him a message? There's an older woman working with him tonight, isn't there? Gray hair, in her fifties, with a bandaged hand."

"Ah, yes, I guess that's the one. They came in a little while ago." He pointed to a reception desk. "I saw them on the security monitor."

"Good. Well, could you tell them—"

She moved so quickly that Nick almost missed it. In midsentence, one hand flew up, caught the edge of the door, yanked it out of the guard's hands. At the same time, she shoved her other hand in his face and sprayed the Mace. When he cried out and slapped his hands over his eyes, Vera pushed him inside and disappeared through the door.

Clutching his wounded hand against his stomach, Nick was at the door within seconds. Inside, he saw Vera give the groping guard another quick shot of Mace. The man tore at his blinded eyes, stumbled backward. He called out for her to stop even as she grabbed the handgun from his waist and drove him back. Then she forced him behind the long granite reception desk, pointed the gun at him, and ordered him to sink to the floor. When he was down, she threatened him again and, keeping the pistol trained on him, ran to the front door. With a flick of her hand, she opened the latch.

"I'm glad you're on my side," said Nick, entering. "The Sovs don't know what they lost."

She hurried back to the guard. Nick leaned out the door, signaled to Anatoly and Larissa, then followed after Vera.

Standing above the guard, she said, "Just cooperate and we won't hurt you."

The guard, his figure crumpled, his hands still to his eyes, moved his head up and down.

Now that he was in, Nick realized that the lobby was leaving them far too exposed. Even with the tinted glass, it was like being inside a fishbowl.

"We have to get him out of here before someone spots us." To the guard, he said, "Is there a janitor's closet around here?"

"Yeah." His voice was weak, scared. "Down that way." He pointed past the elevators. "First door down there."

"Good. Give me your keys," ordered Nick. "Are they for the entire building?"

"Yes."

The man wiped his eyes on his shirt one more time, then unfastened the collection of keys from his belt. Vera bent down to him.

"Your eyes will be fine. Now, which keys will get us into the main part of the building?"

The guard indicated three keys, one for the elevator, two more for the hallways. Then she demanded to know where Stevens was. When he refused, she pressed the gun to his head and repeated the question.

"The same place you were, on B-5."

"What about the FBI?" said Nick. "There are some people with video equipment. Where are they?"

"I think . . . I don't know for sure . . . on the fourth floor down. B-4. But I don't know if they're FBI. Mr. Stevens just told me there was a special crew there and to do anything they asked."

Suddenly there was pounding at the door. Nick spun around, saw the figures of Anatoly and Larissa there. He motioned at them to wait.

"Maybe we should have them stay in the car," said Vera.

Nick stood still. "What do we do now? How are we going

to find your mother and get out of here without being noticed?"

Vera looked out the doors, past her brother, and to the large outline of the hospital across the street.

*"Ya znaiyoo."* I know, she said, the muscles tightening around her eyes.

## Chapter 55

He pounded on the door with the heel of his fist. "It's Stevens. Let me in."

Low, garbled words were exchanged inside, a chair moved, and a person quickly came over. The door was unlocked and pulled open. Denise Lawson stood there.

Not giving her time to speak, Stevens stormed in. "Where's Hughes?"

Lawson said, "That's what we'd like to find out."

Stevens froze. "You mean he's not here?"

"No. We were expecting him back over an hour ago. I thought he was with you."

"Well, he's not. I don't know where he went."

The other FBI technician, Mark Howard, glanced over but did not get up. Earphones on his head, he paid close attention to the video monitor and the recording units. Stevens looked over at the TV and saw the image of Luba flipping through one of the lab reports.

Lawson motioned toward the VCR. "We have plenty of her on tape. All we're waiting for is the arrest."

"Damn." He shook his head. "Where the hell can Hughes be? Have you checked with the office?"

"Not yet. I was just about to."

"Give them a call. Find out if they've seen him. And tell

them to get their asses over here right away. They promised a full team."

"Yes, sir."

Stevens paced back and forth. "Shit, this whole arrest was supposed to take place an hour ago and no one's here to do it. I have it all set up. Major Petrov is waiting in another office. The arrest is supposed to be made tonight and by God they'd better do it."

"Yes, sir."

While Denise Lawson dialed Hughes' office, Richard Stevens stepped up behind Mark Howard. There was a clear shot of Luba on the video monitor and over the speaker came the rustling noise of her busy work. The Russian woman was seated just to the side of the terminal where Vera had worked. Clearly shown were a full roll of magnetic tape and the stack of lab reports.

"That's a good shot," said Stevens to Howard, who partially slipped off the earphones. "You're showing her with all the material." He pointed to the round disk on the screen. "That tape contains all the specs on the GALA-1."

"Yes, we—"

*"Ya nichevo ni ponimayoo,"* muttered Luba over the speaker.

Mark Howard cut himself off and turned up one of the dials. Except for the rustling of papers, Luba was now silent.

"She said she wasn't understanding anything." Stevens laughed. "That's why the arrest has to take place tonight. There's no way she can do that work, and I don't know if I can get her back again."

All he wanted, however, was a considerable amount of commotion in the room. He wanted it filled with Luba, Viktor, himself, and a handful of FBI agents. That way no one— Tommy Lichton in particular, who'd be watching—would notice him taking the computer specs and slipping away.

"Excuse me," said Denise Lawson, telephone in hand. "Mr. Hughes isn't at headquarters. Should the agents come over right away?"

"Absolutely." Stevens started for the door. "I'm going to take Petrov down there now. Undoubtedly he'll say something to Luba about working for the Motherland. Just be sure and get it all on tape." He checked his watch. "Can they be down there in fifteen minutes?"

She repeated his question into the phone, and then said, "No problem. In fifteen minutes there will be a half-dozen agents down there, another half-dozen in the lobby."

## Chapter 56

Vera held open the double door as Nick rolled the cart out of the hospital and into the night. The wheels passed from the smooth linoleum, over the ridge of the threshold, and onto the gritty concrete sidewalk.

They both wore blue hospital jackets that they had stolen from a linen room. As soon as they were outside Vera started to unbutton hers.

"Keep it on," said Nick. "We just want to go across here nice and slow and look like we know what we're doing. Just like we're working."

They proceeded away from the building, the contents of the large plastic bin bouncing along. At the corner, Nick and Vera waited for the walk signal, directed the cart down the wheelchair curb, and across the smooth pavement. They came up and onto the plaza on the other side, and headed directly for the front door of DataResearch.

Vera gasped. "Look."

In the distance, a crowd was moving down the sidewalk.

"The game must just have finished." His eyes flicked from side to side. "Hurry."

Up ahead in the lobby he saw the figure of Larissa. Smoothing a wrinkle in her jacket, she wore the guard's white shirt, blue tie and suit. Behind her Anatoly was removing keys from a ring.

## THE RED ENCOUNTER

"Looks like they didn't have any trouble with the guard," said Nick.

Anatoly and Larissa spotted them coming and hurried to the entrance. Holding the door open, the blonde looked with horror at the large container.

"Is that it?" she said, making a face.

*"Da, da,"* answered Nick.

Anatoly took hold of one of the handles and helped maneuver the container through the doorway and into the building. They went directly to the elevator lobby.

"So what did the guard tell you?" asked Nick.

"Everything. We tied him up in the closet and he told me everything," said Anatoly. "I know exactly where to go and what to do."

Vera pushed the button for the elevator. "It's just a matter of timing, then."

"Take this." Larissa quickly slipped her Rolex watch from her wrist. "It's the exact same time as Anatoly's."

"And these."

Anatoly handed Nick three keys, which the guard said would override the security system along the way.

"Don't forget to use them or all the alarms will go off."

The elevator door eased open and Vera and Nick rolled the container into it. At once a deathly smell rose out of the cart and filled the lift. Nick put his hand to his nose, hoping at least that the thing wasn't already too old, that it was still malleable enough to get in place.

As the elevator doors began to shut, Anatoly said, "I'm going to take the stairs down. Good luck." He looked at the gun in his hand, then shoved it through the closing doors. "Here, you might need this too."

"I'll stay at the front desk for five more minutes. And then I'll get the car," said Larissa. "See you out front."

## Chapter 57

Anatoly hurried down the emergency stairwell to the fourth floor. He stopped at the heavy metal door, took the knob in hand, and listened. Twisting the handle, he pulled open the door and peered down the hall. It was empty and, like industrial night-lights, only half the fluorescent bulbs quivered with life. Yet Anatoly knew of the activity here. Halfway down on the right, in room B412, two agents were filming his mother at work.

He simply had to duck down the hall, enter the maintenance room on this floor, do his work, then leave as swiftly as possible. Without being seen or caught.

Anatoly clasped the guard's ring of keys in one hand, cracked the door open farther, and slipped out. He heard the whirling of tape and machinery and froze like a rabbit. He looked left, then right. The maintenance room was down there, toward the double elevators.

He wasted not a moment in this open territory. His body hunched low, the key in hand, he rushed down the hall and hesitated only a split second at the door. With a nervous glance at the elevators, he twisted the lock and slipped in.

The room was cool and dark. He was still. When Anatoly was sure the silence meant emptiness, he felt for the light switch and flooded the room with the glare from a naked bulb. He spotted at once the circuit-breaker box. He crossed to the concrete wall on which it was mounted and swung open the metal covering. His eyes ran down the black knobs, stopping at one near the bottom. He reached to the switch, rested his finger on it, and checked his watch. Three minutes. And then he'd turn the circuit breaker off for ten seconds. No more, no less.

If this was going to work, it all depended on exact timing. If either he or Nick and Vera were moments early or moments late, they'd all be caught.

# Chapter 58

Luba was in there, behind that wall. Nick could sense her presence. Vera could too. They dared not speak, but Nick knew from Vera's eyes. Yes, Nick responded in his mind. Your mother is there. I hope to hell this works.

He smiled, clutched the guard's gun in one hand and touched Vera with the other. They were just outside the room on the fifth floor, down where Vera had worked at obtaining the secrets of the GALA-1. Rolled up near the door was the large black plastic container they had stolen from the hospital. The stench that wafted out of it reminded Nick of both a high school science lab and an uncleaned kitty-litter pan. So this was what awaited them all, perhaps this very evening.

Vera held Larissa's Rolex watch and the seconds melted slowly away. Finally, the third minute dissolved into the second. Two minutes. That was all until they forced either success or failure. Nick wanted to talk to her, tell her how much he cared for her, how sorry he was. But he couldn't. Luba might hear. If Luba heard them, she might turn, come to the door, open it. And then the agents videotaping her would know. They would surely be caught.

Vera touched his wrist. One minute to go, after which they only had ten seconds to get in there and out. They couldn't be late but they couldn't be early either.

They moved to opposite ends of the container, pushed aside the dirty linen on top. Vera studied the watch on her wrist, her head bouncing along as she counted the seconds.

As the time neared, she raised her hand, the fingers spread wide. Then she began to pull down her fingers to mark the seconds. Five. Four. Three. Two. One.

"Now," she said, her voice shattering the silence.

They each took an audible breath of air and reached into the shallow plastic grave.

## Chapter 59

Denise Lawson and Mark Howard stared at the video monitor as if it were a gripping soap opera about to reach its long-awaited climax. They were both settled deep in their chairs, necks craned forward, mouths slightly open. They watched as the Russian woman flipped through page after page of the lab reports. Periodically, she'd jot something down on paper, flip back, then moan and shake her head. Clearly, she was unable to do the work. But it didn't matter. Within minutes, Richard Stevens and Major Viktor Petrov would enter the room. Moments after that, a team of FBI agents would swoop into the room and make the final arrests.

The atmosphere, as fragile as a glass ornament, shattered when the electricity went off. In a single instant every light failed, the VCR tapes ground to a halt, and the TV faded from color, to black and white, to gray, to black.

"Oh, shit," said Denise Lawson into the void that now surrounded her. "Mark?"

It was as if she had closed her eyes and failed to open them, only darker. There was no light to seep in from anywhere. They were buried beneath the street, buried beneath this building, without a single source of light.

Mark Howard's voice came out of nowhere. "We didn't get nuked, did we?"

## THE RED ENCOUNTER

Denise Lawson touched the arms of her chair. Slightly reassured, she began to move. But where? She gazed in the direction of the TV. Reaching out, she felt a table, a pencil, and then found the monitor. The glass was warm.

"Where's the phone?" she asked.

"Behind you somewhere. You used it last."

"No I didn't."

"Yes you did. When Stevens was here."

"Oh . . . you're right." She paused. "You know what, we better get out of here. There might be a fire. The stairwells should have emergency lights. I wonder if the electricity is out all through the building."

"Man, I wonder what the Russian woman is doing. Probably freaking out but g—"

As if by magic, the lights popped on. Denise Lawson turned to her workmate. She had never noticed that mole buried beneath his right eyebrow or the slightly crooked nose, perhaps the result of a fight.

"That was weird," she said.

"Look."

The video monitor went white, then filled with colored dots. A picture emerged, filled the corners. The Russian woman sat there, her back to them, deep in concentration.

"The lights must not have gone off down there," said Mark Howard.

"Yeah."

Denise Lawson studied the figure on the screen. There was something different about her. Was it the way she was sitting?

"She's moved or something."

"Well, she's not moving a bit now. She must be concentrating pretty damn hard."

"I think we better call this one in, see if anyone can tell us what happened."

Mark Howard pushed back his sleeve and checked the time.

"Hang on a second. Stevens ought to be going in there any minute with the Russian agent. Let's see what happens."

But there was something wrong. Denise Lawson knew it. What was it, though?

"Hey, wait a minute. Is that what she was wearing before?"

Tommy Lichton was so stunned he couldn't move. What was happening? How did those two get in there? And where was the FBI? Didn't they see on their cameras what had just happened?

Frantic, he hit switch after switch. Screens on his video monitor flicked by showing him nothing but empty corridors and rooms. Where was Hughes? The halls, the lobby should have been filled with FBI agents. There was no way anyone should have been able to get downstairs. Tommy cursed himself. He'd been so nervous that the Russian woman would try and flee again that he hadn't checked anything else, hadn't seen anyone enter the building.

"No!" he shouted, rising.

They were going to escape. He couldn't allow it. He had to stop them. In a rush, he charged over to the other side of the white room and flung open cabinets and drawers.

There was a gun here somewhere.

## Chapter 60

Richard Stevens and Viktor Petrov rode the elevator down, their eyes fixed on the digital numbers over the door. When the number five lit up, the lift stopped and opened. The two men stepped out, but they hadn't gone more than a yard when the Russian slowed.

"Richard, are . . . are you sure about all this?"

"Absolutely. Everything's all set. I'm not sure what Mrs. Volshevetz has come up with but . . . we'll see. In any case, what Vera obtained from the computer itself is more than plenty."

Stevens cut himself off and studied the deeply lined face of the Russian. Viktor seemed to ponder each of Richard's words, then gazed down the hall. He turned back to the American and eyed him, thought Stevens, almost suspiciously.

"You really think it will be enough?" asked Viktor as if he were testing him one last time.

Stevens gently took hold of Viktor's wrist, squeezed it, and nudged him on. Just a few more feet, that was all.

"Plenty. Don't worry. Your people will be quite satisfied."

They continued down the stark corridor, the walls of which resonated with the dull sounds of their steps. As they walked along Stevens glanced over at the Russian and cast him a forced smile. He just had to get the Russian in the room, make sure there was plenty of commotion when the FBI arrived.

"You'll see that Mrs. Volshevetz is a bit nervous," he said, his voice low. "She was eager to help and I'm sure she's done her best."

Eyes straight ahead, Viktor nodded. "In any case, I'll get the specs and . . . and . . ."

"And be on your way."

Viktor turned abruptly to him. "Yes, back to Moscow."

Caught off guard by Viktor's seemingly angry attitude, he said, "Viktor, I promise. Just a few more sales after this and in a year's time the two of us will take off."

"Sure."

Stevens slowed as they neared a room near the end of the hall. He reached out with a loose fist and tapped twice on the door. When there was no response, he took the knob in hand and twisted.

"Mrs. Volshevetz?" called Stevens as he pushed on the door. "I'm back."

He glanced in and saw the woman, her back to him, still concentrating on the lab reports. She did not move, neither to flip a page nor to mark something down, not even to greet them.

"Hard at work, I see," said Stevens. "Hope you're having good luck."

He entered the room, Viktor right behind, then shut the door. As he crossed to the side table and picked up several bound lab reports, a thick, odd odor seeped into his nose. He glanced around the room.

"These are some of the lab reports right here, Viktor." Handing the papers to him, he stared at Luba. "We can photocopy anything Mrs. Volshevetz finds." He stopped, giving her a chance to respond. He was met by her silence. "So, have you been able to find anything?" he said to her back.

The woman did not say anything.

"Any luck, Mrs. Volshevetz? Have you found anything yet?"

There was no response, no movement. Stevens eyed Viktor, who appeared equally perplexed.

"I have the gentleman who is going to secure the release of your grandson." He paused. "Mrs. Volshevetz?"

It was then that he realized that something was missing. The large, round magnetic disk with the prints of the GALA-1 encoded on it. He had left it right on the table next to the lab reports.

Quickly, he crossed the room, came up directly behind her.

"Mrs. Volshevetz, where are the prints?"

He reached out and placed his hand on her shoulder. It was stiff. Slowly he pulled on the shoulder, causing the chair to swivel around. He looked down, expecting to see the face of Luba Volshevetz.

Instead Stevens saw the lifeless form of a strange woman. Her skin yellow and rigid, her expression was one of a lifetime of pain, misery. A deep sound climbed out of his throat, and the dead body fell out of the chair, wrapping its stiff arms around his legs.

## Chapter 61

The scream from below meant only one thing. The corpse they had stolen from the morgue—the body of the woman who had committed suicide—had been discovered.

"Hurry," said Nick, clutching the gun in his good hand.

Vera led the way carrying the precious tape, with Luba behind her. Nick moved on only when he was certain no one was chasing after them. Bounding up the steps two at a time, he quickly caught up with the two women. They pressed on, hurrying as fast as they could.

Suddenly, as they climbed to the landing on the fourth floor, a door flung open. A dark arm appeared. Vera stopped. A man stepped out before them.

"Anatoly!" called Luba.

"Is everything all right?" he asked.

Vera grabbed her mother's arm as if to pull her along. "They found the body."

"We don't have any time to waste," said Nick, glancing back down the stairs. "In five minutes this place is going to be swarming with FBI."

Anatoly jogged down several steps and took his mother by the other arm. They raced past the third-floor landing, up to the second. Only a few more flights, thought Nick, and they'd reach the main lobby. Their only chance would be to find the lobby empty. Larissa would be right outside with the car.

Minutes later they stood on the first-floor landing. Nick, his breathing deep and heavy, pressed his ear to the door. All was quiet.

"Sounds good," he said to Vera, who stood just behind him.

He inched open the door and couldn't believe it. The lobby was empty. Unable to believe their luck, he pulled the door wide open. He glanced up and down the glass-enclosed room, saw no one, and stepped onto the granite flooring.

"It's clear. Let's get the hell out of here!"

Vera, Luba, and Anatoly pushed out, followed after him, wasting not a moment in crossing toward the building's entrance. But just as they were nearing the slab of granite that served as the guard's desk, a bell chimed behind them. Nick turned, saw one of the elevator lights flash on. Nick glanced toward the front doors, then back to the stairwell. There was no time to advance or retreat.

The elevator eased open and two men charged out. They jerked to a stop when they saw Nick, Vera, and the others. Vera immediately recognized one of them—the one with the pistol in his hand.

"Richard Stevens!"

"Is the other guy KGB?" asked Nick.

"Yes, that's Major Petrov."

And then, before anyone could move, a side door was flung open. Gun in hand, a tall man with a deep tan and dark hair burst out. He glanced over at Richard Stevens before turning and leveling his pistol at Nick and the others.

"Who's that?" asked Anatoly.

"I don't know, but you better get down!" shouted Nick, shoving them all behind the granite reception desk.

## Chapter 62

Unable to believe it, Denise Lawson slowly turned her head back toward the video monitor. The camera was still trained on the corpse.

"My God," she said, closing her eyes.

"What happened?" groaned Mark Howard, also unable to look at the color image. "Who did that?"

"I don't know, but we've got big trouble." Denise Lawson spun her chair around and reached for the phone.

Howard took a quick look at the screen, and said, "Oh, Jesus. Is that TV or real life?"

"This is great," said Denise Lawson, shaking her head as she dialed. "Theodore Hughes is nowhere to be found, a Russian woman has disappeared, we have a dead body on our hands, and if that weren't enough—" The other end of the line was picked up. "Hello, Denise Lawson here. The prints to the GALA-1 were just stolen. Yes. Not more than five minutes ago. What? No, I don't have any idea who took them, but whoever did still has to be in the building."

## Chapter 63

Seventh Street was bumper to bumper with cars. A sellout Twins game had just ended and over fifty thousand screaming fans were pouring out of the dome, onto the sidewalks, and into their cars.

Once again Larissa cursed America for having such a terrible mass-transit system. If just half these people tonight were boarding a train or streetcar or bus instead of individual cars, then she wouldn't be stuck in this traffic jam. There were so many cars that she could only get the nose of her Saab out of the parking place. She couldn't move another inch. To make matters worse, there was an accident up at the corner and cars were stopped dead all around.

"Damn!"

She slammed her open palm on the steering wheel. DataResearch was just across the street, on the north side. She was on the south. Even if she could get out of the parking place, there was no way she was going to be able to cut across four lanes of stopped cars. She'd have to work her way around the entire block, which, at this rate, might take a half hour. And then what? They'd never be able to drive directly out of here.

Larissa jabbed the gearshift, reversed the car into the parking place, then climbed out. Her ears were greeted by choruses of cheers and shouting, honking horns, and the blare of an impromptu and drunken marching band. Glancing at the intersection, she saw three police cars with flashing lights grouped around the two tangled autos.

She cut around the front of the Saab, wove in and out of the stopped cars, and toward the plaza of DataResearch. She just hoped that they had rescued Luba from the basement room, that they were all still free, that she could find them. At least, she thought, there were people everywhere—more than she had ever seen on the streets in America. They were going to have to flee on foot, and perhaps the huge crowds would make their escape possible.

Nick fired a single shot and the two men retreated into the elevator. The man by the stairwell door aimed his gun at Nick, but then Stevens edged out of the elevator, fired a single shot at him, spun around and fired twice toward Vera and the others. Nick ducked back as the bullets struck the edge of the reception desk and chips of granite went flying. He felt Vera, right behind him, sink her fingers into his waist.

"Vera, who's that other guy by the door? Is he with Stevens?"

"I—I don't know. I've never seen him before."

Behind Vera, Luba muttered, *"Bozhe."*

Nick cradled his wounded hand against his stomach, glanced into the night at the enormous throng of cars and people filling the street. It was only a matter of minutes before the shots were heard and both the police and the FBI descended on them.

"My fun quotient's crashing," said Nick. "A game of sudden death isn't exactly how I planned to spend the evening."

## THE RED ENCOUNTER

Searching outside for any sign of the dark blue Saab, Anatoly said, "I hope nothing happened to my car."

"Anatoly!" scolded Luba, slapping him on the shoulder.

Vera scowled. "Did you forget everything you learned at Pioneer Camp?"

"Let's not get all prissy about Uncle Lenin, Vera."

Searching for his wife and car, Anatoly slowly pulled himself up. No sooner did the top of his head appear above the granite desk than another shot was fired. Anatoly dove for the floor, landing awkwardly on his left arm. When he sat back up, he felt his wrist. Pushing back his sleeve, he exposed his Rolex, the crystal broken and the hands smashed.

"Ruined, and I'm up to my Master Card limit."

The man from the stairwell emerged yet another time. He slipped sideways, trying to get a clearer shot at them. Before he had taken two steps, however, Stevens shot twice.

"Holy shit," said Nick.

The man cried out and was thrown against the wall. One of the bullets caught him in his right arm, and the gun flew out of his hand. Desperate for shelter, he lunged back to the side door and, dripping blood, disappeared before Stevens could shoot again.

"They got him!" said Anatoly.

Nick glanced over at the elevators and saw Petrov taking aim.

"Down!" shouted Nick. "They both have guns!"

Nick struggled to think of a way out. There were two men in the elevator, each with a gun. The authorities would surely be here any minute and then all of them would be apprehended.

He searched the lobby for another exit, then peered around the granite desk again. Stevens was stepping out of the elevator. But, pistol in hand, he again was not aiming at Nick. Rather, Nick could see that he was pointing the gun to the left.

Nick looked to the side, expecting to see the wounded man. Instead he saw no one. He turned further. Outside he saw a blond woman rushing directly to the front door.

"Larissa!" screamed Nick.

* * *

She was staring toward the corner trying to tell if the police or FBI had been alerted yet. And over the sound of the people and cars outside, she didn't hear anything. She didn't feel anything, either, except a chilling whoosh of air past the side of her head. At first she thought a bat had dived out of the night sky. But then she heard shards of glass smashing on the stone, turned, and saw the four of them huddled behind the reception desk. Her first reaction was to run forward. Her second was to see what they were hiding from.

That is when she saw the tall man with the curly hair leveling his gun at her a second time.

She dropped to the ground, ducked back, and this time heard the shot, the quick pierce of the bullet through glass, then nothing. She dropped her purse and ran for the red metal sculpture. Taking cover behind one of the iron beams, she looked back. Anatoly, Vera, Luba, and Nick were there. Inside. Trapped by two men.

She turned back to the street. At the corner, near the scene of the accident, two policemen stood beside their empty cars. Their idling vehicles were pulled right up on the edge of the plaza, just beyond the light of the streetlamps.

Nick stood behind the granite desk, steadied the gun on his wounded arm. Squinting, he aimed at Stevens' chest, squeezed the trigger. The other man spotted Nick, whirled around, fell back into the elevator. The bullet slammed into the wall, ricocheted, and smashed into the opposite wall.

Nick crouched, but only slightly and not enough. Stevens reached around the corner, fired another shot. Nick fell to the ground and behind him another window disintegrated into shards.

Vera pointed outside and shouted, "Police!"

Lights flashing white and red, a police car roared across the open plaza. Racing through the dark, it swerved around the metal sculpture, barreled directly toward the entry.

This was it, thought Nick. Stevens and the Russian on one side, the cops on the other. There was no way out.

But the police car did not slow as it neared the building. Rather, as if it were charging the building, it gained speed with each moment. And as it neared a lone figure appeared behind the wheel.

Anatoly gasped, "My God, it's Larissa!"

Hunched over the wheel, she drove directly toward the sheer glass wall. Then, like a rock hurled through a window, the entire police car shot through the wall and into the building. Splinters of glass tore through the air, smashed on the granite floor, and the car landed in the lobby of DataResearch like a beached whale. Larissa punched the accelerator again and the tires spit glass into the air. Leaving a patch of burnt rubber and ground glass behind, the car charged directly toward the reception desk.

A shot rang out. Stevens had recognized the driver and was firing at Larissa. The car veered to the left, back to the right, then finally braked to a crying halt right behind the desk. Nick jumped up; he fired at Stevens and Petrov as they emerged from the elevators.

Anatoly, his head low, lunged for the police car's front door. He tore it open and grabbed his mother by the arm. "Keep down!" he shouted as he threw her onto the front seat and jumped in behind her.

Vera scrambled to the back door and opened it. "Nick, come on!"

She threw in the prints, dove onto the floor of the back seat, and turned around. Nick, still waving the gun toward Stevens, hurled himself back. Vera grabbed him by the shoulders and dragged him in. Larissa slammed the accelerator to the floor and the police car took off, the back door flapping open and closed.

A bullet pierced the rear window, shot through the inside, and out the windshield. Another struck the trunk with a dull thud.

*"Derzhi!"* Hang on, cried Larissa with a wild look on her face.

She whipped the car around the other side of the revolving doors and toward the other wall of glass. In a single moment, the vehicle punctured the structure and sailed out of DataResearch.

Through a shower of glass Nick saw Stevens and Petrov running across the lobby. Behind them, the unidentified wounded man emerged from the stairwell and groped for his gun. Then to the side, racing around the edge of the red steel sculpture, a green car appeared with a single blue light flashing atop it.

"FBI!"

Larissa twisted the wheel away from the other car and toward the sidewalk along Fifth Avenue. Gawking pedestrians—fans from the baseball game—suddenly realized that the police car was charging them. They turned, ran, screamed. Luba peered over the dashboard, shook her head, ducked down again.

Jabbing the horn, Larissa shouted, "Out of the way!"

Behind, Stevens and Petrov ran onto the plaza and directly into the path of the FBI car. The vehicle skidded to a halt, barely missing Stevens. He and Petrov ran to each of the side doors, yanked them open, and by gunpoint pulled the agents from the car. Once Stevens was behind the wheel and the Russian agent seated next to him, the green car was after them again. The wounded man staggered through the shattered glass wall and fired twice, while a police car at the corner turned on its flashing lights, spun around, and headed off in pursuit.

"Crap," muttered Nick.

Anatoly looked ahead. "Look out!"

A man on the sidewalk was paralyzed with fear as the car zeroed in on him. The edge of the building was on the right. Another group of people were fleeing to the left.

"Go there!" shouted Luba, pointing to a gap between a lamp post and a fire hydrant.

"What do you say in English, Nick?" Larissa's face blanched white. "Oi, *da.* Holy Shit."

There was nowhere else to go, and Larissa clutched the steering wheel and leaned forward. Scraping the lamp post, the car hurled itself through the hole, onto Fifth Avenue. A brown Oldsmobile veered to the left, out of the way, and Larissa wrenched the steering wheel to the right.

## THE RED ENCOUNTER

From the back seat, Nick looked through the windshield at the mass of cars before them. Like magic, the screaming sirens and flashing lights forced a path to open. Cars pulled to the side, jammed themselves bumper to bumper and door to door. Nick watched the street open before them, almost like snow being plowed aside. He turned around, hoping the way would close behind. It did not. The green car, its lone blue light flashing, skidded sideways onto the street. That car started after them and then the police car sped off the plaza and onto the street.

"They're still coming!" said Vera.

The traffic at the intersection of Sixth Street thickened, their pace slowed. Stevens and the Russian would be on them in minutes.

"Turn here!" said Nick.

Sixth, a one-way street from the center of downtown, carried few cars. Larissa turned onto it, pressed the accelerator to the floor. Seconds later, the green car headed around the corner. Nick looked back and saw the Russian agent leaning out the car window.

"They've got a gun on us again, Larissa. Swerve back and forth!"

Pushing the wheel to the left, pulling it back to the right, Larissa drove in a screeching S-shape all the way down the street. From behind, a shot burst into the air, disappeared into the night. Nick took the gun, leaned out the window, the wind tearing at his hair. He braced himself on the door with his wounded hand, aimed back at the tires of the green car. Squeezing the trigger, the gun exploded. Almost miraculously, he hit a headlight, which burst and shattered into darkness.

"Larissa!" cried Anatoly.

Up ahead, a group of pedestrians was trying to scurry out of the way of the seemingly out-of-control car. Running back and forth, they didn't know which way to go. Larissa swerved, hit the curb, turned left onto Portland. It was a broad one-way street and they were going the wrong way. Horns blared, panicked drivers yanked their cars to the side as the police car headed directly at them.

Weaving in and out of the cars, they headed toward the

Mississippi. Somewhere behind were Stevens and the Russian in the green car. And behind them, lost in the sea of cars, was the second and perhaps third police car.

When they came to Washington Avenue, Larissa called, "Nick, which way?"

"Straight, toward the mills!" he shouted, seeing the open land ahead.

A cop at the corner saw the blazing lights of their car and halted all traffic at the intersection. With a stiff arm, he waved them through, only to be confused by the assemblage of people in the squad car. The officer shook his head, spotted the chasing green car and held traffic for it also.

From the back, Nick said, "Anatoly, turn off the lights and the siren."

He fumbled with a panel of switches as the car hit a bump and shot off Washington Avenue. Luba cried out as the car heaved into the air, then landed on the narrow paved road. A wasteland of buildings and railroad tracks lay before them, yet blocking the way ahead was a train loaded with grain.

Vera looked to the right. "There's a road over there." It was the one Stevens had taken the first night she'd met him. "You can go down and circle around the mills. It comes out on Third Avenue."

The car bounced from pothole to pothole on this smaller, unpaved road. Nick looked behind. Stevens had turned off the pavement and was closing in. The police car, caught back in the traffic, was still trying to make it through the intersection.

Like mirrored reflections of one another, the identical gray grain cars were lined up one after the other. Finally, the pattern was broken by a lone caboose, shortly after which the road curved over a crossing. They bounced over the tracks, and around them a series of solid concrete silos burst into the air. Directly ahead were piles of sand—barged up the river and soon to be mixed into concrete—and beyond that the Mississippi.

"The road goes between that last silo and the sand," said Vera.

The car's headlights were trained on the gap. But Stevens was now across the track. A shot rang out. Almost simultaneously the right rear tire exploded into bits of rubber. Larissa screamed as the car writhed from side to side. Together, Larissa and Anatoly held the wheel, trying to keep control. But they swung too wide and the car charged into a pile of sand, sinking at once up to its chassis.

Nick clawed at the handle. He bolted out the door. Gun in both hands, he crouched and fired.

"Get out!" Nick shouted to Vera.

He scanned the night, searched for the closest protection. Directly across he spotted a small wooden door that led into the base of the mills.

"In there!"

The green FBI car swerved to the right, taking shelter behind concrete pilings that held the sand. Stevens and the Russian agent jumped out, aimed their guns, and the black pistols exploded. Nick tried to hold back, not to fire unless it was absolutely necessary. Three shots, that's all that were left.

Vera, the prints still under her arm, scooted out and kept low. The front door was thrown open and, crouching, Anatoly, Luba, and Larissa slipped out. Crawling through the sand, all four of them made their way around to the front of the car.

"Nick!" yelled Vera.

Keeping his gun trained on Stevens, he slipped backward. He shouted to Anatoly. "I'll cover you!"

Anatoly checked Nick and Stevens, then bolted across the open black space. Stevens steadied his gun on him. Nick fired, and the other American ducked back.

Anatoly hurled himself against the cracked door. Nothing happened. His eyes white with panic, he threw himself again and wood cracked and splintered. Kicking, he forced his way in.

Nick crouched behind Larissa, Vera, and Luba. "You three go next. I'll be right behind you." Nick peered over the car toward the two men. "Okay, now!"

Kicking up sand in their wake, the three of them went first, Nick last. Stevens fired, missed. Nick fired back, heard another bullet race past his head. He aimed, almost pulled the trigger, then stopped before firing the last one.

Just ahead, he saw Vera and the others disappear into the mill. Cradling his wounded hand, he ran as fast as he could and dove into the doorway. He tripped and tried to shield his left hand as he came to a hard landing on the wooden flooring. Behind him, Anatoly pushed shut what remained of the door. Inside, it became dark, black except for what little night light seeped through the broken door.

"Nick . . ." Vera reached for him.

Gun in one hand, his other throbbing with pain, Nick stood. He immediately noticed how the floor had quickly stained his hands and clothes. Rubbing his fingers together, the thick scent of oil filled his nose.

"I saw a stairway." Anatoly reached into his pocket, took out something, and moments later held a lit match. "There, all the way at the back."

In the flickering light, Nick glanced around at the wooden structure attached to the cement silos. Rusty diesel motors and barrels were scattered everywhere. This must have been a power room—an add-on to supplement the water power from the falls. And then he saw a black, tarlike line of oil that had oozed from one of the machines. That was what Nick had rolled on.

He looked up, saw the shriveling flame burning down to Anatoly's fingertips.

"Anatoly!"

But it was too late. His skin scorched, Anatoly reflexively shook his hand and dropped the match. It dimmed as it tumbled through the darkness, almost went out by the time it hit the floor, but landed red-hot and struggled back to life. The floor took to the heat instantly and a blue flame burst across the floor like brandy in a pan.

"Oi!" screamed Luba.

Greasy black smoke slithered into the air and the fire poured itself across the floor, lapped at the splintery walls. It was only a matter of seconds before the staircase ahead would be blocked and they would be forced to retreat outside.

Pushing forward, Nick shouted, "Go!"

As they skirted the flames and moved toward the interior of the mill, Nick heard a noise from outside. Glancing back, he saw Stevens and the Soviet agent kicking apart the door, making their way in.

Larissa started up the steep stairs, Luba then Anatoly right behind her.

"Maybe the flames will stop them," said Vera to Nick.

"I—" Nick spotted a gun trained on them. "Vera!"

She ducked and a bullet slammed into the wooden wall. Stevens was about to fire again when reflexively Nick spun around and fired back. Stevens dipped behind a wood column, then reappeared. Nick squeezed the trigger, letting loose nothing more than a metal click.

"Come on, you sucker."

He fired again and again. Still nothing, he threw the gun into a bin of junk and ran after Vera. Another shot pierced the air, slammed into a wooden column just behind him.

They clambered up the steep wooden staircase, the heat and the smoke rising after them. Behind, Nick heard Stevens and the Soviet knocking over a metal drum, struggling to make their way past the flames.

Climbing deeper and deeper into the night, they struggled blindly up two flights of stairs until they reached the second floor. Anatoly felt along the wall until he came to a small steel door. Grunting, he pulled at a large steel lever. Anatoly yanked open the door just as Larissa struck another match. A pile of moldy grain cascaded out, followed by a large rat.

"Oi," said Vera.

Noting that the door was set in a wall of concrete, Nick said, "That must be the base of a silo."

Luba peered down the stairs at the orange glow, then quickly said, "They're coming and . . . and the fire's getting very big."

Vera rushed over, saw the two men scaling the steps. Behind them, the fire crackled, engulfing the ground floor. Smoke rose as thick as a London fog.

Nick spotted an old barrel in the corner. "Vera, help me." To the others, he said, "Go ahead, we'll catch up."

As the others started up another flight of stairs, Nick and

Vera tipped an old flour barrel on its side. They rolled it to the top of the staircase, slipped behind it. When Stevens and Petrov came around the corner, Nick and Vera shoved the container forward. The barrel rolled and bounced down the steps. Stevens shoved the Russian back, and seconds later the wooden barrel crashed into a wall and exploded into kindling.

Nick, clutching his wounded hand, and Vera, the specs in hand, ran up the next flight. On the third floor, Anatoly, Larissa, and Luba were desperately groping along the walls for a way out. On the right Larissa discovered another steel door set in concrete. To the left Luba stumbled into a large room filled with the deep shadows of machinery.

Suddenly, an explosion burst from below. The floor beneath Nick shifted, buckled. He reached out to brace himself, wondering if the whole mill would cave in.

"Ah!" cried Luba, reaching vainly for support.

Metal chutes and wheels squealed loose and collapsed. Nesting pigeons and rats screeched out. And from other rooms Nick could hear windows shattering as if sprayed by a machine gun.

Then, with a grumbling, boards and metal equipment settled back into place.

Waving a cloud of dust away from his face, Anatoly said, "That must have been a fuel tank."

Larissa, who had fallen backward, stood at the edge of a wall. Coughing from the dust, she tried to see what lay beyond.

"Look, another building."

Without a word, all of them rushed down the hall. When they reached a large door at the end, Nick was brushing the sweat from his face. The fire's heat made him feel as though the air itself were melting like hot wax.

Nick, Vera, and Anatoly kicked in the door, led the way over the broken boards. In a few steps they found themselves on a wooden landing overlooking a three-story-tall room. From the light of distant windows, Nick could make out large steel wheels, turbines, cutting blades, and crisscrossing chutes.

Nick looked down, saw a thick gray rat scurrying over

## THE RED ENCOUNTER

Vera's foot. She kicked at it, sending it screeching off the edge and to its death below. Then she kicked at another and another as they raced past her. But it was impossible to stop them. Shaken from their dens by the blast, a line of grain-fed rats scurried from the burning mill behind, through the broken door, and down the stairs.

Nick lunged toward her, leaned against a railing. As he reached for Vera he felt sharp claws and a furry body scamper over his hand. He jumped as if shocked, only to land on the back of another rat, which shrieked into the night.

Grabbing for Vera's hand, he said, "Let's get the hell out of here."

Helping Luba, Vera and he kicked aside a handful of rats and started down the stairs. Somewhere outside Nick heard the scream of siren after siren. Squad cars. That meant fire trucks couldn't be far behind.

"Hurry!" shouted Anatoly. Last on the landing, he saw the hallway behind him smolder with smoke. "This building's going to catch any moment." He spotted the figures of Stevens and Petrov. "They're right back there!"

"Come on!" shouted Vera.

The stairs were covered with a molten flow of rats that poured from the mill and its silos. Screeching and clawing, the creatures were afraid only of the growing flames, knew only that they would soon burn. The rodents clawed over one another, tumbled downward.

As Anatoly, Larissa, and he rushed after the two women Nick swung at a rat that bit at his calf. He hung on to the splintery banister as the staircase dropped to the large milling room below. Behind, Nick heard Stevens and Petrov coughing, then kicking their way through the busted door and onto the landing. Nick swung around on a flight of stairs and glanced up. Through a tangle of columns and boards he saw Stevens raise his gun, then drop it. There was no way he'd be able to hit any of them.

Another explosion thundered into the night, rocking the brittle staircase. Nick lurched forward, grabbed on. Glass shattered like falling icicles. He watched in disbelief as the brick wall behind bulged out, buckled into pieces, and smoke poured through the gaping wound. Forget about the police, thought Nick. The entire row of mills was going to go, and unless they escaped they'd burn along with everything else.

On the ground floor, Nick hurried everyone beneath the staircase. He peered upward, saw the two men pushing their way down. Then his eyes darted through the smoke and all across the massive room. But he had no idea which way led to freedom. He saw rats swarming off to the right, away from the main room.

Nick grabbed Vera's hand. "That way!"

The others followed as Nick led the way beneath a ledge and behind a row of barrels. Running in the same direction as the rats, they made their way to the far wall. Across the room Nick spotted another set of steel double doors. Another building, another mill might lie behind that brick wall. Perhaps a way out.

A shot fired, tore through the air. Stevens and Petrov were on the floor now.

"Keep low!" shouted Vera.

They wove in and out of machinery, ducked behind metal chutes. Nick looked back, saw the flames embracing the staircase they had just come down. Smoke billowed out, filling the room like steam in a steamroom. But he couldn't see what he was looking for. Stevens and Petrov had disappeared. They were hidden somewhere in the confusion of equipment and flames.

Anatoly and Larissa rushed ahead to the large steel door. Nick lingered, trying to spot the two men. He'd have to distract them somehow, keep them back until they made it through the doors.

"Mama, stay behind this post," said Vera, hurrying up to the door.

Anatoly, Larissa, and Vera all took hold of a lever. They tried to slide the door back, but with no success.

"It's locked from the other side," said Anatoly.

Nick heard steps. He grabbed an iron rod, lifted it overhead. If only he still had a gun, he thought, as his eyes desperately scanned the room. But he didn't and . . .

Something moved. His eyes flicked to the side. It was Petrov. But he wasn't staring at Nick, he wasn't about to

## THE RED ENCOUNTER

fire. Instead the Soviet agent was looking to his left. Nick followed the man's glance and saw Stevens. The tall, curly-haired man stood firmly erect, his pistol in both hands leveled at the steel door.

"Look out!" Nick screamed.

Anatoly spun around just as a shot fired out. His eyes opened in horror and he tried to drop to the floor. But it was too late. A bullet caught him in the forehead, twisting him to the side. A large red stain burst across his head, and he fell to the ground.

"Anatoly!" yelled Vera.

She lunged toward him, forgetting about Stevens. Nick turned back. Saw the tall man, his gun in both hands leveled now at her.

And just as he heard the shot, he screamed, "Vera!"

He closed his eyes for just a moment. He could have done something, something more. . . .

Terrified of what he would see, he slowly looked over. But she was there. Alive, standing. Unable to believe it, he spun back around, certain that Stevens would fire again. Richard Stevens, however, was no longer standing. He lay instead on the floor, his body crumpled in a dead heap, his gun harmlessly beside him.

A wave of shock and relief swept over Nick. He turned further, and there, only ten feet away, was the man who had killed Richard Stevens with a single shot: Viktor Petrov. Unable to move, the gun hung from the Russian's limp hand.

"He forced me to—to work for him, to do this," he mumbled, his face white, his eyes red. "He—he blackmailed me. Hughes, I mean."

## Chapter 64

Tommy Lichton was smiling. He felt hotter than he'd been all summer. You couldn't get any closer to the mills than he was. It was too hot, the smoke too thick. He was back on a pile of sand, some fifty yards from the burning mills, and the whole black night glowed red. This was as close as anyone dared go. Even the firemen had given up on saving the buildings, resorting instead to wetting the surrounding structures.

He adjusted the sweater wrapped around his arm to conceal the flow of blood. On foot, he'd pushed through the crowds and followed the stream of sirens that led from DataResearch to the mills. He knew they were in there and, to his relief, he knew none of them would be coming out.

He glanced about. He should leave before he was noticed, before questions were asked. Reporters and television crews were arriving at the scene like ants drawn to honey. The sirens and blaring lights, however, were hardly noticeable above the roar of the flames.

In front of him, a fireman was dragging a long hose from a distant truck. Lichton hurried forward.

"Is anyone in there?" he asked, just wanting to make sure.

He laughed. "There?" He shook his head. "Hell, man, if there is, there's no way they're coming out."

That, thought Lichton as he turned away, was all he wanted to know. It meant the specs were destroyed, along with all the people who could possibly trace Stevens' dealings back to him. Nothing had gone according to plan, but at least he wouldn't be implicated, at least he wouldn't be accused of anything.

Overcome with a mixture of satisfaction and disappointment, he started back toward town. His wound burned. He had to get the bullet removed, and then things would slowly settle back to normal. Perhaps in another six months or so he could try some other way of trapping the Russians as they tried to steal his computer.

# Chapter 65

Behind Nick, Larissa fell over her husband's body and sobbed in bellowing waves. Luba outstretched both her good and bad hands, screamed, then dropped to her knees at her son's side. The two women tried to rouse Anatoly, tried to force life back into him, but it was hopeless.

Stunned, Nick turned back to the KGB agent. "What—what are you talking about?"

Almost by magic, the gun slipped out of Viktor's hand and dropped to the floor. Not paying any attention to the encroaching flames, the Russian stepped over to Stevens' body and knelt beside it. He felt the neck, found no sign of life, and sat back and drew a deep breath. One hand resting on the body, he gazed up at Nick.

"Richard and I were ... were lovers," began Viktor. "Agents of your country found out about us and confronted me. I told them I wanted to defect, but they wouldn't let me. They wanted to know who was behind Richard, who was supplying him. They said they'd give me asylum only after they knew who his source was. I had no choice. They said that if I didn't do exactly as they said, they'd tell my superiors in Moscow. You don't understand. The KGB would have killed me."

Vera's face slowly twisted in despair. "Oh, Lord. Oh, my

Lord. All—all this was for nothing. And now Anatoly's dead."

Nick reached out, placed his hand on her shoulder. It was, however, as if he were touching a table or a wall or anything without life or hope.

"No—no matter what I did," she muttered, "there was never any real chance my family would be freed. The FBI let the KGB do this to me just—just so they could—could . . ." She trembled. "I wish I'd never come to America. I just want—want to go home."

Suddenly, the staircase collapsed, spewing red cinders and fumes. Fiery boards shot into the air like hurled sparklers, and the fire, more liquid than ever, engulfed everything in its path.

Nick grabbed Vera. "We've got to—"

"Why, Nick? There's no hope. There's not even a way out." Shaking her head, she added, "And there's no way Gennady and Vladik will ever . . . ever be released."

The fire was snowballing, uncontrollably feeding on the innards of the mill. The way back was completely gone, a pile of bricks and flaming wood.

Beyond Luba and Larissa, Nick saw a row of rats streaming along a solid brick wall. The plump creatures ran, their eyes beaded in terror. But they didn't hesitate, didn't doubt.

"That's our ticket out of here. No one knows this place better. Come on." He took Vera by the arm, then turned to Viktor. "If we get out of here, I think I know a way to free Vera's family. Will you help us?"

Beads of sweat rolling down his cheeks, Viktor nodded. *"Da,"* he said, casting a last look at Stevens.

They crossed quickly to Larissa and Luba. Vera and Viktor lifted Luba to her feet while Nick gently took Larissa by the arm, raised her. The blonde shook her head, her wet face a mass of painful contortions.

"No, no, I can't leave him!" she screamed, refusing to move.

Nick stared briefly at Anatoly's face, wrapped his arms around Larissa and forced her on. Finally she turned away from her fallen husband, put her head on Nick's shoulder.

She sobbed, stumbled along. As they made their way around the corner, she reached back, cried out.

*"Tolichka!"*

Nick pushed her around the corner just as a large beam collapsed. It fell on the legs of Richard Stevens, crushing them, setting his clothing afire. Nick took a last look, saw that Anatoly, too, would soon be nothing more than ash.

"Nick," shouted Vera, her arms around her mother, "which way?"

The stream of rats flowed along the base of the solid brick wall.

"Right!"

In the lead, Vera, Luba, and Viktor headed toward the far corner. Suddenly there was a snap. Viktor looked up, spotted a beam burning through directly above them.

"Look out!"

He threw his body against them, pushing them back and to the floor. Part of the roof collapsed, sending columns and beams crashing only a few feet away. Frantic, Vera tried to get up, only to be pressed back down. Something clawed at her, scrambled over her side. A half-dozen rats, their teeth yellow and sharp, were tearing over her in their frantic escape. She struck at them with her fist, rolled away, crushing one underneath her, then bolted to her feet.

All around the rats screamed, sending out a signal. In panic, they spun around, shot in every direction. Within seconds, however, they were scurrying back along the brick wall, this time in the opposite direction.

Nick saw the creatures running deeper into the building and knew it was their only chance. He pulled Larissa around, half carried her onward. Viktor and Vera huddled over Luba and quickly followed.

"Nick, are you sure?" called Vera.

"Just run!"

The smoke grew thicker with each step that they retreated into the depths of the mill. Fed by the fire, the air glowed gray, and soon they couldn't see more than a few yards ahead. Larissa, still sobbing, leaned on Nick, choked for air.

Always following the stream of rats, they stumbled

along. They came to a hall, rushed down it. Abruptly the corridor ended in a solid brick wall.

Nick clawed at his throat for fresh air. The heat sucked the oxygen out of the air, out of him. Glancing to the floor, he saw a line of rats disappear one by one through a crack at the bottom of the wall. Nick rushed over, kicked the creatures out of the way, and stomped on the floor. It was hollow.

"Vera, Viktor, over here!" he called. "You two," he said to Luba and Larissa, "keep those things away."

At first the two women didn't understand. Then, as if they were battling for their lives, they kicked at the rodents and forced them back. With Luba and Larissa stomping and screaming behind him, Nick wedged his fingers into a crack in the floor. Vera and Viktor hurried over and grabbed hold. Together, they pulled. The nails squeaked, tore at the old wood. The opening grew larger.

*"Raz, dva, tri."* One, two, three, shouted Vera.

Under their effort, the board snapped back and broke loose. A dark hole appeared below, seemingly with no bottom.

"Another one," called Nick.

The three of them grabbed another board, pulled it back, until it, too, broke free. The sound of rapidly flowing water emerged from the hole. Unable to believe it, they pulled loose another and yet another board until a strong, steady rush of water poured beneath their feet. Strong and cool, the water rushed through a concrete channel beneath the building.

Nick shouted, "Let a few of them go!"

Luba and Larissa stepped back, and as soon as the way was clear two rats scurried forward. Without hesitating, they threw themselves into the hole. They plunged into the water, bobbed up, and were washed out of sight.

Nick smiled, almost laughed. It was an old water sluice that once fed the mill.

Looking up, he said, "Anyone care for a dip in the Mississippi?"

# *Epilogue*

Eleven days later, Nick sat in a tenth-floor apartment, gazing calmly out over the Atlantic. Through the dirty glass he studied the fine line where the dark water met the blue and white sky. He then lowered his eyes to the sand and wide boardwalk of Brighton Beach. Hundreds of people strolled in the warmth of the late afternoon. Those who were not Soviet Jews were American Jews. The few who were not part of either group did not live in the area.

The thick smell of borscht and fish and meat and fried *piroshki* rolled through the apartment, surrounded Nick and blocked out the ocean's saltiness. He heard chattering voices in the kitchen. He looked across the chipped linoleum floor. A long table, surrounded by the twenty or so chairs collected from neighbors, was filling rapidly with food. Strange women—all trusted immigrants—ran back and forth between the table and the steamy kitchen.

Vera's hand descended on his neck and began to rub.

"You look calm . . . but you're tense."

He nodded.

"Me too." She could not, however, hide her excitement. "Afterward we'll really relax . . . eat and drink and dance."

There was a steady knock on the door and Nick and Vera and all the women in the kitchen froze. A short woman with rusty red hair and gold teeth wiped her hands on her apron and went to the door.

Not making any move to open the lock, she said, *"Da?"*

"It's Sasha."

As she twisted open the lock, the woman with the red hair nodded to Nick and Vera, then looked back into the kitchen. At once Luba emerged. Not coming with them, Vera's mother was expending all her nervous energy on the celebratory feast.

Nick rose, felt Vera's hand slip into his, and crossed to the doorway. He glanced at Luba and she rushed over to him. He hugged her, felt the soft folds of her body press against him, smelled the sweet Red Moscow perfume so liberally applied.

"Nick, *dorogoi.*" Nick, dear, she said kissing him. "What would we have done without you? *Xoroshi chelovek, tee. Sami luchi.*" You're a good person. The very best. "You're like—like a . . . son to me."

Over Luba's shoulder Nick saw Larissa lingering at the edge of the kitchen. The tall blond woman smiled as much as she could. Only her loss could never be replaced. Anatoly's remains lay among the charred ruins of the mill, perhaps already bulldozed away.

Nick kissed Luba on the cheek and pulled back. She began to cry. A light covering of bandages were all that covered her left hand, and she used the cloth to dry her eyes.

"*V'cevo xoroshovo.*" All the best.

"To you too," he said. He turned to Vera. "Ready?"

"Yes."

From a side table, Nick picked up the two blue plastic containers of magnetic computer tape. A Soviet cuckoo clock on the apartment wall struggled to sound the time as he and Vera stepped into the hall. It was 4:45. The exchange would take place in fifteen minutes.

Emerging from the apartment as if from a prison cell, Nick and Vera were greeted with almost silent grunts from two Russian men. They followed them to the elevator and rode down to the ground floor. As soon as they were outside, both Nick and Vera gasped, turned around, and basked in the sunshine and warm air. It was the first time they had been outside since they'd arrived.

Almost simultaneously, four Russian men emerged from a gold Mercedes-Benz, alternately pushing and pulling a fifth man, Viktor Petrov. Nick tensed when he saw the KGB major and he grabbed Vera's arm, pressed it in a silent signal. Though Petrov had also been hidden away, it was obvious that it was not in an apartment with an ocean view and a bottomless refrigerator. His face was white, drawn, his eyes red and glassy. Nick guessed that once a deal had been struck with the KGB, the Soviet émigrés had shown little mercy. Not only was it the rarest of opportunities to have complete power over one of the KGB's own, it was also one of the few chances to learn who among them was an agent for the Fatherland.

Nick, Vera, Petrov, and the six Russian men made their way around the corner of the apartment building. Nick hoped this was one of the final scenes in the exhausting drama. Their escape from the burning flour mill in Minneapolis had been as close as it was wet. By the time they had reached the East Coast, Anatoly's connections had everything set. It was simply a matter of waiting.

Nearing the boardwalk, Vera stepped up to Viktor.

*"Spacibo. Bolshoie spacibo."* Thank you. Thank you very much. "I'll never forget."

Petrov said, "I'm sorry this couldn't have been sooner."

"And I'm sorry about . . ." She eyed the immigrants who led them on. "I hope they weren't too . . ."

He shrugged it off. "Goes with the job."

Nick moved up next to Vera. "What's going to happen?" he asked Viktor.

"Once I return? I don't know. It depends if they still trust me back in Moscow. Maybe I'll do some work for your people. Maybe I'll stay. I really don't have much . . ."

They climbed the steep stairs to the boardwalk and the sounds of the ocean and thousands of immigrants washed over them. Behind them, the promenade continued for another half-dozen blocks. Ahead of them the planks continued for miles until, on the horizon, they met the faint shape of Coney Island's ferris wheel.

It seemed as if almost all of the area's forty thousand Soviet immigrants were out. Studying the people on the boardwalk—strolling along arm in arm, playing chess, drinking vodka, and laughing—Nick thought how this was the perfect place to meet. Should there be any problem, Sasha and his men would simply have to call out. An army of immigrants would be upon the KGB's men in moments.

When they were within a hundred yards of the Café Moskva, Nick nudged Viktor.

"Here."

He handed him one of the reels of magnetic tape.

"You're sure this is the right one?" asked the Russian.

"Positive."

As they neared the café, Sasha and his men slowed. The exchange was to take place in front of the restaurant, right out in the center of the boardwalk. Sasha signaled everyone to stop. He checked his watch. They should be here any moment.

One of the magnetic disks still underarm, Nick turned to Vera. She was staring down toward the café, her eyes searching, full of hope, full of life. The ocean breeze reddened her cheeks, tousled her hair.

"Vera . . ."

He embraced her, pulled her as tightly against him as he could. When she kissed him on the cheek, he understood, even accepted, that the passion was gone. He let her go, then stepped back.

"Goodbye."

"What? Aren't you coming back for dinner?"

He shook his head. She started to protest.

"Vera, look."

He nodded past her toward the café. The stark figures of three men emerged on the boardwalk. Partially hidden between them was a shape of a taller yet thinner man and the dwarfed outline of a child.

Vera gasped. She grasped Nick by the arm and sunk her fingers into his skin. It reminded Nick of Luba's birthday party when he and Vera had stood by the picture window. Again, she seemed to be drawing energy from him in order to be strong enough to pull away.

He kissed her on the cheek. "You'll be all right."

Staring at the figures, she relaxed her fingers and finally let loose of Nick. She took a step forward, only to be stopped by Sasha's thick arm.

"Let them come to us." The heavy Russian nodded to Viktor. "Okay. But just a few steps."

Viktor, the blue plastic container of magnetic tape in his

## THE RED ENCOUNTER

hands, began to walk slowly forward. When he had gone but ten feet, he stopped and lifted the tape above his head. The men on the other end understood, parted, and allowed the taller man and the child to move forward.

"Not too fast," called Sasha to Viktor.

As Viktor slowly made his way forward so did the man and boy. They all took one step at time, cautious of the situation, fearful of ruining it at the last moment. Finally their movements quickened until, when they passed one another, the man and the boy broke into a run.

"Vladik, Gennady!" cried Vera.

"Mama, Mama!"

Nick was moving backward, away. By the time Vera reached her husband and son, he was some thirty feet from Sasha and the other Russians. He stopped. Vera and her family had melded into one, a ball of laughter and tears. Their son lifted up between them, Vera and Gennady embraced and kissed and let hope carry them away.

Within moments, Sasha and his group of Soviet immigrants banded around Vera and her family, shielding them from Viktor and the KGB. Past them, in the shadows of the building that housed the Café Moskva, Viktor, the computer tape under arm, was quickly hurried away by his Soviet comrades.

Nick tried to see Vera, but she was lost in a swarm of family and immigrants. He shook his head, smiled, turned, and was on his way. He had taken only a few steps, however, when a young child stepped in his way. The boy, no older than four, looked at Nick, then pointed to a dog.

Proudly he said in Russian, *"Gav-gav, av-av."*

Nick grinned, knelt down to him. "Right. And do you know what a dog says in English?"

The boy smiled, shook his head.

"Bow-wow."

The boy laughed. He looked to the east, across the ocean. Then he searched the boardwalk but could not find what he was looking for.

"In Russian, horses say *Ee-go-go.*"

Nick lifted his head and shook it. "Neigh . . . neigh."

The boy laughed more. "Do you want to come to my house for dinner?"

It was Nick's turn to laugh. The boy was so young but already he was a real Russian. He was so eager to like, to be liked, to take someone into the privacy of his heart.

"Thanks, but I can't."

"Oh." The boy reached out and touched the blue plastic case. "What's that?"

Nick gazed over his shoulder, saw that Viktor and the KGB had disappeared from sight. With Viktor, however, were not the real specs to the GALA-1, but a blank reel. The Russian knew it too. It had, in fact, been his idea to arrange a trade with the KGB; Vera's husband and son in exchange for him and the specs. Over the phone he had vouched to his superiors for the authenticity of the tape, then hung up and told Nick that he'd somehow deal with the matter once he was back in Moscow. Perhaps, he said, he'd ask for permission to further pursue Stevens' reputed source; the man who had supposedly supplied Richard with technical data was still unknown to both the KGB and the FBI.

Nick scanned the boardwalk further and realized that Vera, her family, and the others were gone too.

"*Shto eto?*" repeated the boy.

"This?"

Nick snapped open the case that held the real copy of the computer specs. He had held it overhead, sealed in its blue plastic case, when they'd jumped into the water sluice and been washed into the Mississippi. It had remained perfectly dry, and he had intended to return the copy to the FBI. Instead, however, he reached in and took hold of the end of the tape and handed it to the Russian boy.

"It's a toy. Here."

"I—I can play with it?"

"You can have it." Nick set the open case on the wood. "Just take the end of this tape and run like you were trying to get a kite in the air. Go as fast and far down the boardwalk as you can."

The young boy laughed, looked around as if he were about to do something terribly wrong, and then took off in a burst of energy. Effortlessly, the tape unwound from its container, flapping behind the boy.

"Run!" called Nick, watching the child dodging in and out of the *babushki*.

He stood, laughed, and felt oddly calm. For once he knew exactly where he was headed, where he wanted to end up. It was time to start home.

# 3½ MONTHS ON THE NEW YORK TIMES BESTSELLER LIST!

Blackford Oakes, the hero of WHO'S ON FIRST is back in a daring Cold War mission...

# MARCO POLO, IF YOU CAN
## WILLIAM F. BUCKLEY, Jr.

"Operates exactly as a good thriller should...It demands to be devoured quickly, then leaves the reader satisfied."
*Houston Chronicle*

"Buckley's latest is a dashing historical chess game."
*Washington Post*

"Delightful, diverting and provocative...a suspenseful tale of intrigue."
*King Features*

"Whether Blackford does unspeakable things to the Queen of England (SAVING THE QUEEN), restores by hand a German church (STAINED GLASS), or fails to stop the Soviet Union from launching the first space satellite (WHO'S ON FIRST), each novel crackles...MARCO POLO, IF YOU CAN is superior." *The New York Times*

**Avon Paperback**     **61424-3/$3.50 US/$4.50 Can**

Buy these books at your local bookstore or use this coupon for ordering:

Avon Books, Dept BP, Box 767, Rte 2, Dresden, TN 38225
Please send me the book(s) I have checked above. I am enclosing $_____
please add $1.00 to cover postage and handling for each book ordered to a maximum of three dollars). *Send check or money order*—no cash or C.O.D.'s please. Prices and numbers are subject to change without notice. Please allow six to eight weeks for delivery.

Name _____
Address _____
City _____ State/Zip _____

Marco Polo 5-85

# The Provocative National Bestseller

# WHO'S ON FIRST
# WILLIAM F. BUCKLEY, JR.

"Timeless thriller ingredients: murder, torture, sex... Soviet defection, treachery. And there in the middle of it all is good old Blacky: charming, insouciant, escaping one dragnet after another without rumpling his trenchcoat." *Boston Globe*

The cunning and sophisticated hero Blackford Oakes is back in a new adventure involving a beautiful Hungarian freedom fighter, Blacky's old KGB rival, a pair of Soviet scientific geniuses, and the U.S.-U.S.S.R. space race.

"A fast-moving plot.... As in all good espionage novels there is thrust and counterthrust.... Mr. Buckley is an observer with a keen wit and a cold eye."
Newgate Callendar, *New York Times Book Review*

"The suspense is keen and complicated.... Constantly entertaining." *Wall Street Journal*

"A crackling good plot... entertaining." *Washington Post*

**AVON Paperback**     52555-0/$3.50 US/$4.50 Can

Buy these books at your local bookstore or use this coupon for ordering:

Avon Books, Dept BP, Box 767, Rte 2, Dresden, TN 38225
Please send me the book(s) I have checked above. I am enclosing $_____
(please add $1.00 to cover postage and handling for each book ordered to a maximum of three dollars). *Send check or money order*—no cash or C.O.D.'s please. Prices and numbers are subject to change without notice. Please allow six to eight weeks for delivery.

Name _____
Address __3401_____
City _____ State/Zip _____

Who's On First 5-85